P9-DSY-907

BY ROBERT ANDERSON

Plays

Tea and Sympathy
All Summer Long
Silent Night, Lonely Night
The Days Between
You Know I Can't Hear You
When the Water's Running
I Never Sang for My Father
Solitaire/Double Solitaire

Novel

After

AFTER

RANDOM HOUSE

NEW YORK

AFTER

ROBERT
ANDERSON

Copyright © 1973   by Robert Anderson

All rights reserved under International and Pan-American Copyright Conventions. Published in the United States by Random House, Inc., New York, and simultaneously in Canada by Random House of Canada Limited, Toronto.

Library of Congress Cataloging in Publication Data

Anderson, Robert Woodruff, 1917–
After.

A novel.
I. Title.
PZ4.A54945Af [PS3501.N34] 813'.5'4 72-11439
ISBN 0-394-48536-X

Manufactured in the United States of America

First Edition

FOR TERESA

AFTER

ONE

For months I had awakened hoping that Fran had died quietly during the night. Quietly. I was terrified of her dying in the agony of cancer. For five years I had been terrified of her pain, or rather, of my having to confront her pain, helplessly.

I remember one especially difficult night two years after the first operation (she had seen to it that there were not too many difficult moments for me). But this night she was depressed and felt she wasn't making any progress, and she had blurted out, "I think I have cancer and nobody's telling me." The doctors had all said, "Don't tell her!" and I don't think I had the courage to tell her anyway. I have never been good at confrontations with the truth. (The first Christmas of the Depression, when I was young, and I knew we had very little money, I asked my mother to get a lot of small ten-cent-store toys and wrap them up so that we could have the illusion that nothing had happened.)

But that night Fran had cried, and I had tried to comfort her. And I had lied, saying that I knew no more than she did. And I suggested that we make an appointment with the doctor so that he could tell us both the truth. (These had been my instructions.) "He won't tell us anything," she had said, and she had cried. And I had held her in my arms and suggested that she take a sleeping pill. "What good will that do?"

I could not face this ultimate truth with her any more than I had been able to face other truths with her during our twenty-one years of marriage. We had had few confrontations, gliding by our times of crisis, swallowing our hurts and resentments and moving on. Good friends have subsequently said that she must have been grateful that I hadn't forced us to face her dying together. I don't know. I have imagined the scene a thousand times, wishing that we had had it. But we didn't. In the end, I think, we both knew the truth, but never faced it together. It was very lonely that way. Everything we did and said in those five years was done and said in the shadow of that unspoken truth.

Our son, David, had not approved of this. "I would want to know."

"So would I."

"Then why don't you tell her?"

"I don't think she really wants to know. Five times we have made appointments with the doctor to have him tell us the truth, and five times she has canceled those appointments."

So I had hoped that I would find that she had died quietly during the night. I had heard of other men whose wives had died in their arms, spitting blood, turning blue, gasping for breath. I couldn't have stood that. But, of course, I would have. "I." Always the "I." How often I tried to get rid of the "I." Her first operation, when her breast was removed, the doctor had thought the operation would be a matter of an hour, the cyst, benign. But the hours had dragged on and had told me the truth. And I had sat there in the hospital sun room clutching her watch and wedding ring, which the nurse had brought me in the third hour. They seemed then like "remains," tokens for the survivor.

Other families had been waiting, and during the day surgeons had arrived with "Everything's fine" and they had disappeared together down the hall. Until at four o'clock, I was the only one sitting in the sun room from which the sun had gone. After the fifth hour, I had found myself in a booth in the men's room crying. Men of my background and training cry alone in toilets.

Towards evening, when they told me Fran was on her way down from the recovery room, I said to myself, "I will block out my reactions. I will simply be there when she first opens her eyes, when she asks the questions." I wanted desperately to be away from the place. I did not know if I could share the first moment of awareness with her.

And then suddenly, "Chris, they took it away."

"I know. I know. But you'll be all right. You're well."

And for a year we lived with that illusion, a gift from the surgeon, who already knew the truth.

I have gone over it again and again, and still do to this day, some years later. Should she have been told? Would we have found more comfort? And later, was it an indication of something that was between us, or wasn't between us? I played God, trying to arrange her years, those when she was still able to get around, in a way I thought she might want them if she knew she was going to die, but in a way she wouldn't have had the heart to arrange them if she had actually known.

Now after five years she was almost totally bedridden, lying in our oversize double bed, her neck in traction, the head of the bed raised on blocks to accommodate the pulleys and weights, or on rare occasions, when she could move around, wearing a neck brace that she called her horse collar. Her neck had gone, her back. When I prepared her for the wheelchair, she sat on the side of the bed and I would prop her up with my head while I strapped on her corset and braces, trying to make jokes about it, but wanting instead to press her scarred and beaten body to my face and cry. I never cried in front of her. Perhaps that is why I cried so much after.

Sometimes we still slept together in this large bed. And some nights I would sleep in my workroom, my writing room, which was connected to our bedroom by a bathroom. We lived in an old farmhouse in Connecticut, and it was almost impossible to get nursing help, and certainly not at night, and the last operation on her pituitary had left her with a constant need for water and bedpan. Wherever I slept, I slept lightly. I became like a mother who could hear her child cry anywhere in the house.

There were mornings when I would wake up by her side and look at the bedclothes covering her, and there would be no movement, no rise and fall with breathing, and I would lie back and hope and hate myself for hoping. I would lift myself up and look over and down at her face, hoping and afraid, and her eyes would open drowsily and look at mine. I would feel great joy and relief and I would smile. And she would pout kiddingly and murmur, "I had to take the damned pills."

Various bottles of pills littered her bedside table. She hated to take the Demerol because it left her dopey, but sometimes she had to take it for the pain. Red-letter days were no-Demerol days, often ending in the evening in discouraging defeat. "I've got to take one." And whimpering not so much at the pain as at the defeat of her hope that she might never have to take it again.

"Water," she would murmur, licking her dry lips. "I drink so much water." And I would get up and refill the large glass and replace it on the table, putting the bent tube in it so that she could drink by just turning her head towards the table.

There were two village women who came in and "helped out." They had cleaned for us from time to time, and now they alternated so that five days a week there was someone to clean, prepare lunches and "baby-sit," as Fran called it. They could rarely stay to make dinner, as they had families of their own.

We could have stayed in our small apartment in New York City, the *"pied-à-terre"* we used whenever Fran was acting in a play or when I had extended conferences on my books. It would have been easier to get help there. But somehow it was better in the country. Dying and death were part of the basic rhythms of nature there. In the city they seemed like unpardonable offenses against its obsessive vitality.

Though from time to time I would leave her for a few hours, I really wasn't happy anyplace else, and I couldn't wait to get back to take up my duties. When I was away from her, the idea of her dying swept over me and I couldn't stand it. But oddly, in her sickroom, she wasn't dying. It was a place of enormous activity, visitors, telephone calls, letters, things to be done, with her incredibly gallant soul presiding over it all. Perhaps also I was happiest there with her because we hadn't been as close for years. Though we were fiercely proud of each other's careers, they had led to many lonely times of separation, she away making films or on tour, I away doing research for my books or in seclusion, doing the actual writing.

These last years had brought us very close together.

Perhaps not in the way one would want, but we knew that something important had been forced on us by her sickness. Something more than physical closeness, a sense of mutual dependency.

She had had to be dependent in so many ways, humiliating for a proud woman. It must have been a cruel and devastating experience for her to lie flat on her back and hold off asking for something—a drink, a cigarette, a handkerchief, the bedpan. I'm not sure I could have allowed her to do the things I did for her.

The bedpan, for example. Lying as she was, inactive, unable for the most part to get up those last months, her bowels were a problem. For a long while we had moved her each time from the bed to a bedside commode. But finally the effort became too great and she had to give in to the hated bedpan. And the moment of her first succeeding with it, with me helping to hold her broken body steady, was strangely a great moment of love and trust between us. It was a moment of closeness and openness which surprised me. "My God, I never thought I'd allow you to do anything like this." And she half cried and yet half laughed, partly because she had succeeded in functioning, and partly because somehow a barrier was down. Such a private person.

My trips away from the house usually involved getting something for her—a bedjacket, some flowers (though she was sick of flowers people continually sent, and said, "Please, it's too much. Ask them not to send any more flowers.") But she did like the single flowers I would bring her from her own garden. She could see the garden and a good deal of the lawn in an angled mirror I had rigged up outside the bedroom window. Though mostly flat on her back, she could read by means of a "Rube Goldberg" kind of reading stand I had invented which would hold a book open over her head. (I had devised all these inventions so that she could seem to lead a "normal" life from her bed,

[8]

maintaining the illusion that nothing was really happening.)

I read aloud to her sometimes, but I was not very good at it, even with my own work, which I had to read from time to time because one of the things that depressed her was that tending her was keeping me from writing. One day I woke up to see her leaning over me, looking at me. "You know you haven't written anything in months."

What could I write? All I could think of was what was happening to her, to us. I couldn't write that. Only now, years later, am I able even to try to write about it. But sometimes to relieve her anxiety I would manage to write something, and I would read it to her; it wasn't very good because my heart wasn't in it, and she would tell me it wasn't very good and would blame herself for its not being good, and I would try harder the next time.

For the most part during those last years we lived in the present. It is not a satisfying way to live, with no plans, no expectations, no hopes for the future. In the early days I had insisted we make plans, conscious always that they were probably pointless. She read scripts for plays and movies, and thanks to the X-ray treatments which gave her a miraculous two years with almost no pain, she taught two semesters of her acting class in the city and toured with a play, and even I began to deceive myself that perhaps there might be a spontaneous remission. Then just when I had almost come to believe we had licked it, there would be a pain, an ache. We would explain it away as a muscle, a joint which had been overused. But, of course, it wasn't. Later she responded to various other treatments, cobalt, drugs, operations, and again there would be lunatic hope.

But essentially, from the moment I knew she was going to die, everything was "now." Anything I kept from her now, she would never get. "Why are you being so indulgent to me?" And I would have to stop or she would guess. It limits a relationship not to be able to live somewhat in the future. Planning is an important part of a marriage.

There was an episode in Denmark. She had responded fantastically to cobalt treatment, and after the resultant weakness had worn off, we decided to make a dash for Europe. She had wanted a set of Royal Copenhagen porcelain for party dinners. With delight she made her selections from samples on display. Then the clerk said, "You understand, of course, that we can't promise delivery for well over a year."

She looked at me and said, "Oh, well, in that case, I guess we'd better not."

"Nonsense. We've waited this long for it. What's another year?"

She looked at me quizzically. I became logical and gruff about why we should place the order. And we did. And we walked out of the shop with our arms around each other in a strange closeness. In such ways perhaps we shared the knowledge that she was dying by denying it.

The porcelain arrived one year after her death.

We fought later that day. I had not realized how tired she was becoming, and I had proved ineffective in trying to flag down a taxi, and it was drizzling and she became a little peevish, and I snapped back that I was doing the best I could in a strange city, and there was silence in the taxi when I finally managed to get one.

I remember every harsh word I said to her in those years. And though reason tells me that they came simply from strain and were inevitable, I have tried to take them back a hundred times, to ask forgiveness. But I am not forgiven. The survivor is the sinner and cannot forgive himself, and the only person who could forgive is gone.

TWO

It was early in May, and I had been down in the
village to mail letters, pick up groceries, the laundry and
some liquor.

"How are things at home?"

The whole thing was an almost unbearable charade.
People guessed the true state of things, I suppose, but
officially very few of my friends knew the truth. For the
rest, I told them the same stories I told Fran.

"What are we calling it this month, Doctor?"

"Decalcification of the bones. And that's not a lie, because that's actually what's happening."

But those good people from the village who had
dressed up and come to see her, bringing with them her fa-

vorite jams and jellies, home-baked bread, the first snow-drops, had looked at her with awe and fear and had known.

In the early part of the final months, when she could still be carried, I would strap her in her braces and take her riding in the car, and we would stop in front of friends' houses or in their driveways and they would come to the side of the car, full of hearty surprise. "Well, look at this!" as though she were well on the road to recovery.

I knew she enjoyed these rides. They somehow reassured her. But I have often wondered since if one of my motives in taking her "calling" wasn't to display my burden.

I climbed the stairs to her room, loaded with magazines, a book from the library ("Don't bring me a so-called funny book. They're never funny") and her mail. Every day she received dozens of letters from friends, from people she had worked with in the theatre and from some of the hundreds of students she had taught over the years either in the city or as actress-in-residence at various universities. They understood that they would not hear from her, except possibly a short note from me, but they sent a steady stream of cards, notes, funny messages, just something to keep contact.

As I came into her room, she was dozing. Her face was pale, white, skin drawn tight over fine bones, the lips in a smile, peaceful yet tentative. High forehead, hair cut away and scar still showing from her last operation. Her chin cupped in the canvas traction device, the straps running up the sides of her head and over the pulley at the head of the bed. It was the death mask of a medieval saint. Her breathing was shallow and short, little gusts of breath through her lips as though she were cooling her coffee or blowing fluff from a dandelion.

In the middle of the night, months before, "Chris, I can't breathe." I had sat upright and looked at the panic

[12]

in her face, and I too was seized with panic, and a feeling of helplessness. "Put her in a hospital, where she can be taken care of and where you won't have these terrible moments." "She has been in hospitals till she can't stand it. She wants to be home." I went into the next room to call the doctor. I was always going into the "next room," hiding around corners, whispering. Did I fool her?

"This is Doctor Schwartz's answering service. Is it an emergency?"

"Yes, it is."

"Hello, Doctor Schwartz, you don't know me, but I'm a patient of Doctor Morrison's, and he's out of town, and my wife . . ." and on through the whole story, while in the next room Fran was murmuring and starting to cry. And on the other end of the line Doctor Schwartz was arguing with me that in his opinion cancer patients should face up to the truth, and on my end I was telling him that our doctor, our doctors, had thought not, and what were we going to do? He went on to say that what she had probably done was to crack or break a rib, as she had broken other bones, and this was making breathing painful, but there was nothing he could do under the circumstances. Give her some Demerol.

In fury and rage (in other moments I realized that doctors can't rush around to everyone at all hours of the night) I returned to the dark bedroom and told her that the doctor had said "Demerol" . . . and I managed to get her to swallow it with a little water, and I propped her up and held her as she whimpered and gasped for breath. And then she turned and vomited up the pill and her supper and cried in despair and apologized and cried in pain, until finally by some miracle she fell asleep.

As I stood there in her doorway, my impulse was to leave her asleep. Asleep she was not in pain, she was not asking questions I could not answer. But since her last operation, certain pills had to be given at certain times to maintain the chemistry of her body. I put the mail on the bed and touched her hand.

"Mmmm?" She opened her eyes sleepily.

"Sorry, but it's time for pills."

"I just took some."

"Time for more."

"Those damned horse pills?"

"Yes." I fished among the bottles on her bedside table. "I brought the mail."

"That's nice." She reached down without moving her head and felt for the mail and held it above her head.

"There's a letter from David."

"What does he say?"

"I left it for you to open."

"That's a bill. I don't want any bills," and she skimmed the envelope to the bottom of the bed and picked up another letter. "Barbara called and said the party's at seven, but you should come over as early as you feel like."

I put the pill in her hand and held the glass with the bent straw. "I don't think I'll go."

Her hand stopped halfway to her mouth. "You've got to! You said you'd go. My God, you've got to get out of this house."

"I know you won't believe it, but I don't really enjoy those parties without you."

"I've made arrangements with Mrs. Nelson to stay until you come home. You've got to get out, Chris."

She was right that I needed to get out, but I hated being asked "How's Fran?" and having to go over and over the latest lie. I couldn't stand measuring off "improvements" which didn't alter for a moment the inevitable course of her disease.

And parties made me terribly lonely. All the lovely women, soft, healthy, alive. It reminded me of San Diego on my way back from the Pacific after the war, waiting for weeks for transportation East, being in civilization after months of shipboard life, and Fran in the East. It was too much.

"I know it's hard for you to believe, but I would honestly rather be here with you."

"I've made you a damned prisoner here."

"I get out. I was out this afternoon for two hours. I played tennis yesterday."

She started to cry. In another person it would be a petulant crying. In her it was just that everything was giving out. I sat on the side of the bed. It was impossible to hold her, done up as she was with traction and braces, but I put my head against her shoulder to comfort her.

"Please go. For me."

"All right."

"Get loaded. Get drunk. I told Barbara on the phone not to let them all go on and on asking about me. God, you must be sick of giving weather reports. I don't know how you've stood it."

There is no answer to something like that, except something which sounds mawkish. "I've stood it because I love you. I've stood it because what else could I do?"

What I said was "You've got to stop saying that, because I don't know what to say that isn't obvious . . . It's been a terrible time. I don't know how *you've* stood it all. I've stood nothing. You embarrass me even to mention it. But it hasn't all been terrible." I touched her face.

"I know . . . but, my God . . ." She took my hand and looked into my eyes. "Thank you."

I felt uncomfortable. There was so much to be said. Instead I kissed her cheek. How often physical intimacy had been a substitute for real intimacy! Unmentioned resentments which had never been resolved, but some kind of intimacy had been re-established in time through sexual need.

"There's always somebody there who'll want to play

bridge, and you haven't had a chance to play in months."

"I'll go." I smiled and got up.

"And don't rush home. Mrs. Nelson will be here, and if I need you, I've got the phone right here."

I shaved and showered and changed into slacks and a jacket in my workroom. I went back through the bathroom to get her ready for supper and to say "Good night."

"You should always wear blue," she said. "It's so wonderful with your eyes." Whenever she was away from me, on tour or making a film, she would bring me back blue shirts or blue ties or pajamas. "Stand up straight or you'll get a pot. Promise me you'll never get a pot. I'll kill you if you get a pot." And as I moved to her bed to release her from her traction and to put on her neck brace so that she could eat her dinner, she patted my belly with the back of her hand.

I carefully undid the straps under her chin, and holding her head and neck with one hand, slipped on her "horse collar," which permitted her to sit up a little straighter. It made her look like Erich Von Stroheim.

"You know, I think I'm shrinking."

"Shrinking?"

"Yes. I don't know. I just sense it. Soon I'll be just the right size for those pretty children's clothes I've always loved in Georg Jensen's."

"I don't think you're shrinking. How can you tell?"

"I feel shrunken."

"You're supposed to get taller when you've been in bed a long time. At least that's what they always told me when I was in bed with measles or chicken pox."

"Well, I'm shrinking." And she laughed a little hysterically.

I brushed her hair back and tied it with a pink ribbon, then brought her a basin so that she could wash her hands. I put her bedtray on her bed. "There!"

"If I feel like it, I might want to scribble a note or two

tonight, so leave my pad and pen near. Are they near?" She craned her neck stiffly to look at the night table.

"I'll leave them here." I put the pad and pen on a wide table made from a plank, which rested the length of the bed alongside her. Her radio was there. Her phonograph, and her cowbell to call for assistance, along with books and magazines.

I was being honest about wanting to stay home. Although the days were often very hectic—many errands, friends coming to visit, the neighbor lady helping out, alcohol rubs, sometimes the doctor, the solicitous telephone calls—the evenings, when everyone went home, were quiet. In a way we played house in our large bedroom. Gradually over the months this room had become our entire house, and it was as though we were back in Greenwich Village in our one-room five-flight walk-up.

It was a pleasant and cozy farmhouse room. In the winter I'd draw the curtains and light a fire, and we'd have drinks, and then I'd finish making dinner while she listened to the news. During dinner I'd put on a record, and sometimes when her arm got tired, I'd cut up her meat or feed her. And in spite of everything, it was good. It had always been good when we could be like this. We were in a chalet in the Swiss Alps with snow falling outside, or at our cottage at the beach on the Cape. We were "away," alone, as we so rarely had been in our lives.

Sometimes, when I would read to her, she would fall asleep, because she always had some dope in her. If I stopped reading, she would wake up, so I would try to go on reading and gradually trail my voice off. She would wake up and say, "Why have you stopped reading?"

"Because you dozed off."

"No, I didn't. I was listening."

Or I would lie on the bed beside her, and we would watch television. I had built a shelf up close to the ceiling, and put the television set up there so that she could watch it without sitting up. But by and large her interest span was short, and she preferred my reading.

It was the way I had always wanted it. The two of us alone.

"It's a lovely warm night. I'm going to walk over through the fields. You can watch me in the mirror."

She reached out her hand. "Have a good time. Stay as long as you like. I'm feeling pretty good tonight, so I should have a good night. And Mrs. Nelson's here, and will stay all night if you're late. Tell her to turn down the bed in your room."

I leaned over and kissed her forehead whcre the scar from her last operation crossed her hairline. Some hair was growing back just above it. "I love that fringe."

"I don't think it will ever grow enough to cover the scar."

"Of course it will. You'll start a new hair style." And I brushed it down a little and kissed it again.

She squeezed my hand and looked at me with her too-bright eyes and little set smile. "Thank you." I put my face next to hers and kissed her cheek and didn't move for a long moment. I wanted to take her up and hold her and kiss her and stroke her and just press her close in love and desperation. But it had been many, many months since I could do that because each bone was riddled with disease and fragile or cracked or broken.

Only three weeks before we had been sent to a new doctor who might have some new answer. I had had the ambulance come for her and take her to the hospital, and they had put her in a wheelchair, and we had sat in the doctor's examining room answering questions. He had said, "Now help me lift her onto the table." I had said, "I don't think we can do it." "Oh, yes. It will be all right." And we had lifted, and there had been a sound like a shot, and Fran had screamed, and we had gone on and laid her on the table. I had said, "I think we've done something."

He gave her a shot of Demerol and said, "No. Just a tendon or muscle that hasn't been used."

"If we've done something, we're in a hospital now, and shouldn't we . . . ?"

"No, no. Believe me."

He had poked and sounded and said he knew of nothing we could do for her that wasn't being done now. The ambulance had taken her home, and I had called my doctor, and he came, and the leg was broken, but there was no point in trying to set it, since there was nothing there to mend, and since then her leg as well as her neck had been in traction.

Now, saying good night, I gently pressed her face to mine. I had an instant erection for this crumpled, broken little person. And I turned away slowly so that she would not notice.

It had happened often before. Once, when I was giving her an alcohol rub and she was lying on her stomach, and the feel of her, even broken as she was, and the memory. The little purple crosses of indelible ink on her spine, marks so that the technicians administering the cobalt treatment would know where the cancer was, where to aim. And I had wanted to cry for the thousandth time, and I had leaned over and kissed her buttocks, and she had murmured into the pillow and said, "I can't wait for us to be able to get back to the good stuff." And I had gently reached my hand around to her belly and asked, "Would you like it if I . . . ?" and I had begun to stroke her. And her voice became a little querulous. "No . . . no. I don't think I could take it." I continued stroking for a few moments more to see if she wanted to try it. "No. No. But soon we can be together the way we should be." I left my hand there.

"I just thought it might be good for you."

"No. Not yet. It would be too much."

I kissed her buttocks again. "Beautiful."

"Not very." She snickered. She could never take compliments, and now I knew she felt most un-beautiful.

"You can't see, and I can." And I kissed her again, this time on the spine, on one of those purple crosses. I wanted to turn her over and show her my erection, to show her that she still excited me.

Before the breast operation she had worried so and cried. She had felt that after, she would be unlovable. Her first night home I had kissed every part of her body that wasn't bandaged and we had made desperate love through her tears. And she had been reassured.

"Bring me back all the gossip."

"I will." I rose and started for the door. "Are you ready for your dinner?"

"Yes."

"It smells good."

"Hold in your pot."

"I don't have a pot. I'm thin as a rail. That's my problem."

"There's nothing more disgusting than a pot on a thin man." I straightened up and sucked in my gut. "That's better."

I started down the stairs, then stopped and waved from the landing, but she was already reaching for her pad to make sure it was handy.

I gave Mrs. Nelson a few instructions in the kitchen and left. As I reached the middle of the lawn, I turned and looked up at the mirror outside the window and waved, and headed out on the path across the meadow.

THREE

Barbara and Dan Maxwell were our closest local friends. When we had moved to the farm eight years before, we had found them as our nearest neighbors a quarter of a mile away. Dan was an artist who also taught at the college in the next town, where Fran had conducted an acting seminar one spring. He called Barbara "Wife." It became her nickname among the men. There was something amusing and yet very intimate about calling her that. She was a soft and lovely woman, now in her mid-thirties, a great homemaker, very warm and friendly, and it was nice to call her "Wife."

The party was very much as I had expected, and feared. The most conspicuous person there was not there,

Fran. Though she had asked Barbara to keep the guests from talking about her and her health, it could not be avoided. She was a "dear" friend to all of them. They were all concerned about her, and worse than that, they all wanted to make this a great night out for me. I was not allowed to help. I was not allowed to make my own drinks.

But it went reasonably well, and they played bridge because they knew I liked to play (and Fran did not like cards). Sometime after midnight I went to the bathroom off the bedroom upstairs. When I came out, Barbara was at the dresser, leaning towards the mirror putting on lipstick. She looked at me, startled.

"Sorry, the john downstairs was busy."

"I just didn't know anyone was in there." She looked at me a moment. "This is no good for you, is it?"

"I've been having a good time. But I think I'll be taking off now."

"I have instructions from Fran to keep you here till the bitter end." She smiled. "How are things, really?"

"I think her courage is giving out, but aside from that . . ."

"What do they think will happen next? I mean . . ."

"Nobody knows. It's just a question of what it strikes next. And, of course, there's always a chance of what they call spontaneous remission."

She looked at me. "You look awful. I know I've said it a dozen times, but can't you get away . . . at all?"

"I don't want to get away. When I'm away, I feel lonely. I feel she's already gone, and I get the terrible sense of what it's going to be like after. When I'm with her, she's not dying. She's all trussed up, but she's very much alive, making lists of things to do, phone calls, little notes. She's always created life around her. You know that."

We looked at each other for a few moments. The sympathy I was beginning to hate, or rather needed but couldn't handle, came into her eyes. She took a step towards me, and putting her face against mine, patted my shoulder. Suddenly I grabbed her and crushed her to me, clutched her body against mine and kissed her hair and her face and her lips. Then I stepped back, eyes closed, ashamed. "I'm sorry."

She touched my cheek with her hand. "Don't be. My God, after all . . ."

"I know, but . . ." I shook my head, embarrassed. "Thanks, Barbara. I'm sorry. I . . ." She just stood there looking at me in such a way that I knew I could kiss her again, hold her again. But the whole thing had suddenly changed. My impulsive need to hold, to touch, to fondle a healthy body had changed to something else. I was being offered some kind of pity or sympathy which I couldn't take. The situation made me a "privileged person," but taking advantage of the privilege seemed somehow cheap to me.

"I'm going to just disappear. Will you say good night for me?" I looked at her and then reached out and put my hand against her cheek. "Thanks." And I left.

FOUR

I walked over the meadow, confused and embarrassed by Barbara's apparent willingness. My body was
heavy with hunger. It wanted to press against something,
into something. What do you do? What the hell do you
do? Absurdly I almost threw my arms around a tree, remembering many years ago on a walk through the woods
when I had suddenly pressed Fran against a tree and
hugged her and the tree at the same time.

Mrs. Nelson was sitting in the kitchen, asleep in front
of the television set, the volume turned low. I put my hand
on her arm.

"Oh!" She looked around, orienting herself. "I must
have dozed off. Is everything all right?"

"Yes."

She got up.

"Do you want to sleep here, or can I drive you home?"

"What time is it?" We both looked up at the kitchen clock.

"Twelve-thirty."

"I'll drive myself home . . . Everything's fine upstairs. She went to sleep around nine o'clock, I think. I turned your bed down. Did you have a good time?"

"More or less. Thank you for staying."

She put on her bulky cardigan and picked up her enormous purse. "Well, I'll see you tomorrow."

"I do appreciate your staying so late."

"I watch TV one place or the other. Doesn't make much difference." She giggled and closed the door behind her. I stood at the window and watched her drive away, then switched off the outside light.

I poured a drink and found myself pressing against the counter. Something. Anything.

I turned out the light in the kitchen and went into the hall and looked up the stairs at Fran's door, deciding I wouldn't go up to my room just yet. Maybe if I got myself a little more loaded I would either jerk off or forget about the whole thing. I flopped on the sofa.

I had talked to our doctor once, during a physical exam. Casually I had said that though it was unimportant, Fran's being sick was all very rough sexually. I don't know what I expected him to say. He was sympathetic but said that nocturnal emissions should relieve the situation.

It had been so long now since Fran had been able to do anything. After that first night home from the hospital five years ago, we had managed for a while. She would never let me see her naked, but we got to the point where I could joke that I was never a breast man anyway, which she knew was a lie. And she would never again make love

[25]

with the light on or even our "fucking lamp," a small antique silver candlestick we had bought many years ago.

But we managed, she maybe fighting off her many fears with this most living act, and I out of a determination that she should know that she was loved. As she became more undesirable to me as a body (it is somehow shocking to vent lust on a dying body), she became dearer to me as a person, and that made it all possible.

And there had been good periods during the five years, between operations and treatments, when to all intents and purposes she seemed active and healthy, but then with new pains they had decided to sterilize her with X-ray in the hope of stopping the spread of the disease. I had had to sign the paper agreeing to the sterilization, and that night before it was done, we had made long and tender love with no joy but only sorrow, she ending not in orgasm but in tears.

The cobalt treatments left her exhausted, and the sterilization on top of the breast operation left her feeling like a neuter, and nothing I could do could change her feelings.

So for a very long time now there had been nothing. There really could be nothing between us, and for a while there was nothing for me too. And then occasionally in desperation I would return to "solitary practices" of adolescence, ashamed and disgusted.

And then, Sarah . . .

It had been on one of my trips into the city. This time to see my editor. And late in the afternoon he had had to rush out to a literary cocktail party and had left me in his office looking over a contract. His not-so-young, not-so-pretty secretary had made me a drink, and we had started to talk, and like a dam breaking I had told her everything about Fran. We had gone out to dinner, and then to her fourth-floor walk-up apartment in the Village, and though it was obvious that it was pity and compassion and that she was ministering to me, I took it . . . because to lie there naked and fondle and kiss breasts, to make love to a body that could bear the weight and thrust of another body—no scars, no little purple crosses, no bones which might snap . . .

Though I went back to her a number of times, I was ashamed of just using her. She claimed it was not that, but I felt nothing for her except lust and gratitude. Oh, we were tender with each other, but I couldn't interest myself in her life as a lover should, and though I listened and tried to return some of her sympathy, it was all a fake. All I was interested in was lying in bed with her and finding oblivion in her lush body. I wouldn't take her out to dinner the nights I stayed in town. I wouldn't be seen in public with her. She said she didn't mind this, but I did.

I had never been able to bring myself to just pick up a girl and lay her. I hated words like lay, bang, screw. They all seemed to describe things you did to someone, not with someone. Once on a visit to a mining town when I was around fifteen, I had gone with a group of older boys to a crib and watched a young man "screw" a whore. It was my first experience with sexual intercourse, doing or watching. We had financed the exhibition. The young man had just been loitering in the area unable to afford a girl. I could never forget the contempt in the girl's eyes as she lay back lifeless and let it be done to her, and finally her flat "Are you through?"

It had been three months since I had told Sarah that I couldn't see her any more. She had been surprised that I felt any qualms about seeing her. "What you do here has no relationship to what you feel for your wife." But it was impossible for me to disconnect. I came from that generation that was programmed to connect.

"Everyone would understand." But it was not an image of myself I could live with. I seemed to prefer "I don't know how you stand it." I was pained by the hypocrisy of seeming to be a stoic and yet rushing off for a comforting "fast fuck" in dark corners.

Thinking of Sarah, even in rejecting her, I was aroused by the memory of her fleshy, "odalisque" body with its strong odors which repelled and excited me. I turned and pressed myself against the pillows at the back of the couch. And even as I started to let myself go, I felt an irrational resentment against Fran that I should be reduced to this.

Then suddenly I stood up, gulped my drink and headed for the stairs. I could put up with the discomfort and tension easier than the inevitable self-disgust which followed. Perhaps tomorrow I would go to New York to see Sarah.

Though I usually slept in my workroom on nights when I had been out late, tonight I would crawl into the large bed beside Fran and at least touch some part of her body. In her drugged sleep she would murmur an acknowledgment that I was there, and her frail warm hand would tighten on mine, and she would be asleep again in a moment. I would eventually go to sleep somehow comforted by self-righteous thoughts of my own decency.

FIVE

I went to my room, undressed and put on my pajamas, turned out the light and went into the bathroom between our rooms. I looked at myself in the mirror. There was a trace of Barbara's lipstick on my cheek. Had Mrs. Nelson seen it? I wiped off the lipstick and dropped the tissue in the wastebasket and washed my face. Then I took the tissue from the wastebasket and dropped it in the toilet. I left the small night light on in the bathroom and quietly turned the knob of the door into Fran's room.

In the faint light I could see her lying there on her back, her chin cupped by the canvas traction device; at the foot of the bed, the sandbag for the leg traction. I closed the door and moved quietly to my side of the bed, turned back the covers and slid in. So far I had not disturbed her. I lay back, happy that I had made this decision, more comfortable than I had been all evening. The nearer I came to the day when Fran would be gone, the more I realized how much she was the condition of my life.

I slid my hand along the sheet and touched the sleeve of her flannel nightgown. I moved my fingers down her arm to her hand. Her fingers did not close around mine. She did not murmur.

I held my breath, listening for her breathing, the gentle puffing. I heard nothing.

Was she dead? How could she be dead? Only hours before she had been so alive, had said she had had a good day. All the months I had wanted her to die quietly in her sleep. Now the idea was intolerable.

After a few moments I slowly got out of bed and moved around to her side, never taking my eyes off the shadowy figure. I leaned closer to catch her breathing. Nothing. I couldn't see anything clearly in the faint light from the windows. I swung her light away from the bed so that it would not shine in her eyes and lowered it beneath the level of the bed and turned it on.

I looked back at Fran and moved closer. Was she breathing or wasn't she? I touched her hand and tried to find her pulse. There was none. Yes there was. Or was there? It had always been difficult to find her pulse. I moved my finger, pressed harder. There was!

I reached for the phone and dialed the operator to call the ambulance. Then I saw the blue envelope with my name written on it in her beautiful script. I froze. Cradling the phone at my neck and looking over at Fran, I opened the envelope and looked at the note. It began:

Dear Chris:
 If you should come back too soon, please, please, let me go!

[30]

"This is the operator. May I help you?"

I looked at the bottles on the table. The Demerol and sleeping-pill bottles were empty.

"This is the operator . . ."

I hung up the phone and closed my eyes. She had done it! For months somewhere in the back of my mind had been the thought that she might do this. Oh, Jesus! I looked at her and then back at the letter.

> I'm so tired. I know it's just a matter of time, and what's the use? I have so often wished that I would just not wake up one morning. But it hasn't happened that way. Do you remember when we were young, we agreed that if this happened to either one of us, we'd have the decency to let the other one go . . . would even help?
>
> There comes a time for letting go. You know I've always said this about friends and people. Now you must let me go.
>
> I wish I could be with you to comfort you as you have comforted me. It will be easy for me. Hard for you.
>
> You've been so good to me. Thank you.
>
> I've been so proud of the way you've grown and of your work . . .
>
> Don't stay by yourself. See people . . .

She moaned, just a low, small moan. How many times she had said "If I moan a little, it helps. But you shouldn't listen." Now there was this moan from some part of her which was still feeling or dreaming. But another part of her had said "Let me go!"

I wanted her alive in whatever condition, because taking care of her had become my life. But I felt a flash of anger that I should be put in this position. I had wanted her to die quietly, but now I was the one to make the decision. In my fantasies it had all just happened. Now I had to make it happen or at least allow it to happen.

I wanted to touch her. I didn't want to touch her. If she were going to die, I wanted her to die quietly. No struggle. She moaned again. Oh, God, don't wake up! Because only that part of you which hurts and wants help will wake up, and not the Fran who wrote "Let me go."

What would happen? I would call the doctor or the ambulance from the Volunteer Fire Department. The doctor might say, "Let her die." But he couldn't. Once he knew, his ethics would not let him say it. If I called, I could not ask for an opinion. It would be to save her. And what for? For me, really. To save her for more pain and God knows what kind of end.

Only a few hours ago we had joked. We talked. We remembered. What is living but that? She ate. She read. If I brought her back, all this could go on. And I hadn't said "Good-bye."

In spite of her letter, did she really want to be saved? I knew that people often tried to commit suicide to communicate how desperate they were, but they hoped to be saved. Had she done this? Her way of forcing us to face the reality of her death together? Yet she knew that tonight after the party I would sleep in my own room.

I looked around for a clue. A list on her table of things to do, people to call, mostly to help other people get jobs or make contacts. But that was a list that had been there several days.

God, when do you give up? When was the right time? For five years we had fought for every day. New doctors had taken me aside and said, "It will be over soon. Any time." And each time I had looked at them and had said we had fought for every chance, we weren't going to give up. Tomorrow they might come up with something. Who knows? It will be on some "tomorrow." Why not tomorrow?

What if we had given up four years ago when the doctor had said to me, "We couldn't get it all. We told you we did to give you time without this hanging over you."

There had been months free of pain. And then the cobalt and months again, and the operation, heroic efforts. But what about now? The spinal column was going, the leg was broken and impossible to set . . . the ribs. Had she known all this time and held on until *she* knew it was hopeless, there would be no more months, no more weeks when she could be up and about and pretending that everything was going to be all right? "If I drink more milk, maybe these old bones will mend." Could she have said that and known that she would never get well?

But she knew now. And she wanted to die.

And standing there looking down at her, I knew I would let her die. And I started to cry quietly. I wanted to run away, not to be there, not to be responsible for this last act, not to have this last responsibility forced on me. But I stayed. And I knew I would go over and over that moment the rest of my life; wondering why I had let her die.

I didn't want to touch her because that might bring her closer to consciousness, and I couldn't take that. She had not responded to my touch before. And yet I wanted to touch her. To hold her. I wanted to unfasten her from all the contraptions which had imprisoned her for months and hold her shriveled broken little body. In spite of my fears, I put my hand in her hand, and her fingers closed a little, and her eyebrows seemed to go up a little in recognition.

We had had a game we called "Dove." One of us would make a small fist and place it in the other's hand, and the other would make a nest for it with palm and fingers.

I did not want her to stir. I couldn't let her go if she stirred. She moved her head slightly in the direction of the light and frowned. With my other hand, I reached over and turned out the light. I reached behind me and pulled up a chair and sat down and pressed my head against the side of the bed and stayed there until her hand turned cold.

When she was finally gone, and the exact moment was impossible to know . . . she would seem to be gone, and then there would be a small sigh, and then another . . . But when there was no doubt, I let myself cry out loud. I didn't want to live, but I knew I would live. I had glibly written others in their grief, "The last act of love is to survive." I would survive.

Finally I opened my eyes and looked at Fran in the first light, and wished I hadn't. Had the eyes been open all the time, the lips drawn back in a hideous grimace? I wanted to get out and I wanted to stay. I knew I was supposed to close the eyes. Why is that? I knew I had to close the eyes or leave the room and not come back until someone else had done it. Remove yourself from the moment, the act, and just do it! I did it.

But then there was the mouth. I did not want to remember her this way, but it was past wanting or not wanting. This was the way I would remember her. I looked down at the twisted, rumpled body, the body we had tried to patch and keep together for five years. Now it was all over. There would be no more pain, no more moans, no more lies. Now all the ropes and pulleys and sandbags and braces and corsets could be thrown away. The body could be touched, moved, arranged, without pain. I pulled the covers over her face and went into my room and lay down on the bed, and overwhelmed by emptiness and questions I could not cope with, I drifted into sleep.

SIX

When I awoke, it took me some moments to remember what had happened. When I did, I wanted to go back to sleep again. But I knew I should call the doctor. I should call David.

What should I tell them? The doctor obviously would have to know that she had taken the sleeping pills. But would I tell him that I had stood by and let her die? I had, hadn't I? . . . There was probably no reason not to tell him. He had said a number of times, "We'll do all we can to hold down the pain at the end, but you can never tell." I decided not to tell him, since I could hardly admit it to myself.

My guilt took precedence over my grief, and I broke

out into a sweat and played the moment over again. I called the doctor, the ambulance, they managed to wake her, to save her, and now I was holding her, and we were both crying, sharing at last the awful knowledge that she was going to die. Later, but much, much later, when the pain got unbearable, I would even help her, as we had promised when we were young. We would be so close by then, so trusting, that I could help her . . .

But it had not been that way.

And it had not been that way five years before when while making love I had first felt the small lump and had said nothing. Why? Oh, God, why? Instinctive fear. My mother's warning, "You must be very careful of women's breasts"? And then a cancer appeal for funds had listed the danger signals. Such ignorance was unforgivable. But now again, as I had for so many times in the last year, I compulsively played the scene over again. "Darling, this small lump . . ." And we are in time. And . . . and . . .

I closed my eyes tight to block the images, but "the show" had begun, and it would not stop till it had played itself out, and I was left exhausted.

I would not tell David. The doctor would probably not put down suicide if I asked him not to. I could never tell David that I had stood by while she died. I could never tell anyone.

David would probably approve of his mother's taking her own life. Something right and gallant about it. Knowing of her suicide would confirm for David that she knew the truth, and he would have been ashamed and angry that we had not faced it with her.

When the doctor arrived, I showed him Fran's letter, which I told him I had found just this morning when I had come in to see how she was. He said "It was for the best" and that he would put down as cause of death "uremic poisoning" developing from the cancer.

[36]

When the undertaker came, the doctor tried to keep me involved with details in my room, but I looked out the window and saw them carrying Fran away, bundled in a blanket as though to keep her from being cold. I resented their taking her away. These last years she had been my charge, my whole existence. I had had her home with me. Wanderers, we had had a home. She had been dependent on me, and I no less dependent on her. They were taking away my wife and my reason for getting up in the morning. When things had been at their most terrible, I had collected pamphlets on distant tropic islands. And I had fantasied myself on those islands "when all this is over." But now I did not want those islands. I wanted my bondage, my pain, my anguish, my life. And they were taking her across the lawn and away.

SEVEN

I longed to disappear up into our woods, to take
Fran up there to our pine grove and bury her and stay
there with her until I died or found some reason for living.
But instead, in a kind of limbo of shock, I dutifully went
to the undertaker in the next town, made arrangements
and came back to the house. The driveway and street were
filled with cars of friends and neighbors who had lovingly
come to share what I could really only share with Fran.
And because that is what Fran would have done, I took
over the proceedings, making introductions, passing coffee
and cakes, arranging transportation for people up from
New York, answering phones, receiving telegrams, and

comforting those who had come to comfort. "Fran was so fond of you. You were so good to her."

Most of the people were Fran's friends, and mine only by association. For many of them I had always been the rather offish and detached husband who had tried to keep Fran to himself. They knew that I had often resented the particular Fran they had lost, the kind and loving friend who never said "No," who seemed always to put their interests, their problems, above her own. Many of the friends were hurt that some had known and they had not. "Oh, you knew?"

"Yes."

"I see."

The newspapers called to work up an obituary. Months before I had prepared an obituary. It had seemed ghoulish, but I wanted to do it. A first step in continuing her life after death. But now I was embarrassed at having written it all out, and I asked a director who had known her for years to take over.

"What are the plans for the funeral?"

"I haven't made them yet."

"Where will the burial be?"

"I wanted it here on the farm, but the undertaker says it's not allowed."

"Chris, I know how you feel, but believe me, that wouldn't be wise. You might want to sell the place, and . . . After Charlotte died, I never came near our house again. I arranged for someone to sell it and I took off."

Friend after friend came up and took me by the elbow. "I know this is no time to give advice, but—" "Don't do anything sudden." "Get away from here as soon as you can." "Don't be brave. It's got to hit you. Let it hit you now and get it over with." "Get rid of everything. Otherwise, land mines and booby traps the rest of your life." "What are your plans?" "We're going on a cruise. Would you like to come along?"   "Don't be alone."   "Time. Remember time heals all wounds."

I bobbed my head to all this, not knowing what I would do, only sensing that a terrible thing had happened to me and I was absurdly hosting a party.

Barbara took me gently by the elbow and led me aside. "Chris, the undertaker called and said he'd forgotten to tell you that he'd need some clothes. Do you want me to take care of that?"

"I told him I wanted the casket closed."

"Yes, of course. But still he said they'd need some clothes. What about the lovely pale silk she always looked so pretty in?"

Incredible thoughts and images. Silk. I thought of Fran lying in the New England hills in silk and that she'd be cold. How long would I consider her alive? One friend had said, "It takes nine months for a person to be born. It takes at least as long for her to die."

"Let me go up and look, Barbara."

"Are you sure you want to? Mrs. Nelson and I could . . ."

"No. I want to get away for a moment anyway." And we started up the stairs.

I entered our bedroom and stopped. The room had been transformed. The women had been at work. The bed was off the blocks, the medicines gone, the pulleys and sandbags, the reading stand I had built for Fran. Every trace of Fran and her illness was gone.

I was outraged. There seemed to be some conspiracy to take Fran away from me. To pretend that nothing had happened. The room looked like a motel room ready for its next occupant. As I looked around, Mrs. Nelson whipped the leather "horse collar" behind her back. "We've almost got it back to rights again. If you'll tell me what you want done with the clothes . . ." She caught the look in my eye and stopped. "Well, I'll be downstairs."

"Thank you, Mrs. Nelson. I appreciate it. You were awfully kind to Fran." I took the neck brace from her, gently, as she passed. She seemed to want to protest. But she didn't.

Barbara said, "You don't want to go through all her dresses, Chris. It'll be terrible for you. Let me . . ."

But I wanted to. I felt cold inside from being distracted. I somehow wanted to feel the warmth of my grief. I opened the door and looked at the dresses, and immediately turned away. Barbara reached in and took out a dress. I didn't watch her. She closed the closet door.

"I'll take care of this. Why don't you lie down a moment? You're exhausted."

I nodded my head. As she left, closing the door behind her, I caught a glimpse of pale silk.

I sat on the edge of the freshly made bed, wanting tears. I wanted to return to the real situation of only a few hours ago. Fran here, still with me, though lifeless. My charge. "They" had taken her away from me as "they" had done so often over the years.

I looked at the "horse collar" in my hands. I brought it to my face and smelled Fran's odors worked into the soft leather. This should have done it. But all I managed was a few impotent whimpers, almost mechanical, like a finger thrust down the throat to induce vomiting. Then, nothing.

I lay back across the foot of the bed and closed my eyes and waited. Then some part of me, the Fran-social part, began to say, "Your absence will be noted. People down there will be uncomfortable. You're very conspicuous by your absence. Grandstanding. People want to see you, to talk to you about their feelings for Fran. You are what is left of Fran. You have an obligation . . . Later. Later. There will be time later."

EIGHT

David arrived from college in midafternoon. I
was listening to someone tell a funny anecdote about
Fran, and smiling when I looked up and saw him standing
in the hall. I moved towards him at once, and suddenly the
laughter and chatter stopped, almost guiltily, as people
watched us.

David moved away from the hall, instinctively feeling
that the moment of our meeting should not be public. He
was in the upstairs hall when I reached him. I put my arm
around him. Who comforts whom? It is not a question of
that. It's a quick clutching and holding and patting. An
awkward sharing of a loss by two men who had rarely
shown emotion to each other.

We moved towards Fran's room. "I'm glad you're here."

"Gretchen didn't feel she should come. She felt she might be . . . I don't know . . . that perhaps it might be awkward." Gretchen was a girl living with David in Boston.

As we moved into Fran's room, he looked down the stairs at the friends, who had resumed their talking and laughing. "I know it seems incongruous, David, but they all loved her very much, and after they've said how sorry they are, there isn't much for them to do. But they want to stay, to be close. They're telling lovely and often very funny stories about your mother."

David nodded his head. He looked around his mother's room. Someone had added a bowl of fresh flowers since I had been there last. "Some of her friends came in and cleaned it all up while I was at the undertaker's. I was upset when I saw it, but they meant well. The idea was to remove all traces of her. Which is not what I wanted and probably not what you want."

"Where is she now?"

"At the undertaker's. She'll be . . . well, if you remember my dad's funeral, you know what goes on."

"It just seems impossible. I talked with her last night. She called me."

I was suddenly on my guard. I wondered what she had said. "What time was that?"

"Oh, just after seven. She said you had gone to a party. We just talked . . . about . . . things." He shook his head in disbelief. "Were you sleeping in here? What happened?"

"No. You know sometimes I did and sometimes I didn't. She'd made me go to this party Barbara and Dan Maxwell were giving . . ." I was angry with myself for feeling that I had to defend myself for going to a party. He was looking at me with the frown he had had ever since he entered the house. "I hadn't been out at night for weeks, and . . ." I could see that he wished I wouldn't explain. "Anyway, I came in late. Mrs. Nelson had been here with your mother. And I came in here to check on things. Your mother seemed to be sleeping well, so I went back to my room and went to bed. When I came in this morning, she was . . ."

David shook his head. "She was alone then?"

I resented the tone of accusation. After all the years of caring and tending . . . I wanted to blurt out that she had not been alone, that I had sat over there holding her hand. "The doctor says she probably died in her sleep, with no pain or . . ." I was about to say "struggle" but I remembered, heard again, the faint moans, and I didn't say it.

There was a burst of laughter from downstairs. David could turn his emotion against the friends. "I won't have to go down and be nice to all those people, will I?"

"Not if you don't want to. We have to set a time for the funeral. Have you any thoughts?" He shook his head. "What about the day after tomorrow? Are your exams over by then?"

He nodded his head. "I could stay over the weekend. I should be back on Monday afternoon."

"Of course. Whenever you feel you have to go back." It was so like him, at least in his relationship with me, to mark off the limits of his stay, his involvement, before committing himself. His route of withdrawal was always clearly marked and open. As an essentially private person myself, I could understand this. The fear of being committed without time limits.

"We have no burial plot. I was wondering which would be the better place. Here in the village, or down on the Cape. Do you have any thoughts on it?" He shook his head, staring at the bed. "She has many friends in both places. We always loved the cottage down there, but this is

[44]

more home, I suppose, and nearer her theatre friends in New York."

"Wherever you'd like. Did she ever say anything about it?"

"No. A friend died here in the village, and we were at the burial, and she did say something about its being a lovely place."

"She didn't mention anything about being cremated?"

"No."

"That's what I would want."

I didn't answer for a moment. "I know it makes sense, and it's probably what I would want for myself, but it's not what I want for her." He looked at me. How to explain to a rational, logical young man that all the images are terrible, consumed by fire, buried in the earth. Perhaps shock keeps our imaginations from going beyond the moment of burial, and the person remains in our minds forever there in the earth. But when the body is consumed by fire, there can be no blocking out of the reality that all that is left are the ashes. I couldn't tolerate the idea of her not being there, but to go further and cut off so quickly the existence of the shape, the form.

"Would you come along with me to the cemetery and help pick out a place?"

He looked at me a long time, wondering, I suppose, if he should have any part in a procedure of which he disapproved. "If you want me to."

"I know you'll have to turn around and get back to college for your exams, but . . ."

"No. No. I have time."

Just as he was always eager to set the limits of his commitment, I was always anxious to let him know that he was free to go, to leave, to take off whenever he wanted to. Or to come. My father had been so insistent, had made so many and such continuing demands on my time and affec-

[45]

tion that I never wanted David to feel that he *had* to do anything or *had* to be anywhere for my sake. I made it clear to him that I had no compulsion about the family being together for Thanksgiving, Easter, Christmas, Mother's Day and Father's Day. Had he misinterpreted and come to think I didn't really care if he was around or not?

NINE

I told Barbara and Mrs. Nelson where we were going. David went down the back way to avoid the people, and we met out by the driveway. My car was hopelessly blocked, so we went in David's old MG. It was rare for me to sit anywhere but in the driver's seat. I found it difficult to be a passenger. I noticed that when he got behind the wheel and turned on the ignition, David felt more at ease, assured, than he had been since he arrived.

I'm sure that those left behind felt that now father and son would be off alone and they would really talk. But as we drove along, we had nothing to say to each other except small talk.

David had lost his mother, whom he adored. I had

lost my wife. Perhaps we were jealous of each other's right to grieve and yet at the same time did not want to express our grief in competition with each other. Neither of us felt free to impose our sorrow on the other. As the father, I made every effort to acknowledge David's anguish, to draw it forth with sympathy. He was having none of it. I understood. I had never confided in my father.

He pulled the car up alongside the cemetery and we got out. For months I had passed this cemetery knowing that one day I would be stopping, moving in, choosing a plot. When I had driven Fran around those last months, we had unavoidably had to pass it several times, and she had looked long at it each time and said nothing.

It is a beautiful spot, a country burial ground just outside the village, with the white houses and church spires in the distance and on a nearby hill, the Catholic burial ground. It was too bad we had not done this years before or that there had not been some family plot with room for another grave. Less than twenty-four hours ago I had been sitting on her bed joking with her as I tied a ribbon in her crazy-cropped hair, and now we were out here on a New England slope looking for a piece of earth for her to lie in. How sudden! At least I had been with her when she died, had had those hours after to sit there before everything started happening.

I thought perhaps we should have brought a few friends. There was a reason for the chatter of friends, the distractions. When there were many, you could wander off and be alone for a moment till you could get control. Someone else would carry on, pass the time. But not to wander off, to stop and turn and look at the distant hills was to impose emotions on the other. As the father I had the responsibility.

"The central area, as you see, is pretty much filled. They're spreading to the slopes on either side across the paths down there and over there."

Not saying anything, we started down one of the dirt roadways. Elms on either side. I was glad in a way that there was no room left in the center portion where villagers had been buried for two hundred years. The slopes on the other side were almost idyllic. Cows were feeding in the pasture beyond the fence. Hers would be the first grave there. She would be alone. Incredible to think like this. Alone. She was dead. Of course she was alone. I also thought, Fran would not want to be alone. Fran loved people, lots of people. It was I who liked to be alone. Or with her.

I stopped at a small knoll which looked out across the fields. It was a picture-book spot, sheltered by an elm. I turned to ask David what he thought about it, but he wasn't there. He was wandering down the road, his hands thrust in his pockets, ostensibly bending over from time to time to read the names on the crumbling headstones. I turned away so that he would not find me watching him, and walked down to the fence and looked at the cows and at the field beyond. I was not there. As so often before, I had made myself not be there. The father was there, the man responsibly making funeral arrangements was there. But something inside was saying, "These last things I will do that must be done, and then Fran and I will go away together . . ."

Finally, out of the corner of my eye I saw David standing where he had left me. I walked back up the slope. "Did you find any spot you liked over there?"

"This is nice right here." He scuffed the ground.

"Yes, but if you found a place . . ."

"No. This is fine."

"It's a nice spot."

"Yes." And he started back to the car.

TEN

The country church was filled to overflowing. And some of her students had even gathered outside on the steps; people had come from all over the country for the funeral. As my sister and I stood in the vestry before the service, greeting friends and many people whom I had never met before, one young actress who had studied with Fran said, "I knew how important she was to me, but I had no idea she'd been that important to so many people."

My editor was there with his wife. Sarah, his secretary, had come along too. I wished she hadn't. I wanted it to be as though she had never been.

"I'm terribly sorry. Keep in touch, please!"

Finally it was time to go into the church. David appeared from nowhere, having shunned the greetings in the vestry. I shifted into neutral, determined not to be reached, and sat down between my sister and David.

Everything seemed to be arranged to appeal to the emotions which in friends were sad and acceptable but in the immediate survivor impossible and intolerable. So for the last two days I had shut myself off. And I had found that even when I was alone, my emotions were sealed off.

The night before, I had gone to the funeral parlor and asked to be alone, shut in with Fran. "Well, Fran, here we are." But nothing had happened. I had sat there dry-eyed. It was too much of a set piece. It was something that was supposed to be, and it just wouldn't be. As I sat there waiting for my tears, I incongruously remembered we had known this sometimes in our love-making, an anniversary that we had tried to honor appropriately in bed, and we had not felt like it. I left the chair near the coffin, unsatisfied and unrelieved.

Now I looked up and saw the display of flowers and was almost overwhelmed. The church seemed literally filled with flowers. I should have said "No flowers," but I hadn't. Somehow I had wanted but not expected this. It seemed as though her whole life and its importance was being defined by this response.

In a profession so full of bitter jealousies, Fran had been an exception. She was inordinately kind and thoughtful to everyone. She had always seemed to be much prouder of young people she had taught and helped than of her own accomplishments.

At the height of her career as an actress she had made the decision to spend a certain part of each year teaching young people about the theatre—conducting acting classes, directing them in college plays, instilling in them the joy and discipline of the theatre experience. She had one child, David, but many "children."

But this goodness was also tough. She had no patience

with anyone who wouldn't try, who wouldn't work, who was easily discouraged or quit under fire. I remembered once in Washington when she was co-starring in a play which was in trouble, and the director, one of her "children," started drinking and evading the problems and finally decided to withdraw from the production. I sat in the hotel bedroom with the door closed, and listened to her give him a tongue-lashing such as I had never heard from man or woman. He stayed on with the show. He pulled it through. And some years later, when he was directing one of the major productions of the American theatre, and she was in the hospital for the fifth time, he called her to tell her that the curtain was up on the opening night and how grateful he was for that tongue-lashing.

Playwrights who gave up out of town or who wanted to quit writing after a set of unfair reviews, young actresses who despaired of ever doing what the director wanted, stage managers driven to distraction by neurotic, exhausted directors—these were her children. She listened to them, she commiserated for just so long, and then she insisted on action.

As I looked at the flowers and the crowded church, I kept thinking, "She would never believe this." Though I think she longed to be loved, I don't think she ever really knew how loved she was. I had always been proud of what she did and what she was, and especially in the last years, when I knew she was going to die, I had reached out for every small piece of praise and love and appreciation to bring it close to her. In a sense, I had stood there holding the door open, wanting all love and honor and affection to come to her bedside so that she might know who she was before she died.

But this! I sat there forcing my mind into neutral corners. Appeal after emotional appeal was made as the minister and friends talked about Fran, and about us. "An exceptionally devoted couple." "She had the mothering instinct. She left her memorial in each of us." "We each did our best to live up to Fran's expectations for us." I struggled to think about taxes or the buttons on the prayer stool in front of me.

At last it was over, and we moved out of the church and stood around on the lawn and shook hands and kissed, waiting for the undertaker to remove the coffin and get it a quarter mile down the road to the cemetery. "It was a lovely service." "It was just the kind of service Fran would have wanted." "You were always so good to her."

And, "Thank you. Thank you for coming." "No, we never met, but Fran would have been so touched by your coming." "Yes, there'll be some kind of memorial. I'll let you know." "There'll be some food and drinks at Barbara's if you care to drop in."

Since it was such a nice spring afternoon and the distance was so short, we all walked down the road to the cemetery. I could see the hearse making its way far back to our plot on the slope. On the way to the church, I had seen the gravediggers at work and had quickly looked the other way.

As we came to the cemetery, there seemed to be a general reluctance to move in, to approach the ultimate act. Groups moved across the grass by twos and threes, spread out like an infantry company cautiously approaching an objective. "Was it time? Were all the preparations made?" They cast sidelong glances towards the open grave to make sure that as much of the ugliness as possible had been obscured. Some walked in by the dirt roadway which cut through the cemetery. Others made their way between old headstones and marked-off plots. I could see that the casket draped in carnations was poised above the grave, the minister was standing ready, and the undertaker was looking around for me to approach. Most of the friends stayed a good distance away, little clusters dotted among the other graves.

I had not been able to locate David. I had wished that he had brought Gretchen, but he hadn't, and so he seemed very much aloof, in some way critical of everything that was going on.

I now spotted him alone and somewhat away from the graveside. Everyone had stopped moving. It was obviously time to begin. I left my sister and the small group of friends I had walked with and started towards the grave. My head throbbed with the tension of emotion denied. I stopped a few feet from David. He was staring at the casket. "David?" He shook his head no.

He disapproved of this whole procedure, I knew, and would have preferred not to be there at all. I was angry for a moment. I admired and envied him the purity of his feelings and responses, but didn't he know that they were also cruel? There are certain things that one does. There are obligations.

I turned and moved closer to the grave, stopping maybe six feet away. The undertaker looked towards the minister, and the brief words of committal began. I turned myself off and stared out over the casket at the fields beyond, the cows, the dogwood and apple blossoms, the new spring green. I kept myself unmoved by the words of committal, which usually touched me deeply. "Dust to dust, ashes to ashes . . ." I tried to be simply a necessary figure in an arrangement, a stand-in for the person who would later give the part its full emotion.

Then suddenly I was aware that David had moved up and was standing by my side, slightly behind me. And this act of thoughtfulness broke through my defenses, came at me from a direction where I was not protected, and the tears welled up in my eyes, and I had to fight for control. My father would have gripped his hand and embarrassed him. I was simply grateful that David had decided or had been irrationally moved to stand there with me.

The words were finished. The handful of earth thrown on the casket. It was time for lowering the casket. I sensed behind me people turning, moving away. The undertaker moved a few steps and asked me if I wished to remain while the casket was lowered. No, I did not wish to stay, but I would stay. I nodded. I was there to witness. I would witness to the end. I would watch the procedure, absorbed by the mechanics of the casket's descent into the ground.

As it was lowered, I suddenly felt suffocated, as though I were in the coffin alive. I wanted to lunge forward and tear open the lid.

The ropes were recovered, the undertaker looked at me as though to release me. I turned to David and without looking at him, touched his arm and murmured, "Thanks." We started walking up the dirt road, looking nowhere in particular, and I remembered I hadn't thanked the minister or the undertaker. I stopped and went back and shook their hands. The men were standing around with shovels, waiting considerately till I should withdraw.

And I was waiting for them to withdraw, for everyone to withdraw, so that I might return alone and experience the act which I had till now simply witnessed.

ELEVEN

David dropped me at Barbara and Dan's house, and as I watched him drive away, I saw that he turned back towards the cemetery and not towards our house. I felt a flash of anger. He was going back to be with Fran, where I should be, where we both should be.

I didn't stay long at Barbara's. It was all too much, the strain of going over and over everything with the new arrivals. I had no answer for "What are your plans?" Suddenly my energies were exhausted, and I left, heading home through the fields.

I came into the house through the kitchen. David was standing in the shadows by the stove. He had changed out of his blue suit.

"I was just making myself some soup. Would you like some?"

"I ate a sandwich at Barbara's. But yes. If there's enough." It would give us something to do, get out dishes, make some toast, find spoons. "I'm sorry I had to drop in over there. It's just that there were a lot of your mother's friends I hadn't seen in a long time. And many I'd never met at all."

"Sure." He turned off the gas and poured the soup.

"Did you go back to the cemetery? I saw you turn in that direction."

He looked at me in surprise. "No. I just drove around."

I fiddled with the toaster. It wasn't working properly and Fran had asked me to get it fixed months ago. I would get it fixed in the morning. "Everyone over there is planning some kind of memorial for your mother. It's rather overwhelming." They had consulted me on what would be appropriate, and I soon realized, and welcomed the realization, that in a sense, I would be the keeper of the legend.

"That's nice." He went on eating his soup. "What kind of thing?"

"One of the playwrights is dedicating his play to her. Some of her students wanted to set up a fellowship. The place was full of plans."

"She would have loved that. Plans." He smiled.

It was good to see him smile. It was a sharing, almost for the first time, of something of the quality of what we had lost. He went on. "Her lists. Things to be done." He shook his head.

I nodded. "All those people were there today because of her little lists, things to do for people. You know, she never said 'No,' never refused a call for help. We'd be having dinner in the city, and some person would call and say he was having a rough time, could she come over, and

[57]

she'd leave the dinner table and just go . . . One Valentine's Day in Boston, oh, early in our marriage, she was rehearsing in the afternoon, and I had decided to surprise her with a party, just for the two of us, at home. And I prepared the dinner, got flowers, favors, the works. And she didn't show up. She went out for dinner, without calling, with a member of the company. When she came home, she said she had not remembered it was Valentine's Day and that she had gone to dinner with the old actress 'because she needed me.' "

I had meant all this as a compliment to her caring, but suddenly I sensed the hurt in my voice, and I was surprised and embarrassed.

I went on eating for a few moments. "In the last months I've been thinking of some kind of memorial. I know it may sound ghoulish, but it satisfied some need in me, some need to insure continuity, that something would go on."

"Sure. I understand."

"You know your mother got her start acting at college. There was this great teacher there, Miss Allison, and she encouraged Fran, and got her a spot as an apprentice down at the summer theatre in the village where we have our cottage. I thought maybe I'd set up a scholarship for some student to go from the college each year to the playhouse as an apprentice. It's the kind of living memorial Fran would have liked."

"Sounds like a good idea."

"Along with it I'd have deposited at the college a brochure or pamphlet on your mother, so that each girl who wins would know something of her . . . I won a prize at college, The John Amory Award for writing, and I could never find out who John Amory was."

"I think that's a great idea, Dad." There was something preoccupied about his manner. Something almost condescending.

"I'm glad you talked to your mother on the phone . . . that evening."

"Yes."

We just looked at each other for a moment. I nodded. "She loved you so much."

David moved nervously in his chair, embarrassed. "What are your plans, Dad?" I sensed that he wanted to establish what his involvement would be and hoped it would be minimal.

"I have no plans at the moment. But obviously there's a great deal to be done around here. I want to answer the letters and telegrams. All the flowers." Each time anyone had asked me my plans, I had almost panicked, because I had no plans. Plans and projects had been the supporting spine of my life. I was relieved to be able to look forward at least to these tasks, which would to a certain extent structure my time.

"There are printed forms for that, you know."

"I know, but your mother's relationship to all these people was so personal." I dreaded answering the letters, but also looked forward to it, as a way of re-creating Fran, keeping close to her.

"Maybe you should get away." I had said this to my mother after my father's death, when I could no longer cope with her dependency.

"Months ago, I thought when this happened, I'd close the door and disappear to some beach somewhere. Now I don't seem to want to. I don't know."

He rose and took his dish to the sink and ran the water. "Are you going to the beach house this summer?"

"I don't know. As I said, I have no plans. I'll just play things by ear. If you and Gretchen want to use it . . ."

"No. Oh, we might come down from Boston for a weekend, and if you do go there, you could come up and see us. She's going to summer school too."

"Good. That would be nice."

We sat and looked at each other. "I appreciate your coming down." Immediately I realized this was an insult. Why should a son be thanked for coming to his mother's funeral?

"I'll have to go back tomorrow morning. I have an exam in the afternoon."

"You could go back tonight, if you wanted." I meant this out of consideration for him, but the moment I said it, I realized that there were many meanings. I was perhaps irked by his tentativeness about being there, constantly reminding me he couldn't stay. But also, I really *did* want to be alone. I couldn't stand being "social" any longer, and though we were father and son, we were inevitably being social. "You be the judge. I'm going to bed very soon with a couple of sleeping pills."

I could see the war going on inside him. I had fought it often enough in the presence of my father. "I think I'll sleep over and get an early start. I can put in a couple of hours on the books upstairs and then get off around six in the morning."

"Do you need an alarm clock?"

"I've got my old one in my room."

"What about a sleeping pill?"

"No thanks."

I stood up. "I've been preparing this little pamphlet on your mother . . ." Again I knew it sounded ghoulish to have been working on a pamphlet while she was still alive. "Have you any picture you'd especially like me to use?"

"I always liked the one at the picnic."

"Yes. That's a nice one. All right, we'll use that."

"You may prefer another one."

"No. I think that's a good choice." Why was I so anxious to please him? We were in the hall. "Are you going up now?" I put my foot on the first step.

"I think I'll just get an apple from the kitchen to take along."

He was anxious to hasten the moment of our parting. We looked at each other. "Well, David . . ." He obviously dreaded any emotionalism on my part. I put my arm around him and hugged him although I felt his stiffening.

I drew away. "Good night. I may be up in the morning, but if I take the sleeping pills, maybe not." I knew that I would not be, and that if I were awake, I would let him get away without seeing him as I used to lie in bed in the morning as a boy waiting until I heard my father's car drive down the gravel driveway before I would get up. "Keep in touch."

"Yes, I will."

I started up the stairs. "Have you got everything you need back in your room?"

"Yes. Fine. Everything."

"Drive carefully tomorrow. You'll be tired, you know."

"I will." He moved towards the kitchen.

"Good night."

"Good night."

TWELVE

With the sleeping pills, I didn't wake up till after nine. David must be gone. I listened for any sounds in the house. There were none.

I was alone.

I took a deep breath and closed my eyes. Nine-thirty and I wasn't up, getting breakfast, handling bedpans, making arrangements. I felt a sense of relief . . . and a sense of loss. I thought of a friend of ours who had cared for her husband day and night for two years, and when he had died, she had felt so lost she went to work as a volunteer at a hospital for incurables. I could understand.

"You know, Fran has been the patient, but unless you take care of yourself, you could end up the invalid. We've found that depression can make a person susceptible to all kind of illnesses." My brother-in-law, a doctor, had taken me aside after the funeral. The minister, who had been standing with us, had said, "That only happens to people without other resources."

What were my resources? Fran and my work had been my whole life. A solitary who had reached out of his cave and dragged in one other person as a connection with life. The long-distance runner loping alone through the woods, the horseback rider off by himself, the boy bouncing a ball off the side of the barn for hours on end. All my life I had relished aloneness but had been terrified of loneliness.

I lay back knowing I could sleep forever if I wanted to, wishing, in a way, I would. I never had to get up. During the last days of the war when I had been exhausted, I had had fantasies that when I returned home, I was going to sit in the back of a car and let someone drive me for miles and miles and days and days, and I would just look at the scenery or sleep. A strange fantasy for someone who never liked anyone else to drive.

I dozed off.

The telephone woke me. I wanted to rip it from the wall. I wanted to be quiet and alone to try to reach myself. But if I didn't answer, someone would come running to see what was the matter. For a while I would be a ward of the community. I answered. It was Barbara saying I should come over for dinner tonight. I told her I didn't know. Could I leave it open?

I looked towards my desk with the messages and letters and cards. I should make a list of things I had to do. A "Fran list." 1. Answer the hundreds of letters and telegrams. 2. Finish the pamphlet on Fran and get it printed and distributed to friends. 3. Get in touch with the college and the summer theatre about some memorial award. 4. Fran's will. I would have to go to the beach house on the Cape to pick up some of the knickknacks she had willed to her friends.

I felt vaguely hungry. I put on some old corduroy slacks and a sweatshirt and padded down the hall to David's room. The house had the feeling of the day after Christmas. The hustle and bustle and socializing and feeding were over. The house was empty. Fran and I had it to ourselves to discuss the weekend, the guests, to arrive at some estimate of the occasion.

David's room was empty. He had made his bed, tidied up and gone. By now he was probably back with Gretchen, finally talking, confiding. I envied him.

Downstairs in the kitchen I thought perhaps there might be a note from David. There was no note. I shuffled around the kitchen getting my orange juice, cereal and coffee. From force of habit, I got out two glasses, two cups. It didn't make me sad. It interested me. Even amused me. Pavlov's dog.

I sat at the kitchen table, eating and staring, waiting for contact. I felt empty, gutted. I longed for some kind of sensation so that I could feel alive. All my life I had dreaded emptiness, blandness, and had generated feeling when there was none, simply to feel alive. I could not just be. I had to feel.

When would I get back to my own work again? How much I had written to please Fran, to make her proud! "The need we all have to live up to Fran's expectations of us." She had such faith. The first stories. I couldn't stand being in the apartment while she read them. I would walk and walk until I thought she would be through. "Remember, I'm a slow reader."

But what to write? The last five years were like a massive roadblock, packed solid with emotions and material, and yet I couldn't write about them. "Emotion recollected in tranquillity." Sorrow and bewilderment were not tranquillity.

[64]

I almost fell asleep at the table. I went back up to my room and lay on top of the bed and looked out the window. Summer had rushed in while I was involved elsewhere. A few days ago there had been lacy patterns of dark and light under the maples. Now there was deep shadow.

"See people. Don't be alone." But I wanted to be alone. I wanted to wallow in aloneness. I wanted to board up the house and shuffle around and be slovenly and alone with Fran. I had always wanted to be alone if I couldn't be with Fran.

But I also had a need to share this with someone, pour it all out and get it all over with. I needed enormous, unquestioning comfort from someone. For days we had been "celebrating" Fran. Now something childlike within me was beginning to murmur, "Me . . . Me!" I knew there was a great cry of pain and hurt within me. But I knew that someone would have to come and find me. My pride would not let me go out looking for help.

I had once struck a large dog with my car on a country road, and he had limped off and hidden in a culvert. When I reached him, he snarled and bared his teeth, but at the same time he wagged his tail, wanting me to help him. I managed to pick him up and get him to a doctor and save him. I sensed myself as that dog, snarling at anyone who might come to help me, but wanting it desperately.

And inevitably I thought of Jean.

It was Jean I had gone to when I knew Fran was going to die. Jean I had cried with. Jean whom I had loved. I shut my eyes, ashamed. Fran was dying and I had loved Jean. Until I had told her not to write any more . . .

"Darling Chris, I know you told me a year ago you didn't want me to write, and I understood. But you must know that I think about you and what's going on, and if anything should happen, please let me know."

"Darling Chris." It was meaningless.

"Why do you say 'Darling Chris' when you have no feeling for me?"

"But I do. I just don't have the feelings you want and need."

And I had torn up the note and burned it. Angry and ashamed during those last two years with Fran to be reminded of Jean. But though I was ashamed now too, I thought of Jean and that whole time with a welcome rush of warmth and feeling. I turned on my side and pressed my head against the pillow.

That fantastic Sunday night. The year after the operation, when we had thought that everything was all right, and Fran had recovered and was on tour with a play. A Sunday evening party for theatre people, and Fran had called from Los Angeles and had insisted I go to the party, a traditional pre-Christmas party we had always attended together. Jean was in New York, starring in a play. Her husband was away on one of his many extended business trips. She and I had both arrived at the party alone, having known each other vaguely from other such parties. And we had talked the whole time, and I had taken her back to her town house (rented for the run of her play), and she had invited me in for a nightcap, and I had talked about Fran and how we had met and all about our wonderful early days together, and then suddenly we had kissed, and for a half hour had held each other and mumbled senseless syllables, overcome with the suddenness of the passion, kissing and touching and murmuring, sensuous purring, our looks full of surprised smiles. She was the first woman I had held and kissed since my marriage.

And then when it was becoming inevitable that we would go to bed, her son crying down the hall. She rushed away and entered his room seconds before the housekeeper coming from the top floor. There was nothing wrong with the boy. A bad dream. But she returned to the living room a wife and mother, embarrassed by what she had done.

After that for a few months we had met many times, luncheons, suppers after theatre, and it was all made to seem "business" because an item appeared that she was trying to arrange an adaptation of a novel of mine which she might perform. And we were discreet.

But only once again was I allowed upstairs to the living room. As a stranger seeing a lady home, it was proper to invite me up for a nightcap. But as a lover who couldn't keep from wanting to touch her, it was too dangerous, and I was restricted to lengthy good-night kisses in the downstairs hall. "I'm a selfish bitch. I should send you packing, but I can't. I can't love you, but I do love your love."

How had I put up with it? I had put up with it because I needed it. She called what we had a "passionate friendship" and said it was often more important than marriage. I would declare that I would never see her again, that I couldn't stand it this way. And then she would smile at my pain and touch my hand, and it was like a blessing.

The one other night I was admitted upstairs in the living room alone was towards the end of Jean's stay in New York, the night after I heard that Fran was going to die. Several times when Fran and I had talked on the phone from the cities where she was playing, she had complained of pains in her spine. I had urged her to see a doctor, and she had finally asked me to ask her surgeon whom she should see in San Francisco.

I had gone to his office and had told him of Fran's pains, and he had asked me to come back after five when his office hours were over. Then we had sat in the twilight and he had told me the truth, which he had known after the operation. Breast cancer often showed up next in the spine. It was now just a matter of time.

I had walked the streets for hours trying to absorb this information, my eyes wide open yet seeing nothing. My mind registered nothing, neither my surroundings nor what I had been told. It was the mercy of shock which holds off awareness until in some mysterious way the body and mind have prepared defenses against the truth of what has happened.

I had finally gone back to our apartment and cried in despair, and sometime later, drugged with sleeping pills, had fallen asleep.

The next day, after spending another hour with the doctor, determining courses of action, X-ray, further operations, and what we were going to tell Fran, I had to talk to someone, and it was Jean. She had let me upstairs to the living room and I had told her about Fran. The complexity of the moment had bewildered me. Telling Jean, trying to hold back tears but not succeeding, tears because my wife was going to die and I didn't think I could live without her, yet wanting this lovely woman to whom I had poured out my anguish about the loneliness and hurts of my marriage, wanting her to let me make love to her.

After that evening, when she had comforted me, kissed me again, but nothing more, what had been what? What was love and devotion for this beautiful woman and what was anguish at my inconceivable loss?

And it had all ended shamefully a year later. Jean had gone away to make a picture, and when she had finished, she had stopped over in New York, and I had asked her to come to see Fran, who was again in the hospital. She had come and been shocked at Fran's appearance. Why had I asked her to come? She and Fran were only acquaintances. I did not want her to feel for Fran. I wanted her to feel for me. Later that night I had asked her to stay with me, to spend the night with me.

"I can't. It's awful, but I can't."

And I hadn't seen her again. What ridiculous bitterness! She didn't owe me anything. She had let me love her, write passionate letters full of my love for her and full of my sadness about the bad days of my marriage and about Fran's dying. And she had listened to me. I had listened to her too. The unhappiness at that time of her marriage. Unhappiness and loneliness our tenuous bond.

"If I came to you, stayed with you, when Fran dies, you wouldn't be able to stand the guilt."

I felt guilty for the little we had had. But she had helped me survive. For a while she had shared the sadness I should have shared with Fran. Fran, so much stronger, had shared her sadness with no one.

Since then, only that short note a year ago. "When anything happens . . ." I had no idea where she was, whether she was on good or bad terms with her husband. But I knew it was Jean I wanted to see.

I turned and looked at the ceiling. Fran dead four days and I wanted to see Jean. I shook my head. The man shocked the husband. Nothing for two years, still I wanted to be in touch. To touch, to talk.

I wondered where she was. I knew her address in California by heart. I could wire her there. Call? No. She had asked to be told. They would forward the message. I would simply tell her and wait. For what? For her to live out the fantasies I had had of her coming to me, comforting me?

I picked up the phone.

"Western Union. May I help you?"

I gave Jean's address.

"What is the message?"

I had not thought of the message. I had only thought of the comfort and excitement of getting in touch with Jean. I stared out into the room. "The message is . . ."

"Yes?"

"The message is . . . Fran died Thursday." Before I reached "Thursday," my voice started to break, and I couldn't stop myself. I hung up the phone in bewilderment and confusion. Suddenly after three days of holding

[69]

back, this simple declaration of the terrible fact reached me. I turned over and buried my head in the pillow and cried. At first small whimpering sounds of loss and sorrow. And at last wild animal cries of grief and rage and anger.

Some time later, towards the end of the afternoon, I dressed, put on a windbreaker and picked up large pruning shears in the barn and drove the station wagon up our road to the pine grove. The flowers on the grave would be wilted now. I wanted to put a cover of pine boughs over the raw earth.

It felt good having something to do, and in a sense, doing it for Fran. It was like shopping for her in Guam or Hawaii during the war. It made me feel close to her. Then I had not seen her for a year and would not see her for another year, but in many ways we were never so close. Closeness did not depend on seeing each other. Closeness was the idea of the person and the relationship to that idea. In this sense, Fran was still as much with me as she had been when I was in the Pacific. There had been days when I had not heard from her, months. There would be days, months now. But I would go on feeling her presence, the idea of Fran, the idea of wife.

Now I was cutting pine boughs for Fran. And then I would write the notes and letters for her, and finish the pamphlet and establish the memorial. There was no end of things I could still go on doing for her. It was Fran whom I would be with, talk to.

I cut enough for four graves. The activity exhilarated me. Finally, when I could get no more in the wagon, I stopped and drove down back past our house and to the cemetery.

As I approached the cemetery, I saw a car parked at the edge, and looking down tne drive towards Fran's grave, I saw a woman standing there. It was Mrs. Nelson, who had not had a chance to get to the burial because she had been so busy helping out. I was touched but annoyed that she should be there. I drove on by and up to the top of a hill which commands a view of the cemetery and sat there and watched till she left.

Then I drove down and turned into the cemetery and down the long, narrow drive, and stopped some yards from Fran's grave. It was impossible not to visualize her lying there, and the image was troubling but comforting. I was thankful that the morning had drained me of tears.

Now as I removed the mound of wilted flowers, I was just tending Fran as I had tended her for years. I took the flowers down the hill and threw them into the brush. Then I brought the pine boughs from the station wagon and laid them carefully over the raw earth.

A car seemed to pause in the distance on the road. "Leave me alone, please!" It moved on, and I finished what I had to do.

THIRTEEN

For several days I stayed in the village. The whole rhythm of my life changed. I had always been an early riser. Puritanically off to my writing table at eight o'clock. Now I slept late and, like all solitaries, stayed up all night.

Answering the letters and telegrams gave my days some structure and kept me where I wanted to be, close to Fran. I also found myself writing to her "children" in a way which was most uncharacteristic of me. "If I can be of help . . ."

Exhausted and depressed by the letters, but with each one, more in love with Fran, I would then drive to the post office to mail them and then off through the hills to some other towns, where I would wander aimlessly through stores and then go back home.

Though I thought I wanted to be alone, I found myself dropping in on friends in the evenings. I strangely chose friends who knew us least well. With them I could reconstruct our life the way I wanted it, gradually shaping a memory I could live with. At the end of each evening I would look urgently into their eyes, asking (but not in words), "Tell me that I loved her, please!"

With closer friends like Barbara and Dan, I would be more explicit. "You know, I've been wondering if I really made her happy."

"Of course you did."

"If I did, I wish she had let me know." I seemed to need constant reassurance.

After four days I left for New York to stay in our small apartment there. I left to escape the sympathy I needed but was beginning to hate. I also felt it would be an act of friendship to get myself out of town so that voices would not have to be lowered and sympathetic smiles smiled. I should leave, and when I came back, that would all be over.

I told Barbara and Dan and called David in Boston, and packed one suitcase with clothes and one with the letters to be answered, and on Friday afternoon, headed for the city.

FOURTEEN

As I drove down the East Side Drive, I felt my usual excitement in approaching New York. Traffic was all moving the other way, people on their way to the country on this lovely late-spring weekend. I was glad I was going into the city. Cities are lonely on spring weekends, and I wanted to be lonely. No phones. No friends. Free to be lonely, but also free not to be a marked man, free to be simply the "gentleman in the parlor" to whom anything might happen.

I left the Drive at 72nd Street and managed to find a place to park on the street, where I could leave the car till Monday at eleven. I took the two suitcases and approached the house.

We had the third floor in a remodeled brownstone. It was a charming small apartment with a fireplace in the living room and another in the bedroom. But I had come to hate the place because of the number of times in her last months Fran had had to be carried up and down those narrow stairs in a carrying chair. For all the various checkups requiring her presence at the hospital, we had had to arrange for an ambulance to come and get her and bring her back. The stairs were narrow and almost impossible for a stretcher, so they had used a carrying chair.

Except for the night her neck had gone. She had lain all day practically motionless, staring at the ceiling, while I had tried to get one doctor after another to come to see her. It was really not the doctors' fault, it's just that when you have one surgeon for one operation and another for another, and a family doctor who really is out of his area with cancer, you are in trouble. You long for some all-knowing guiding hand who will take over and be on call at all times.

Finally that night the surgeon who had operated on her head had made a generous exception and had paid a house call. He had called for the ambulance at once and arranged for her to go to the hospital. He had told me as he left that this might be very near the end. It wasn't. She lived for many months after.

But the ambulance men had come, and this time they had had to use a stretcher because she could not sit up, and they had found it impossible to put her on the stretcher without jiggling her, and she had screamed and screamed, and they had muttered to me, "For God's sake, why didn't he give her a shot to put her out!"

I had ridden in the ambulance with her, and then at the hospital the room was not ready and she had lain on the stretcher on the floor of the corridor for what seemed like hours, and nobody would authorize a shot because they wanted to make some tests before they put her out, and I stayed kneeling and crouched beside her just listening to her cry and trying to hold her head steady so it wouldn't hurt. Finally they had come to the room and put the head of the bed on blocks and put her neck in traction, and then gone over the extremities of her body with pins. "Do you feel that?" And finally they had put her to sleep.

The apartment was dark and stuffy. We faced south over some lovely gardens, but in the late afternoon the rooms were full of shadows. I opened the windows in the living room. The plants were all right, and everything was tidy. Alice came in half a day a week. A note from her. "Dear Mr. L, I'm so sorry. She was such a nice lady. If you need me extra, just call."

I took the suitcase with the letters into the second bedroom, which I used as a study, and then I took the other suitcase into our bedroom. I looked at the bed. The head was still up on blocks for the traction device. I suddenly realized that I would have to sleep in that bed. In the country I had slept in my study since Fran had died, but there was no bed in the study here. Well, there had to be a first time. That's what I was there for.

I went back to the living room to the bar table and took a swig of gin from the bottle. Fran used to kid about that. In England when I would complain about the weakness of the martinis, she would laugh and say, "You're no judge. Why don't you just ask for a bottle and a straw?"

It was inevitable that for a while everything I did or touched or saw immediately associated with Fran. After all, these were all our things. Each piece had a history of some sort, pleasant or unpleasant. I looked at a lamp I violently disliked and had raised a row over because it was so expensive. I turned away from it. I hated it even more now because my hating it then had made Fran cry.

Why the hell had I done that? Why hadn't I let her do the apartment the way she wanted to? Why was I always warning about the chancy nature of our careers? "We can't live as well as we might like today so that we won't ever have to live as poor as we may be some years from now." God, I hated the sound of my own voice, remembering. Where had that come from? My father: "I have made it a practice always to try to save about half of what I earn." And he had made me do that as a boy with my allowance, and later when I had earned my own money, I had saved what I could. And it had been a damned good idea. It had seen us through these years of sickness when nothing much was coming in.

I hated the self-serving, self-righteous way my thoughts were running. What comfort to her? Of course, it wasn't as though we had stinted in any large sense. After we had started earning money, we had had a lot of things. But they were never enough for Fran. Fran always liked first class. Why the hell hadn't I let her have what she wanted?

I went to the study and turned on my desk light and pulled the shades at the windows. Habit, writing habit, to shut out the sun or the rain or the snow. Without sitting down, I took out the letters and telegrams and flower cards and stacked them to one side. I stood looking at the picture that it made—paper, pens, pencils, warm light. It was a picture that I liked, that I could create any place in the world. It was my place of work, a brightly warm and inviting spot in a shadowy room.

But I didn't sit down. I heard the city through the open windows, and something in me wanted to go out and experience it. Cities always had that effect on me. Fran would want to lie down and rest after the trip, and I would want to hit the streets.

I turned out the light, raised the shades, and left the apartment with a guilty sense of relief.

FIFTEEN

I made Bloomingdale's my destination. (My father had always said, "Don't amble. Always walk as though you had a destination.")

Bloomingdale's had been my walking area for years. I rarely bought anything. I just walked through every floor. It was a covered, all-weather bazaar with enough varied activity and things of interest to take my mind off my work.

In the early days Fran and I had walked through the store many times together on winter Saturday afternoons, often bringing home something utterly useless, just to buy something. I used to say that Fran hated to go to museums because there was nothing she could buy. She always had to bring home a favor from the party.

Now each young couple drifting aimlessly through the store, arms loosely draped around each other, made me homesick for Fran.

After buying a few things, I headed back to the apartment. Some letter paper for the notes I was writing, and a large photograph album. I had taken a great many pictures of Fran during the last four or five years. Movies too. When I knew that she was going to die, I went out and bought new cameras, and started taking pictures of her on all occasions. I had also bought a tape recorder. It had all been a desperate effort to save any part of her I could. Friends and students were beginning to send the snapshots they had taken. I could not yet look at the pictures or play the tapes. But one day I would.

Back at the apartment, there was a stack of mail in front of my door with a note from the couple on the floor below. "We heard you come in but didn't want to disturb you. We are so sorry." That was a true city dweller. I opened the door and went in, put down my packages, turned on the light and glanced at some of the envelopes. Just the return names and addresses, some from abroad, touched me. But I didn't want to read the letters or go into all that now. I felt drowsy, without pills, and I wanted to take advantage of it.

I lay down on the couch in the living room, putting a piece of newspaper under my feet and a light throw over my legs. (Fran's instructions.) It had always amused Fran that I took naps on couches rather than on beds. For me, lying on a bed was too positive an act. It scared away sleep. You're supposed to sleep. No sleep! There was something more like stealing sleep on a couch, holding a newspaper for a few moments and being surprised by sleep. I dozed off quickly.

When I woke up, it was getting dark outside. Lying there, really wishing I could just slip back into sleep, I looked out the window across the gardens and saw families moving about, preparing dinners, making cocktails, one woman dressing. I had looked at her before with amusement and curiosity. She always pulled the shade eventually, but it never seemed to occur to her until she was almost down to her skin. Tonight she filled me with loneliness and longing.

"Get out and see people." It was Fran's voice. "You shouldn't just sit around when I'm not here. It makes me feel awful, leaving you the way I have to . . ." ". . . I like to be alone." And that had been true, to a certain extent. Always, of course, with the knowledge that I was not absolutely alone. Fran was someplace. How much I had been dependent on her to create activity in my life!

I had very few men friends. We had friends together whom we enjoyed together. But if I were alone in the city or in the country, I wouldn't call a friend for lunch or dinner. I'd get a newspaper or a magazine and eat alone.

The telephone rang. I had sworn not to answer phones this weekend. I had come here not to answer phones. It stopped. It occurred to me it might be Jean. Though I had not sent the telegram, sooner or later she would hear and get in touch.

It rang again. Automatically I reached for it. That had been Fran's signal. To ring, hang up and call back immediately. It was my lawyer and oldest friend, Roger.

"I've been trying to reach you."

"I drove in this afternoon."

"Oh. How about coming over for dinner. We're going to sit down in a few minutes. Just us."

"No, thanks, Roger. I just want to be alone. Get caught up."

"You could just come for dinner and leave when you want."

"Thanks, Roger."

A pause. "Are you sure?"

"I'm sure." He knew I almost always said "No" to everything at first.

"How about lunch then on Monday. We have to go over the will and I have to make a date with the Internal Revenue to open Fran's safety-deposit box."

"Really? I'd never heard of that."

"Yes."

"I don't think you'll find anything much in it. Everything of any importance is in mine . . . I think."

"You have no idea what we find in these boxes."

"She had one in Boston too. She kept it for old times' sake."

"Well, we can go over it all on Monday. One o'clock at the office?"

"Fine."

"Sure you won't come for dinner? It smells very good and I've got some Tanqueray gin."

"No, thanks."

"We haven't really seen you . . . to talk."

"I know. We will." Each family of friends wanted their time to "talk out" Fran and resented it if they didn't get the chance.

"I'm not sure it's wise for you to be alone, Chris."

"I just seem to want to be."

"Well, if you change your mind, we'll be in all evening."

I went into the kitchen to see if there were any canned things I could eat. The phone rang again, and I stood in front of it and waited for it to stop, thinking all the time, "Who could it be?" Undoubtedly some of the calls I hadn't answered had been from Sarah. That would have to be faced.

The kitchen was spick-and-span. Nobody had eaten there in a month. I opened the cupboard door and two cockroaches scampered across the shelf and down the crack in the back. In our first apartment in Boston, Fran and I had had cockroaches. When we went out at night, on our return we'd each grab a handful of paper toweling and then turn on the light in the kitchen and go after them.

I closed the cupboard door, put on my jacket, and took a taxi to my club.

SIXTEEN

As I entered the club, the "one drink before catching the train" group was leaving. I checked my coat and went into the bar. Many of the faces I passed were familiar; that is, I had seen them in the club for twenty years, but I had no idea of their names or they of mine. Some I recognized as classmates whom I had not known at college nor since. Fran had occupied most of my time at college. There were a few classmates whom I had known vaguely, and we always smiled and waved or shook hands and said "Hello," but we never broke our stride or said anything more. I ordered my drink and went upstairs to the library.

I sat in a large overstuffed leather chair in the dimly

lit book-lined room and looked through the newspaper. I hadn't the slightest idea of what I was reading. It was like walking through the store. I realized how much of this I had done in the last years. Turning the pages, relating to little or nothing. Marking time. I had related to little because I didn't really know who I was except a man waiting for his wife to die.

I was about to put aside the paper when I read: *New Hope For Cancer Cure.*

I broke out into a sweat. For years I had grabbed at any scrap of news about new treatments or possible cures. Now I didn't want there to be a cure. Not yet. Not so soon after Fran's death. If this actually turned out to be a cure, and I had let her die . . .

Reading on reluctantly, I was back in Fran's bedroom that night, calling the ambulance and the doctor, and he had brought her around and she was alive and we would try this treatment, and . . .

> The investigators emphasized that this development does not mean an immediate breakthrough. It will be at least a year before the drug can be tried on human beings.

I closed my eyes, perversely relieved, and waited for my breathing to return to normal. Of course, even if they could stop the cancer, Fran's bones couldn't have been mended, the spine. She would be alive, but . . .

I needed a drink. Leaving the library, I noticed an older man slumped asleep in one of the chairs, and another across the way with ashes down the front of his shiny coat. I had remembered men like this, of course. I had seen them before when I had eaten a quick meal on the way to the theatre. But now I looked at them in a new light. They seemed utterly without resources. I had thought of coming back after dinner to browse among the books until it was time to go to bed. I decided I wouldn't.

As I went down to the bar for a second drink, the club

had practically emptied except for men like those in the library, the nightly inhabitants.

I decided I would have one more drink, a fast dinner, and then get back to the apartment. I had letters to write. I had things to do, to occupy me. What had happened to these old men? Were they widowers? Old bachelors? What? Old men seemed so much more pitiful than old women. During the daytime I had never seemed to notice them among all the active, vigorous younger men, heading to and from the squash courts, laughing at the bar, rolling dice at the backgammon tables. This was the residue. Did they live at the club? Did they have homes? I wouldn't come back here alone. It would be better to cook something and eat it at home.

I stepped into the bar. Nobody but the bartender at the far end of the bar, reading the newspaper. He got up as I entered, but I turned on my heel and decided to have my drink at the table.

I entered the huge dining room and saw that there was only one old man, sitting at the long table which at lunch was usually the scene of great conviviality. He looked up at me with a hopeful smile.

"I'm looking for George Benson," I lied. "Have you seen him?"

"No. I don't think I know him."

"Thank you." And I walked out, picked up my coat, and hurried out of the building.

God!

Avoiding restaurants where I was known, I found a small place between Fifth and Madison where I had never been.

Business was not particularly good, and I was seated at a small table along the wall. I ordered my drink and felt alone and awkward. Single people should really eat at home or at Schrafft's or in a bean wagon on a stool. Couldn't they find *anyone* to eat with? My God, they must really be creeps! Or does he prefer to eat alone, and if so, he is more of a creep.

I spread my napkin on my lap, and felt uncomfortable without a newspaper or magazine. I had a small breast-pocket notebook I could riffle through, but when I reached for it, it wasn't there. It must be in another coat. I just had to sit there naked.

I sipped my drink and tried not to feel sorry for myself. I had rigged it all this way, to be alone, as I had done so often in my life. There was no need for me to be alone.

Across the room were three people, a man and two women, all in their late thirties. The women were talking animatedly. The man didn't seem very interested. Which one was the wife? It was a game Fran and I had played often. One of the women turned and looked in my direction. She was beautiful. She laughed at something the other woman said, tossed her hair, and suddenly I desperately wanted to touch her.

She had dark hair, a wide face with a sensuous mouth, a womanly figure. I remembered how during the war, the night before I was to ship out of San Francisco, I had had a similar feeling about a woman sitting in front of me in the bus. I had wanted to reach out and touch her hair, to hold her head close to me. And now this woman. I stared at her unashamedly. I wanted to be enveloped by this woman. I wanted to be passive and have her make love to me. I wanted to be warmed by this unknown woman who was all woman and to tell her about Fran and how terrible it had all been.

I continued to stare, and she looked away from her friend for a moment and looked at me. She had dark beautiful eyes. Could she have any thought of what I was thinking? I wanted her to know. I continued to look. The curve of her breast under her sheer blouse made me wretchedly homesick for a woman's body. As she talked, she seemed kind and responsive. I began to fantasize. She was not the

[86]

wife. The others would have to leave early, and she would stay on. And what would I do?

The woman looked away from her friend again and towards me. I continued looking at her for a long moment, then dropped my eyes to my glass and took a sip. My heart was beating rapidly. I wanted that woman desperately. In my anguish I had always turned to a woman. But this was more than anguish. True, the husband wanted comfort, but the man simply wanted the woman. I felt a warmth and excitement, and began to get an erection.

I looked up again, and she was looking at me, just for a moment, then her glance went back to her friend and she answered some question. I continued to stare at her. She turned towards the man and said something to him. He looked over at me for the first time, and I flushed and looked away. After a moment I looked back casually, and the second woman had twisted around to look at me. The man looked sternly at me.

From time to time after that, when I glanced at their table, I noticed that the woman was looking at me, but would look away when I caught her at it.

What would I do if she stayed behind? I had never picked up a girl in my life, that is, in a public place. A certain ongoing part of me was taking over. It was responding to the city and the situation and my need. Hunger had made me finally get out of bed that first morning alone. There was something rueful in my awareness of the paradoxes and contradictions.

I lingered over my coffee. Perhaps they would leave first and she might cast a last look back. But they didn't leave, and I began to feel foolish dawdling over coffee. I looked at my watch. It was after nine. Safe to go home. Five to nine were the hours of anxiety when I was alone. After nine it was all right to go home to an empty apartment, buy a newspaper on the way, glance at it, have a couple of drinks, watch a few minutes of television, and the day was safely over. When I was alone, to have nothing to do between five and nine gave me a sense of panic.

I would have to learn to cope with it. Start reading. How long I had hoped for time to read for myself, books I needed to read and wanted to read. The last years I never seemed to find the time. Now I was alone and could read to my heart's content. But somehow I didn't want to read alone in the apartment.

I got up from the table, now risked a smile at the woman across the room, and handed the hatcheck girl my check. As I put on my raincoat, I looked back, and the lady was looking at me. I left. Perhaps she was not the man's wife. Perhaps if I had stayed. As I walked away, I thought I might go back to that restaurant another night. She might come there often. I felt excited. I had been "the gentleman in the restaurant."

SEVENTEEN

Back at the apartment, I was restless with
thoughts of the woman, but I went into my study, turned
on the desk lamp and created "my world" and started answering the letters, writing about the last years and Fran's
spirit and gallantry, and soon I had transferred my longing
to Fran.

After a couple of long letters, I was tired and drained
of emotion. The phone rang, and I let it ring itself out.
There could be no emergency that would involve me.
David? Yes, something could have happened to him, but
he had Gretchen, and I doubted if I would be called until
the emergency was over. Sarah?

I sat on the couch with my drink and put my feet on

the coffee table. Of course I would have to start answering the phone and I would have to start making calls. What did other people do?

I started thinking of other people who had lost wives or husbands. I had some special friends, eight or ten years older than I was, and I always checked them out from time to time, birthdays, wedding anniversaries, to see how they were holding up, how they were meeting various crises, success, failure, children, divorce, middle age. But in thinking about them, I had come to realize that death was not an abstraction but something that happened to individuals and individual relationships, and the reaction depended on the individual and his relationship to the person who had died.

One friend had gone completely to pieces and had committed suicide. Another had shocked everyone by marrying immediately. I thought about that for a while. I couldn't imagine standing up there and saying "I do." In a strange way it would be a final death for Fran. She still lived as my wife. "My wife and I" was still Fran and I.

And yet, what about my feelings for the woman in the restaurant? That was something else. I closed my eyes and thought about her, her mouth, the curve of her breast, and suddenly she was naked and multiplied by ten, and I was embraced, held, holding, touching, touched, engulfed in flesh.

I got up and poured myself another drink and stared out the window. All the curtains were drawn. I stood over my desk, saw my address book and picked it up and went in and settled down on the couch again. The first page or two, there was nobody I wanted to call, to see. Had our lives been made up of keeping in touch with people we really didn't care about? I could remember good and friendly times we had had with them all, but I didn't want to call them. I wanted something much more primitive or much more complex than I could find with friends.

The phone rang again, and I picked it up. It was Sarah.

"I called earlier, but there was no answer."

"I was out. I've just come in." I was angry with her for calling, and thoroughly ashamed at being angry. I sounded distant and disinterested, and I was ashamed of that. This girl had comforted me, had helped me to forget my troubles in a bath of sensuousness. She was ready to help me again. She couldn't understand that though I desperately needed to hold and be held, it was different now. Now there would be something ongoing about it, and I couldn't feel that way about her. And I was angry with myself all over again for having "used" her.

"I tried to call you in the country this afternoon."

"Yes. I drove in this afternoon."

"Am I calling at the wrong time? Is it embarrassing for you to talk to me now?" What the hell did she mean? That I would have someone else here with me now? Some woman? What was I getting upset about? That's what I wanted. Some image of a woman who didn't know me, who hadn't known Fran, who would just listen to me say how much I had loved my wife and how lost I was and who would believe it all and would be compassionate and passionate, and let me lose myself and find myself in some complex way in her body.

"What do you mean?"

"I just wondered from the way you sound. If someone else is there, I could call tomorrow."

"I'm alone."

"Would you like to come over for a drink?"

"It's late." (It had been late before when I had called urgently and had begged to be allowed to come over.) "I'm writing letters. You know. All the letters people wrote about Fran."

"You could get printed cards for that."

"I don't seem to want to."

"You shouldn't sit around in that apartment alone. Could I come over tomorrow and cook you up some dinner?"

I began to feel sorry for her, and I knew what happened when I felt sorry for a woman. Once, when I was a freshman in college, I had gone to a dime-a-dance place, and during one set, a relatively unattractive girl was the only one left with no partner. Some men standing near me kidded each other, saying, "There she is. Just for you." Another one said, "That dog?" I thought she looked terribly lonely and hurt out there, and I went out and gave her my tickets and danced with her. Perhaps I am always projecting my terror at loss of pride. Obviously this girl couldn't have cared less that she was left alone. When she started to dance, she ground her belly and pelvis against me, chewing gum and looking the other way all the time. The whole thing had been ridiculous as she maneuvered me into a dark corner and ground herself into me until I had an orgasm.

"Sarah, I'd like to be alone this weekend. There have been so many people." But at the same time I had a vision of the club and the restaurant alone. And I knew I would have to see her sometime to explain, to end it.

"Well, if you change your mind, I'll keep free tomorrow."

"No, don't do that."

"I've got a lot of manuscript reading to do anyway and I'm finishing a new short story of my own. Just let me know in time so that I can get some food. My kitchen is being ripped apart, so it will have to be yours."

Sarah had not been to my apartment. Some nicety had kept me from letting her come. What I had done with her, I had done away from my life. It had no connection with my life. I didn't want her to come to my apartment now. "This place is a mess. The kitchen hasn't been used for months. If we do anything, we'd better eat out."

"I could come over early and clean it up."

"No . . . Look, Sarah, I really did come here to be alone with myself. Get through these letters. I don't want to sound rude, but . . . I think it's best that way."

There was a pause at the other end. Normally I would have softened such harshness by saying, "We'll do it later." But I didn't.

"If you don't mind, I'll check with you tomorrow. You're walking wounded now, and by tomorrow night you may need someone to talk to."

Her nursing instincts sensed a sick person, wounded prey. I would need her desperately. Wounded people, ostracized people, often became the willing prey of solicitous people they normally wouldn't spend time with. I decided I could always just not answer the phone. "Okay. But if anything else definite comes up, don't turn it down."

"Nothing else will come up. Don't stay up all night writing those letters now. Go to bed."

"Okay."

"Good night." And she hung up.

I felt trapped and angry with myself for leaving the door open at all. I finished my drink in a gulp. Perhaps I'd wait a half-hour, then call her back and say that I'd just had a call from David, and I had to leave in the morning for Boston. But I knew I'd have to handle the thing better than just running out.

I finally decided that I would call her in the morning and invite her out to dinner. We'd go to a small restaurant near her place in the Village, and we'd talk, and that would be that. The few times when we'd been together, we'd always met at her apartment and stayed there. I didn't want to stay there this time. Anyway, she said her kitchen was torn apart. And I didn't want to be seen with her. I flushed with embarrassment. Why not be seen with her? My God, it was obvious why not. My wife was dead a week, and here I was in the Village . . . But I was in the Village, wasn't I? So why shouldn't I be seen? With Sarah. The hypocrisy of it all sickened and confused me. What did I care what people thought? I cared. It was vitally important to me and to Fran's memory and the memory of "us" what people thought.

I walked into the bedroom. I had forgotten to take the bed off the blocks before I went out. I didn't feel like doing it now. I also did not want to sleep in that bed. Not yet. The paradox of wanting to stay close and yet not too close. I moved a pillow into the living room, threw a blanket on the couch, and decided that for tonight at least, I'd stay there. I took a couple of sleeping pills, undressed, and turned out the light, and thought about the woman in the restaurant, and let her make love to me till I went to sleep.

EIGHTEEN

Sarah's street in the Village was depressing. This time I noticed it. Before I had just put my head down and hurried through the block.

There was a liquor store next door to her apartment, and other times I had stopped to buy a fifth. This time I didn't. The fifth had been necessary the other times. A drug to my conscience, a prelude to complete abandon, a bedside companion. This visit was going to be different.

Other times there had been a tension, a driving sexual urgency which had tumbled us onto the bed with animal groans and clutching hands and arms. I felt no urgency now. Nothing. Only embarrassment which anesthetized me completely.

She had said, "You always are so ready. You leave me nothing to do for you . . . Come over sometime when you are not so ready. Trust me!" And she told me of a man who had been with her, who even though he stayed inside her, would insist on bringing himself around with his hand at the end. "So untrusting. Would you trust me? Just lie there and trust me?"

I had told her I didn't know. I had always been chagrined not to be ready. I had thought it somehow insulting not to be ready from just the idea of the woman, the touch. Fran had given it significance too.

Sarah said it was not trusting, not being willing to be really naked, and she said something I laughed at, but it was true. "A man with a hard-on is not naked."

I rang the hall bell, and after a few moments Sarah buzzed and I entered the building. The grime and peeling paint and smells of cooking depressed me. At the top of the stairs Sarah's door was ajar. I knocked, and she called out, "Come in."

She was in the bedroom. "I was just changing."

Although Sarah had not done much to fix up her apartment, it was definitely a woman's, and I felt both homesick and uncomfortable the minute I closed the door.

Sarah came down the short dark narrow hall buttoning her blouse, a blouse that I had unbuttoned on other occasions.

"You didn't say where we'd be eating, so I'm not dressed up." She kissed me lightly on the lips.

"I thought we might eat at the place around the corner." I was not known in this neighborhood. It was unlikely that we would meet anyone who might know me.

"That place has dreadful food." She buttoned her cuffs. "You know what I'd like? I'd like to go to Luchow's."

"I don't know as I feel like anything that"—I hesitated—"that big, you know." I was appealing to her understanding that I wasn't emotionally ready for a big public place like that, while I knew what I meant, and was embarrassed.

"I'd just like to get out of the neighborhood. I know, what about Charles? That's quiet, and they have booths, so you wouldn't feel surrounded by a lot of people."

I could have gone on turning down all her suggestions, but it was obvious that she wanted us to be out in public. It was almost a dare, a challenge to my hypocrisy. I was coming to see *her* now. Presumably I wanted to see *her*. Therefore we would be seen in public.

"Pour yourself a drink and come in while I finish putting on my face." She headed back to the bedroom. "The kitchen's a mess, but the ice thing is working. I'd like just some vermouth on the rocks."

I had hoped that we could have gone out immediately. The memories of my other visits to this place when I had wallowed in her bed were now too painful. I brought the drinks into the bedroom. She had taken off her blouse and was in her bra and skirt.

"If we're going to Charles, I'd better put on something a little more fancy." She turned and smiled at me as she raised her arms to slip into another blouse.

If she had been any other woman, I would have taken her in my arms and we would have tumbled onto the bed. I think that is what she wanted. I put her drink on the dressing table and sat in the one chair, behind and away from her. I wanted to go into the other room, but I couldn't do this.

"How are you getting along?" I saw her eyes in the mirror. They were kind.

"Okay, I suppose."

"You shouldn't stay alone all the time, you know."

"I seem to want to."

"You'll get morbid."

I shrugged my shoulders. "I'm just doing what I seem to want to do. And I seem to want to be alone." I felt this was too unkind, so I added, ". . . Mostly."

"I've read parts of the pamphlet you've been writing on Fran and your marriage."

"Oh. I haven't finished it yet."

"Chuck gave it to me to read." She looked at me in the mirror. "It's lovely. Of course, with the kind of marriage I had, I found it slightly unbelievable, what you had together. But it's lovely."

Something inside me flared up in defense, but I only said, "I thought a lot of her friends would like to have it."

"I never told you, but I once went with a man, a stage manager who had worked with Fran. He said she was nice."

I was offended by the tepid description "nice." It seemed so insignificant for the Fran I had been remembering.

I watched her put on her lipstick and remembered her carefully removing it so that it would not be on my shirt or neck, or "anywhere." She looked somewhat like the woman in the restaurant, dark, lush, sensuous. I thought I could see the large reddish-brown nipples through her blouse. It was just memory.

She caught my eyes in the mirror and just sat there, perhaps waiting for me to come up behind her and cup her breasts and press my hardness into the side of her face and wait for her to reach for the zipper.

After a moment she snapped off her dressing-table light and stood up.

I helped her on with her coat. She said, "You look tired. You need taking care of." As she opened the door, she noticed something on the bookcase. "Last time you were here, you forgot your pipe and tobacco. I meant to send it to you, but then felt it might . . . lead to problems." I reached for them. "You can take them when you come back. You don't want to lug them around."

I had hoped to avoid coming back, and I paused for a moment, then said feebly, "I might want to smoke after dinner."

"A pipe at Charles? You'd better not." I took them anyway, and we went down the stairs.

I had never eaten at Charles with Fran, though I had been there a couple of times on business. But I was not known. As we were shown to our booth, I glanced quickly around the room to see if I recognized anyone. And I felt cheap doing it.

After we had been served our drinks, Sarah looked at me and smiled. "You know, around the office there's a great deal of speculation going on about you."

"What do you mean?"

"It's not really appropriate to discuss now, but life goes on, and . . . anyway, they are wondering if you would get married again and who you might marry." I frowned. She went on. "I know, but it's inevitable. I went to a funeral last month, and as I came out, I saw the widow being helped to her car by a male friend of long standing, and someone next to me said, 'That's the new husband.' People are just that way."

I smiled at the gruesomeness of the story and shook my head. "I feel very much married to Fran right now. In some sense, I feel almost more married than before. A greater sense of responsibility . . ." I really didn't want to go into all this with Sarah, but it might help her to understand my attitude towards her.

She looked at me as though wondering if she should say what she was about to say. "Do you know Spender's lines 'At first you did not love enough, And afterwards you loved too much.' The first part doesn't apply to you, as far as I know, but the last part is worth thinking about."

I was upset at her constant small references to my feelings for Fran. "Maybe."

"It'll make it very hard for a real live girl."

The waiter brought the menus. After we ordered, she went on. She couldn't seem to get off the subject. "You have an interesting time ahead of you, do you know that?"

"What do you mean?"

"I was a very innocent girl when I married. And while my marriage lasted, I guess I had my head in the sand. But when it blew up after five years, my eyes were opened. Suddenly I was showered with luncheon invitations from my friends' husbands. And I was on their lists to call when wife was out of town visiting family. More married men came scratching at my door."

I wondered if she realized how she was making me feel. She must have, because she went on. "Oh, you're not included. I don't mean the way you came. Please understand that. You were different." And she touched my hand. "But these others. I saw the underside of most of my friends' marriages, and it wasn't pretty. It's given me a rather jaundiced view of marriage." She sipped her drink. "I don't know about you, Chris, but I don't think I'd ever try it again. I'd settle for a nice long love affair." She looked into her drink and fished out a twist of lemon. "Of course, I'm being realistic, at thirty-five that's about all I'm being offered." She smiled at me.

I wanted this to be over as soon as possible. I knew I was supposed to say something pertinent. I had just had an offer, an offer which embarrassed me. I had come out of courtesy and obligation to try to let her know that things were different now. I had hoped that she would have sensed by my small signals that things were different. Instead she had just suggested a long-time love affair.

One afternoon in her bed she had said, "You don't need to apologize. You don't need to apologize at all." And she had laughed. I had never thought of myself as much of a lover, and when I had come too fast for her one time, I had mumbled something, and she had said, "At the risk of turning your head, you have nothing to apologize for at all. You'd be surprised . . ." and she stopped and shook her head. "You're very thoughtful. Shall I go on, or have I reassured you enough?" And she had smiled. Her compliments had aroused me again. I had been surprised that I had been up to her needs and demands. There was a certain grossness about her which excited me.

Later that same afternoon she had looked at me a long time and said, "I'm going to break all the rules of our relationship, but I'll go crazy if I don't." And after looking at me again for a long time, with a kind of fear, she had said, "I love you. I God-damn-it love you." She had hugged me, and I had turned cold. "Don't answer! Don't say anything! Forget it!" And I had managed to smile at her and kiss her and stroke her face lovingly.

Now her offer of a love affair had been left hanging. I didn't answer it. Or rather, I did answer it by branching off into some discussions on love affairs and marriages. "After a while there's nothing ongoing about a love affair, and I've found that any relationship requires something ongoing." I talked about marriage, and inevitably to some extent about Fran and me.

"Yes, I read all that in your little book. But as I said, your relationship was unusual . . . almost unbelievable."

She knew I was rejecting her, and in retaliation she attacked marriage more and more, and I defended it. Then we made the transition to talking about our writing, and I talked to her about her use of her feelings about sex and love and marriage in her writing. And she attacked my feelings about love and marriage not as they actually were, but as they appeared in my work. She knew I wrote close enough to the center of my feelings so that she could attack me by attacking the attitudes of my characters.

"I always feel I would like to dirty your men up a little. Mess them up. Do you understand that? Does that make any sense to you?"

"Yes, it makes some sense." I wanted to say to her that I would like to give some of her brutalized characters some feeling of sentiment and affection. But I didn't. It was she who wanted to hurt me for not accepting her offer. I just wanted to retreat with the best terms possible.

And I *had* sometimes felt some kind of hypocrisy in me and my male characters. I had come to Sarah from a sick wife. A special privileged category. But had I come so innocently? Hadn't Fran's illness been something of a self-righteous excuse for something I had wanted to do?

"Why don't you put one of your men in bed with someone like me and have him do the things we did together. He'd still be a nice man. At least I think so."

After dinner it was only nine-thirty. I didn't want to talk any more. I couldn't just deposit her back at her apartment. I suggested a movie, though I didn't feel like one. But it would keep us quiet for a couple of hours and pass the necessary time.

After the movie we walked back to her apartment, and at one crossing I took her arm to help her, and she responded by pressing my hand to her side and up to the edge of her breast, with her elbow. I kept my hand there. It would not be much longer.

"What are your plans?"

"I'm going back to the country. There's a great deal still to be done. Then I thought I might just go away someplace. I know you think it's not healthy, but right now I have so much to straighten out inside my own head that I find straightening out my other relationships almost impossible." I had unexpectedly added the last part. It had just seemed to follow, and she accepted it as an explanation of my attitude towards her that evening.

"I understand." She pressed my hand.

"Then I'm going up to New England to Fran's old college around commencement time to hand out a prize and scholarship I've set up there in her memory. And then I should go to the cottage at the beach."

"You have a lot to do."

"I seem to want to clear this all up, wind it up, and then get away. Disappear." That word "disappear" had kept cropping up when people asked me my plans.

I wanted to leave her at her doorstep, but that would be too much. As she opened the door, she said, "Come up for a nightcap?"

I looked at her and smiled. "Not tonight. I really am very tired." I hoped she would not press further.

"I understand. Well, anyway, come up for your pipe. Oh, no. You took that, didn't you? Took all your belongings." She smiled.

"I'll go upstairs with you."

As we climbed the stairs, we made small talk.

"Drop me a card from wherever you disappear to."

"I will."

"And you have my number."

"Yes."

"I'll see you when you come to the office."

"Yes, of course."

"Though I'm thinking of switching jobs, get something that will give me more time to write. Don't tell anyone yet."

"I won't."

She opened the door and looked at me, a wondering, longing, sad look. I suddenly felt great compassion for her. How many times had she been left like this? And I wondered, "What if right now, standing there, she had put her arms around my neck and said 'I'm so God-damned desperately miserable and lonely. Please come in and stay with me and sleep with me.'" What would I have done, and what would I have felt? I would have done it, of course. And I would have enjoyed it if that's the way it had come about. She didn't ask me.

"Good night."

"Good night." I leaned down and kissed her.

She looked at me and smiled, no longer trying. "What you're in for the next few years! Promise we can get together sometime, in the distant future, and you'll tell me all about it."

I smiled. "Yes, sure. We'll compare notes." Now that she was not pressing, I felt tender towards her. This had been a terrible evening, but there had been warm and good ones, and we should part on that note. I embraced her, held her close, not kissing her. "Thanks, Sarah. I've got such fouled-up, confused feelings about everything now, guilt and sadness and loneliness, and I don't know what. But you know . . . back then . . . in a way you saved my life."

She held me tight for a few moments, then she kissed my cheek. "Thanks. But you don't owe me anything. I had a wonderful time." There were tears in her eyes. "Good night." She moved inside the apartment and half closed the door. "Keep me in your telephone book." And she smiled and closed the door.

NINETEEN

On a fine day in mid-June, I drove up to Fran's college just outside Boston to make the award which I had set up in her memory. It was too soon, really, for this kind of pilgrimage, but I wanted to go. If the award was in memory of Fran, I wanted the winner to know something of who and what Fran was. To this end, I had been working on a collection of pieces about her, pictures and articles and a few of her letters. I intended to have them kept at the college so that each girl through the years could glance at them after she had won the prize.

I pulled up at the Inn, took out my two suitcases, one filled with letters about Fran which I had not yet answered. "For God's sake, Chris, just throw them away.

Those people don't expect an answer." But I needed them.

This Inn had many memories for me. As I checked in, I heard the jukebox from the dimly lit bar where after rehearsals of college plays Fran and I had shared our dreams and ambitions and confessed our sins. I had come out from Cambridge often to act small parts, and sometimes she had come to Cambridge to act in our plays.

As I signed the register, I remembered that I had a key back home to Room 16. We had had a habit of keeping the keys to hotel rooms where we had enjoyed ourselves through the years. I forget how Fran finally managed to sneak up to Room 16 the night she opened in *Saint Joan*. It had been an exhilarating night. She had been terribly effective and she was "high" with the excitement. I was staying at the Inn over the weekend (I saw all the performances) and after we had escaped from the cast party and were in my car holding each other and kissing, she had said, "I'm coming up to your room." As I say, I'd forgotten how she managed it. It had something to do with the ladies' room being on the second floor. I smiled. Fran always found a way to do everything she really wanted to do.

We didn't make love that night. She would not let me in her, and did not until we were married. Oh, over the months I begged and pleaded and cajoled and pretended that I was going to force myself on her, but she didn't want that and she was very positive about it. We had a marvelous time anyway, lush with sensuality and discovery and humor and just feeling loved and in love. We experimented endlessly and found all kinds of ways of exciting and satisfying each other. She introduced me to a way she had said was "very European," but she would never tell me where she had learned it. Though she did tell me that she had had an "all the way" affair with an older boy. And he had left her. And I told her about a girl and a married woman who had "indoctrinated" me. "She did a very good job." And she laughed.

Fortunately they did not give me Room 16 or any other room we had occupied on our many returns to college. As I climbed the stairs with my suitcases, I nodded to parents who had come to see their daughters graduate. The daughters all looked so young. It was impossible to believe that Fran and I had been this young. I turned a corner in the corridor and surprised a boy and girl kissing. I smiled and said, "Sorry." And they laughed easily, and suddenly I was miserably lonely for Fran and for our youth, which had been our best time.

TWENTY

Those of us on the stage stood as the girls marched in for Prize Night. There was no uniformity of dress. This was not Graduation. It was the more informal occasion of giving class poems, class orations and the prizes for excellence.

As the girls sat down, the lights in the auditorium lowered, and the program began. We looked at the girls, and the girls looked at us, faculty and guests.

A phrase of my mother's came to mind. "The priceless gift of youth." I had never really known what she was talking about when I was young. It hadn't seemed a gift at all but a burden until I met Fran. I had longed to be older and mature and poised and self-assured. But now in my early forties, I knew what she had meant. Even those girls who were not really pretty were beautiful with youth.

I looked along the rows, and I thought how nature repeats herself! I could almost name each girl for her counterpart in Fran's class. I felt like smiling at them in recognition. Pat, the studious one. Myra, the poet. Mimi, the seductress. Rachel, very much involved with settlement houses, with really no time left for frivolous things like combing her hair. Fran, the actress. I stopped. She *did* look like Fran. She had what always had been described as Fran's "heart-shaped face." I wondered if she could be the one who had won the drama prize. It was uncanny. I kept looking back at her. I thought, "I never should have risked coming here. It's too soon. But perhaps if I just read the words I had written I can get away with it."

One of my friends had laughed and said, "I'm beginning to be attracted by my daughter's girl friends, and that's bad." How easy it was to be attracted by them! I felt as young as they looked, actually younger than I had felt at their age when I had been a kind of hypochondriac . . . until I met Fran. Then all symptoms had disappeared. I remembered that one outspoken friend had remarked on it. "You know, you used to more or less fade into the woodwork. What the hell's happened?" Purpose. Direction. No lonely nights and weekends of wandering, snooping, attending countless movies alone, but a girl on the other end of the phone, work done quickly so that I could get to her, evenings not dreaded for their emptiness but anticipated for their possibilities. I had had the feeling of being suddenly liberated from the prison of my inhibitions. Everything was possible.

My eyes looked further back in the hall, and there were the young men. Their young men. Was I ever that young? Not alone, but together with Fran I was that young. In a sense, she had given me my youth. I looked for myself in the rows of young men, but I could find no one.

Oh, I would have liked to have identified with that tall ruddy-faced young man with all that lustrous hair, but honesty wouldn't permit it. I still had a mop of unruly brown hair, but that was about it.

Now the heart-shaped-face girl was coming down the aisle to receive a prize in higher mathematics. Fran couldn't add the figures in her checkbook. Her body was nothing like Fran's. She would run to fat later on. Fran could still wear the clothes she wore on her honeymoon. The ribs were the test. You should always be able to see your ribs, was her contention. And no bra. If you wear a bra, the muscles get lazy. Of course, after the operation . . .

Finally . . . "This evening we have a new award which we haven't had on Prize Nights before. It is in Drama"—I sat up and reached in my pocket for my notes—"for the most promising actress in the graduating class. And we're honored tonight to have with us the donor of the award, the novelist, Christopher Larsen, who will present the award, and, I hope, say a few words about the woman it honors, Frances Larsen."

I started from my chair to approach the lectern, when she went on. "I think it might not be inappropriate to announce at this moment that the Trustees of the college have decided that our new theatre, which you all have seen under construction across the campus, will be named The Frances Larsen Theatre."

There was a burst of applause at this announcement, and I was left moving to the lectern with a lump in my throat. It was unfair to throw this at me when I had everything under control.

I started to read what I had written, trying to think of anything but what I had just heard and what I was saying. "Thank you, President Brewer. I just wanted to tell you, perhaps, the 'Why' of this award. It is a frankly sentimental award. As many of you know, Fran came to college here, studied acting here, and played in many plays under the direction of your beloved Miss Allison." I turned and bowed towards a spare little lady who had given Fran most of her fierce standards, who had always been proud of her, and who had always kept in touch. The audience applauded, and she waved her hand in an embarrassed little gesture.

I continued. "Fran went on to be an apprentice the summer she graduated, at the Chapel Playhouse on Cape Cod. I was an apprentice, too, that summer. It was there that she blossomed into being a fully accomplished actress, and it was there that she persuaded me to give up acting and become a writer."

The laughter made it easier. "Fran always believed that the only way to learn to act was to act. So this award is appropriate. A full scholarship with room and board at the Chapel Playhouse this summer and a small amount to help pay for a cold-water flat in New York or someplace else next fall." I looked at the slip of paper which Mrs. Brewer had given me as I approached the lectern. "The winner this year is Marianne Chappelle."

I looked out into the semi-darkened auditorium to see which one would be Marianne Chappelle. Somehow I had not seen her as my eyes had wandered over the rows, or I would have known. The first thing you noticed was "style." She was tall and slender and held herself beautifully, almost like a dancer. Her dark hair was worn in her own particular style, not the style of the day. And as I moved to the edge of the stage to help her up the stairs, I saw her large dark eyes, and they were filled with tears. She smiled at me as she took my hand to be helped. The entire effect of her was striking. I led her to the lectern, handed her the envelope and stepped aside.

She smiled desperately and looked at a small piece of paper she had crumpled in her hand. "Thank you." And I knew she was never going to make it. Tears started coming to my eyes as I tried to smile encouragement. "I . . . I can't tell you what this means . . . what this . . ." She bit her lip, turned to look at me helplessly, and then walked rapidly off the stage into the wings and disappeared. She did not run. She walked, and beautifully. The sympathetic audience burst into understanding laughter and applause to cover her confused exit. I returned to my seat.

When the ceremonies were over, Miss Allison made her way to me and put her arm around me and kissed my cheek, and said gruffly, "Thanks for the nice words. You didn't have to."

"I wanted to. Fran always said you were the most important influence in her acting life."

"Fran always was too generous with her praise, but that was Fran." She kept her arm around my waist as we walked to the side of the stage. "Look, this is all rough for you, I know. But it means a lot to us all. Thanks."

"I wanted to come."

"Because Fran would have done it, I know. But it must be one hell of a strain. That girl has great promise. Sorry she muffed it up there, but ever since she's known she was getting the prize—we had to tell her so that she could make summer plans—she's become very involved with Fran and her life, and she identifies with everything that's happened to you and Fran, and . . . well, I guess it was just too much for her."

"That's very touching."

"Well, she's read all the things you sent up, and the things you've written about Fran, and of course we already had a raft of material on her."

"She's very striking. Fantastic features for the theatre."

"No one part of her face is beautiful except those eyes, but it all adds up to an impression of beauty. I think she's going to be great." We were leaving the building. "You look as though you could stand a drink, or several.

Some of the members of the department and a few of the better students are coming to my house for whatever they can find. Would that be too rough on you? Just say so, if it is."

Miss Allison's house would be a difficult one to visit. Fran and I had met there when I had come from Cambridge to try out for a play (to meet girls, really). And we had often rehearsed in her large oak-beamed living room, and matchmaker that she was, Miss A had managed to leave us alone in the house a number of times, had turned it over to us to cook meals for ourselves. We had lain entwined for hours and hours on the couch in front of the fireplace . . .

She looked up at me. "No? All right. Some people want to run away, never go back. Some don't want to run away."

We started across the quadrangle in the direction of her house. Fran had really been deeply influenced by this no-nonsense yet terribly considerate little woman, who had spent most of her life living other people's lives. "I seem not to want to run away, at least yet. I'm staying in the house. I'm going over her things. I also seem to talk about nothing but her. Maybe it's a way of holding on awhile longer."

She put her arm around my waist again and studied the path as we walked. "I'm going to say something very tactless, so forgive me. But I don't know when I'm going to see you again, so I can't be too nice about my choice of time. But I hope that you find some nice woman and marry again."

She must have felt me tighten. She looked up at me. "I said it was the wrong time, but remember it six or eight months from now. You adored Fran, and that was good. And you will go on adoring her. And that will also be good. I've been reading what you've written about her. And it's lovely and true. *But* you've given her credit for everything you ever did, inspiration, et cetera, which is touching and understandable at this moment. But it simply is not true. You know, you mustn't make a life out of tending a legend. Now I'll shut up, and let's go get drunk."

TWENTY-ONE

A dozen or more of Miss A's "kids" were already in the house when we arrived. Those who had been at Prize Night had changed into jeans and sweaters. They were in full charge of the party.

Miss A sang out, "Look, everybody. This is Chris Larsen. You all know who he is. If you want him to know who you are, take care of introducing yourselves. But not until he's had a drink." And she led the way into the kitchen.

I smiled and said "Hello" to the students we passed. They smiled back. I knew the ropes of this kind of evening from talks I had given at other colleges. When I had my drink, it would be up to me to break the ice. Probably none of them had read anything I had written. Tonight I was strictly Fran's husband, and I would do what she would have done, go up to each one and, parrying questions about myself, find out the special interests of each and encourage her or him in that interest.

We entered the kitchen, where Fran had taught me the basics of cooking. A few girls were getting things ready. "Christopher Larsen . . . Debby Thompson, Bonnie Rogers (a very funny comedian) and Helen Margolis, my right-hand everything . . . Where's the booze?"

I tried to talk to the "funny comedian" and ask her what she had played, but she was shy. "Oh, Miss A exaggerates. I had this funny part in the last show. So I was funny."

"It was a nothing of a part, and you were funny. So, you're funny," Miss A shot at her. "However, she's off to get married, so that's that. I hope your husband likes a funny girl. I imagine it would be a great asset in marriage."

She took me by the hand and led me out of the kitchen and towards her study-library. "I've got a gift for you."

We entered the study. Books, pictures, model sets, costume sketches, a jumble of theatre objects. "That's a model of the theatre. Fran's theatre. That took you by surprise, didn't it? I was mad as hell about holding the announcement till tonight. I told them about Fran, how sick she was, but they wouldn't. I wish she could have known."

I stood and looked at the model of the theatre and frowned. I had found this a way to block emotion. The next moment I had a headache, and took a drink. "It looks great."

"It's not what it should be, but then, like most small college theatres, it has to double as lecture hall, concert hall and movie theatre. We're just lucky it doesn't also have to serve as a gymnasium and annex to the infirmary." She went to her desk and picked up a large manila envelope. "Don't open this now. And don't open it ever if you don't want to. But I've gathered together the pictures of Fran when she was acting here. And the ones of you too. You looked very good in tights. I'm sorry you weren't inclined towards older women." She smiled and handed me the envelope. "Now I'm going to see if Marianne has arrived yet and send her in to you so that she can thank you properly."

"Look, please. She doesn't have to . . ."

"Just stay here," and she left.

I had just about decided to risk opening the manila envelope when Marianne Chappelle was standing in the doorway with a drink for me.

"Miss A said I was to bring you this." She had changed into blue jeans and a faded scarlet turtleneck sweater, and her dark hair was down around her shoulders.

"Thank you." I took the glass and put the empty one on a table.

"She said it would give me a chance to make up for my incredible clumsiness at the ceremony."

"Oh, that was charming."

"I had something all written out, but then . . ."

"I understand. Congratulations again."

"It was bumbling, and I can't stand bumblers. I wanted to say something about your wife. I'd done so much reading about her and you, and it was my responsibility to say something about her."

"I'm very touched that you wanted to."

Her large dark eyes looked at me with such challenging intensity that it was difficult to return her look. There was an air of concern, as though she were saying, "How are you, really?" It was all I could do not to reach out and touch this girl.

"What parts have you played here?"

"Oh, the inevitable for someone of my height. Rosalind in *As You Like It,* Joan in *Saint Joan.*"

"Fran played Joan."

[117]

"Yes, I know. Though Miss A was very discreet, I kept thinking that in the back of her mind she was saying, 'Why can't you do it the way Fran Larsen did it?' " Again the lovely smile. I had forgotten about beautiful girls.

"I'm sorry I didn't see you."

"I've read all the pieces you've written on Fran. I'm sorry, but that's what we call her here, since she's more or less the patron saint of the Drama Department."

"That's nice. That's fine."

"I'd like to know more. You know, with the poetry prize, it's the obligation of the winner to write a paper on the poet in whose memory it's given."

"That seems a rather arduous task . . . But I'm getting together some material, a kind of scrapbook."

"I'd like to see it."

"And I have some tapes." She never took her eyes off me. It was as if she had been saying very intimate things to me.

"Will you be down at the beach cottage this summer?"

I looked at her for a moment. "I don't know. That's going to be the hardest place to go."

"I can imagine. I feel I know it all by heart."

"How?"

"From what you've written about it."

"It's just the way we left it in a hurry last year. The beds are probably still unmade. We never had anybody help down there. No intrusions."

"I'll be down there at the theatre. If you don't want to go, I could take care of things. Send you anything you might want. I should do something for my scholarship." She smiled, and her eyes talked and questioned and seemed to plead. I had never seen such expressive eyes.

"Thanks, but no. I want to do it myself."

"I understand."

"I may not get there till fall. But I'll get there."

There was the beginning of tears in her eyes, though she was smiling at me, and again I wanted to reach out and hold her. Tears and this lovely girl. I had the most terrible body hunger, an almost uncontrollable desire to hold her. The loving and inconsolable husband of Fran Larsen, keeper of the flame, survivor of the beautiful marriage, had no other desire than to hold this lovely girl who looked at him as though she wanted him to tell her everything. I cherished the concern in this girl's eyes. I wanted to tell her that I was exhausted, burned out. I wanted to tell her how much I had loved my wife and how much I needed to make love to her.

"Here is what I was going to say tonight." She handed me a crumpled piece of paper. "It's not the same as saying it, but at least you'll know I meant to say it."

"Thanks." I started to open it.

"No. Don't look at it now. I'll feel silly." She put her hand on mine to stop me.

"Well, has she made amends?" Miss A had returned.

Marianne quickly withdrew her hand. "I've just given him what I meant to say."

"If you get to the Cape this summer, drop in and look at her. She's good. And this one isn't going to get married." This embarrassed Marianne. I remembered that Fran had said she was never going to get married—then one day she married me. "Incredible dedication. The purest girl I ever met." And she pointed a finger at Marianne. "I don't mean her love life. I don't know anything about that. Ha-ha. But I mean purity where it counts." Completely flustered, Marianne blushed and looked at me, wondering what I would think. "I leave you nothing to say. Good. Then get out and mingle with your peers. Your puppy dog is waiting just outside the door." She patted Marianne on the shoulder and kissed her on the cheek. She turned to me. "I used to call you Fran's puppy dog, remember?"

As Marianne retreated, she said to me, "I'm going to write you a proper letter."

"When she learns how to spell." Miss A shooed her from the room. As she went into the hall, I saw a young man's arm go around her waist. "Fran would have been proud of that girl. She shames me with her dedication, her discipline. Did you see the way she holds herself? Fantastic. Such style. Absolutely ruthless with herself. It'll take her weeks to get over not having said her little speech tonight." She sat down on the couch and patted the place beside her. "Now, let's talk."

TWENTY-TWO

After two weeks at home in Connecticut, I headed for our beach cottage on the Cape. One more "duty call" to make before I "disappeared." The compulsion to disappear was overwhelming. Not just to disappear geographically but perhaps to disappear as Chris Larsen, his attitudes, his history, his strengths and weaknesses.

During the two weeks there had been constant invitations to dinner, picnics, movies, cookouts. Some I had accepted, and some I had not accepted, thereby offending and losing friends. Others had simply dropped in. "We were passing and saw the lights." So that finally if I wanted to be alone, I closed the garage door and sat in the kitchen in the dusk without turning on a light.

I had found myself staying in bed longer, withdrawing from the empty days. There had been times in my life when I had managed to doze away whole days and weeks rather than face the anxiety of emptiness. The letters gave me something to do, and I welcomed them. I was a writer and I should write. I would have to start earning a living soon. But I could think of nothing but Fran, of the last years, and I didn't have them in enough perspective yet to write about them.

I had often envied men who had to get up and go to an office and busy themselves with business routines. I envied them more now. Their business obligations seemed to me to provide them with at least a framework for their otherwise possibly shaky lives. I ran over assignments which had been offered me. I must check with my agent. Get out of here. Get an assignment in a foreign country, if possible, where nobody would know me. I would go to the Cape to set all that in order, and then . . .

I stopped to shop in a town ten miles from our beach cottage, in a place where I was not known. I then approached our entrance by a back road, avoiding our village and the houses of friends.

I had dreaded this visit, yet knew it had to be made, almost longed to make it, longed to keep finding the pain, thus keep contact with Fran. During the years of illness I had ticked off the times and places which I knew would be difficult after her death. And this place was always the hardest. It would be the place most dominated by her absence.

At the entrance to our drive, I stopped and swung open the gate, started to look in the mailbox, then decided against it. All second- and third-class mail stuffed into the box. If I removed it, Bessie, the mail carrier, would know I was there, and the news would be around town in an hour. I drove the car through the gate, got out and closed it, and started down the twisting avenue of pines that led to the clearing and the cottage and the water beyond.

This cottage had been our first real home. We had bought it with the first money we had saved and with the help of my father. At first Fran had not liked it because it was run-down and ramshackle, but her best friend had talked to her and told her how essential it was for me to have a place away from our lives in the city. And this was all that we could afford at the time.

The morning after the first night we spent in it, we had had a fight. She had said "Call the real-estate agent and tell her to sell it." I forgot what it was, the smell from the kerosene hot-water heater. I don't know. But I had insisted that we keep it, and as she fixed it up, she had come to love it.

I knew we needed someplace of our own, away from our small five-flight walk-up in the city, with its incessant going and coming of Fran's friends and students, someplace where we could be alone. And it had been just that for us. Over the years it was a place to which we had brought our jangled nerves, our differences, our murderously conflicting schedules, and on the beach, in the water, in the simplicity of the house we had been able usually to touch base again. We had been lovers in this village when we had been apprentices at the summer theatre. We had sometimes been able to be lovers again when we came to this cottage.

Even after we had basically moved to the country and only kept a small apartment in the city, this was still our place to get away to. We would instinctively sense that it was time for us to get to the cottage, recharge our batteries while driving through the winding roads. (She always loved to "tour"—"Look, Chris, there's a road we haven't taken!")

I could never explain why, but at the cottage we always seemed to be so much better suited sexually. In the city, days and weeks would go by, anxieties over work, hers and mine, would build up, time schedules would make any kind of moving together impossible. We would meet each other coming and going. Yet we were so ambitious for each other, so proud of each other, that we would try not to notice the loneliness of our marriage.

Then sometimes we would grab at each other, knowing that it had been a long time since we had made love, knowing that somewhere in our make-up we wanted it. And often it had not been at all satisfactory. Frantic, distracted, a "thing" we did together with an unspoken promise of a more relaxed and real and meaningful coming together at some later time. Keeping the franchise.

Resentments would grow, inevitably. Bad timing, poorly concealed accommodations to each other, transparent excuses. Yet when we got in the car and drove towards the cottage, it was as though we could sense that things would be different up here. We had the memory of intense times of love-making, days naked on the beach, the sensuousness of salt water and sun. Up here we seemed to be able to cope with the simple problems of the cottage and the more complex problems of ourselves. It was, in a sense, playing house. And perhaps we were both better at that than at keeping house.

I drove out of the woods and there the cottage lay, down by the water. The grass had not been cut. Frank was waiting to be asked, as he had waited every year. "You want me to cut the grass again this year?"

I stopped the car and just sat there. The wall had not been finished. Last fall, when we had left here so suddenly, Frank had promised it would be fixed by spring. It was force of habit to check the chores we had left to be done. When we had driven up from the city on Friday nights, arriving after dark, before we would go into the house, we would explore the grounds with flashlights or use the lights of the car to see what work had been done in our absence, to see if the roses had started to bloom, if the shelves had been put up in the shed. Each nail driven, each plant planted, each stone laid on a wall made it more ours.

And sometimes in the summer we would take off our clothes and run into the water and then hurry shivering back into the cottage to start a fire. "Why can't it be like this all the time?" Often I would feel like spoiling it by saying, "It could be, if only . . ." But I didn't say it. It all seemed so petty in the light of our joy at that moment. And she didn't say whatever it was she might have said. We asked questions. We never faced the answers.

I got out of the car, leaving the door open, and walked through the high grass and around to the front of the house and the wooden deck facing the beach. Fran's "birthday roses" were in bloom. Roses which came out almost without fail within a day or two of her birthday. Frank had apparently cultivated around the bushes. And he had cut a small stretch of lawn by the side of the house. Why had he stopped?

The late-afternoon sun felt warm and good. I don't think I could have stood it if Fran had died in the winter. An odd thought, but one that had occurred to me several times. Still, I shivered and needed a drink.

I went around to the back door, took the key from under the rock. Ants were crawling all over it. I opened the door and stepped in. The house was dark and chilly and smelled of dead mice. I went to the kitchen cupboard and took a couple of swigs from the bottle of bourbon, opened a window, turned up the thermostat to kill the dampness, and went outside again.

I walked around the outside of the house, peering in the windows like some trespasser. A ground hog scampered from his home beneath the shed across the lawn and into the field beyond. Fran had hated ground hogs and always wanted me to shoot them. I had tried once, but had only wounded it and hadn't been able to find it to put it out of its misery. I never shot another.

I sat on the railing at the edge of the deck and looked out at the long stretch of empty beach and the water. My head was aching. I needed another drink, but I didn't want to go inside again until it was warmer. Although it was summer now, I had felt cold ever since Fran's death. I could have asked Frank to come in and turn up the heat for my arrival, but then people would have known I was here.

What did I hope to accomplish here? Some final burning-out of the wound? One last and terrible encounter with the pain? And then it would be over? Cold turkey? Or some compulsion to stay close to Fran, secure and hurting.

I went around to the car, took out the provisions, entered the house and closed the door. The kitchen was a mess. I had kept it more or less clean that last month we had been up here, but the last day we had left in such a hurry. "I've got to get to the hospital, Chris. The pains are very bad." Then the long and painful ride into the city for the final operation.

I opened the refrigerator to put away the things I had bought, and there were the remnants of our last month. How much she had eaten then, and still skin and bones. Breakfast and then a midmorning something, lunch, tea, and then dinner and a nighttime snack while I read to her. I hardly seemed to get out of the kitchen before she would giggle apologetically and say she was hungry again.

I dumped everything into the garbage can, took the bourbon and moved into the living room, which Fran had made so bright and cheerful. It was still a little damp and I started a fire and then sat back on the large country couch. "Well, Fran, here I am. Here we are."

Fran's presence had always been with me. Other girls I had known disappeared from my thoughts when they were absent. There was no "idea" connected with them. Lively, beautiful, desirable, interesting. Fran was always more than that, an idea, a set of values and aspirations. A soul. It was not important that she be there in person. She was always "there." As a matter of fact, often more "there" when not actually present, diminished slightly by dailiness. Now dead, therefore, more "there" than ever.

A friend who was trying to comfort me had told me that his wife had been dead ten years and he could hardly remember her face. I couldn't believe it. Or perhaps it was Fran's being an invalid, in my charge for those years, my child, in effect, as well as my wife that put some kind of indelible stamp on her image, on our relationship.

I looked unseeing into the flame. "You never looked back, Fran. When we kissed good-bye on street corners or at airports or stations, you always turned away and walked on without looking back. I always stood there for a while, or kept turning to see if you were turning."

"Let go, Chris. Let me go."

I was so much more dependent on you than you were on me. Except for the last years. But I don't mean dependency in that way, physical, taking care of. I was dependent on you for the quality of my life. The endless hours I hung around rehearsal halls, or the stopping by to take you to lunch or dinner between rehearsals or your classes. I seemed to have no life independent of you. It was my work and you. But that had been my understanding of what marriage was. Or simply my need.

I would like to have one person I could talk to, talk and talk. Try to go through everything, sort it all out. But there is nobody but you. And after a while we didn't talk much about what mattered. How often there were things I wanted to say to you, but I waited till you were away or I was away, and then I wrote them to you. And we never mentioned the letters when we were together again. So open in my letters. My letters from the Pacific, not about the death and destruction around me, but about us. "We must try"   "When I get back, let's just be alone for a while and try."

But you were always more formal, barely humoring the ardent man in the letters, perhaps not trusting him in real life. Your letters full of what you were doing and "I miss you." My letters full of tortured emotions and longing expressed in sexual terms which embarrassed you, though I explained that officers censored each other's letters without reading them.

I looked around the room. This room had been our world for two months last summer. Taking care of you, washing you, cooking, massaging. I refused all offers of help from women of the village with nursing experience. For so much of our lives we had been unavailable to each other, it was as though I wanted to make up for it all in the time we had left.

Voices and images and memories began to drift back.

"I'm not going to get better gradually. One day I'm just going to wake up, and I'll be able to walk, and I'll be well." When all hope has gone, there has to be something.

"You must not tell her unless she demands to be told. It is not something you force on a patient just because it is your theory she should know. If she wants to know, have her make an appointment with me. I have had more experience in telling patients these things. As her doctor it is my responsibility to tell her."

The night here in the cottage when she had asked for the truth, perhaps the third or fourth time (Oh, Jesus, that night!), and finally she had calmed down and had eaten her supper and taken a Demerol. I had washed the dishes and gathered things together for my trip to the village dump. She was stirring as I passed through the living room. "I'm just going to the dump. You all right?" She had nodded. "I'll be back and read to you."

She had smiled. "That will be nice."

I put the garbage can in the station wagon and drove off into the twilight to the dump.

It had been raining for two days, and I hadn't been able to get out, and now I was out and away from the questions I could not answer. After stopping at the dump, I suddenly found myself taking the turn away from the beach, away from the cottage, and soon I was driving with almost suicidal recklessness through the twisting country roads, exhilarated by the risks I was taking, unable to stop. I drove on and on, inviting Fate at every curve. Finally it was dark, and I was calmer, and I turned back towards the cottage.

As I emerged from the woods into the clearing, I saw no lights. Fran would be asleep where I had left her. I stopped the car, got out and took the garbage can into the kitchen. Then I heard weeping. I went into the living room and turned on the light. Fran was not on the couch.

"Chris?"

I turned to the deck, and there she was on her hands and knees in the dark, sobbing.

"What's the matter?"

"Where were you?"

"I was at the dump."

"But you were gone so long. You've never been gone that long."

"I just drove for a while. What are you doing out here?"

"I was frightened."

"Of what?"

"I don't know. I just didn't know where you were."

I was angry, and hated myself for being angry. I had just wanted to drive, had had to drive for an hour, and she had punished me by doing this. Not punished, for Christ's sake. She was helpless, frightened.

As I helped her into the wheelchair and back inside the house, I murmured over and over, "I'm sorry. I'm sorry. I just wanted to drive. It was so beautiful." Her tears finally subsided, and I settled her on the couch, and after a while I read to her till she felt tired enough to go to bed.

Every cruel, unkind, short word came back to me. "Chris, maybe it would be better if you put me back in the hospital." One morning when she wanted breakfast before I was really awake.

"No. No. Just give me a minute to get awake."

People wondered at the care I took of her. I wondered at their wonder. She was going to know that she was loved. Let that be her last knowledge in this world. Why had I been so anxious to have her know this?

This internal dialogue had gone on ever since Fran had died. I had total and instant recall of every moment of cruelty.

I got up and shuffled towards the bedroom. The bed was still unmade. Last fall I had hastily thrown a cover over it. A pair of her shoes tossed in a corner. As we were leaving hurriedly, having made contact with the doctor and the hospital . . .

"We have to take my shoes."

Sharply. "We can't take them all. I want to get you to the hospital as soon as possible."

In tears. "I want to take my shoes."

In anger I had gathered together the ten pairs of shoes we had carried back and forth from the city, though I knew she would never wear any of them again, would never walk again. Of course I understood their meaning for her, for God's sake. I wasn't stupid. But I was tired and beyond my limit. She had said we could leave this pair of shoes because she wore them only at the cottage, and I had tossed them angrily towards the closet.

Ashamed and guilty, guilty of everything that was wrong with our marriage, even guilty of her death, I leaned against the doorway to the bedroom and started to cry. I cried for I don't know how many hours until I finally fell asleep.

[130]

TWENTY-THREE

Sometime the next morning I woke up, against my wishes. I felt drained. I didn't really allow myself to come fully awake. I was vaguely aware that I needed to go to the bathroom, but it could wait. The sun was up. I could see it on the beach and water. I didn't know what time it was. I didn't care.

I woke up again sometime later. Half asleep, I got up and shuffled into the bathroom. I stumbled back to the bed. I felt like some very old people I had known, crumpled on their beds. "Go away!" That's all that they had been able to say, and they had meant it. They were not asking for pity, or for someone to insist on staying. They genuinely wanted to be alone. They didn't have the psychological energy to make or endure social contact.

I lay there on my side, staring into middle distance. I had reached the depths I wanted to reach. Surely there was no further to go. But I had no will to start up again.

I became aware that I was hungry. I hadn't eaten last night. I had drunk a lot, and maybe I'd wolfed some crackers, but I was hungry.

I moved through the living room into the kitchen. I put some water in the coffee pot, took oranges from the refrigerator, and was about to squeeze them when I looked out the window towards the beach. Sitting on the railing at the edge of the deck was a girl. I just stood there and looked, resenting the intrusion. Were the kids from the village taking over this beach, knowing I wasn't here this summer? I looked up and down the beach. Deserted.

She turned and looked in the direction of the house, and I saw that it was Marianne. Were the apprentices at the theatre using the beach? Sometimes Fran and I had invited them down for a beach party after a performance or for an occasional afternoon swim. Perhaps it was just Marianne who was using it, and maybe the boyfriend who had been lingering in the hall waiting for her that night at Miss A's. I felt annoyance at the intrusion, but at the same time I was once more aware of what a lovely girl she was. Black hair, white T-shirt, faded blue jeans, bright orange towel on the rail beside her.

I didn't want to be rude. She had been so very touching after the award ceremonies, but I didn't think I could stand watching her and her boyfriend running down to the water, clowning, and finally lying out in the sun on that orange towel. She must have seen my car. Why didn't she knock?

Not knowing what I was going to say, I opened the door onto the deck and stepped out. She heard the door opening and jumped off the railing and came towards me. "Hello."

"Hello."

"If you want to be alone, just tell me to go away. I've been coming down here afternoons to swim and sun. Today we have the whole day off till we strike the set tonight . . . Perhaps I should have gone away when I saw the car." She was looking at me again with that concerned look.

"No. No. I'm glad you've been using the place."

"How are you?" That small frown.

"I'm okay." I obviously didn't look it.

"It's a beautiful place."

"Yes."

"How do you like the job I did on your lawn?"

"Did you do it?"

"Yes, but this is all I managed before I broke the mower . . . And I dug around the roses."

"Thanks. Usually a man does this. I guess he thought I wouldn't be coming down this summer . . . You looked as though you were waiting for someone."

"Me? No. I just come alone." She flashed her radiant smile at me. "I would have cleaned up the house for you, but I couldn't get in. And I remembered what you'd said to me about the people who had done that . . . before."

"The key is kept under the flat stone near the back door."

"When did you arrive?"

"Late yesterday afternoon."

"I didn't get here yesterday. May I see the house, or would you rather I didn't?"

"It's a mess."

"I peeked in the windows. It looks lovely. So bright and comfortable."

"I was getting myself some breakfast."

"I wish I'd known when you were coming. I would have laid in some things."

We moved towards the door. "I stopped at the market on the way."

"It's a sweet village."

"I shopped up the coast. I didn't want anyone to know I was here."

Just inside the door she stopped and looked at me seriously. "Then I shouldn't be here."

"No. I'm glad you're here." I started to show her the house.

She paused before the production photographs of the plays Fran had done, studying them carefully. "I saw that one. It's the first play I ever saw."

"It's all a mess. We left very suddenly. Fran woke up one morning and wanted to get to a hospital."

"If you'd let me, I'd like to help set it straight. Only what you told me to do." She had the gentlest voice.

"It's not required for your award, you know."

She smiled. "I know, but if you'd let me."

"I don't know how long I'm going to stay."

She looked around quickly with a frown. "Oh?"

"I'm not so sure it was such a good idea coming down."

"You look very tired."

"Well, I need a shave and I fell asleep in these clothes . . ."

We moved back towards the bedrooms. She barely looked at Fran's and my bedroom. The bed was still unmade, the shoes on the floor. We moved into the other room, where I had spent the night.

"This is the guest room, or really, my study. We didn't have many guests down here. It was the place we came to be alone." She looked over at the almost empty bottle of bourbon on the night table and moved to the

[134]

windows. "Most of the rooms open onto the beach or ocean. Get up in the morning and run right out and take a dip, skinny."

"I've been doing that. I mean, swimming skinny. There doesn't seem to be anybody around." She looked at me with that smile. And I just looked at her, and her smile died slowly and that frown took its place, her eyes never leaving mine. I reached out and touched her face, barely touched it, and shook my head. She moved her head slightly and kissed the palm of my hand, and with an animal groan I took her in my arms and crushed her to me.

Her arms went around me and held me to her tightly, as if this had been something she had been wanting to do. With short, quick movements she kissed my head, my cheeks, my eyes. Her intensity took me by surprise. My body surged with desire. My hands stroked quickly up and down her back, clutching and pressing her against me. It was all urgent for both of us. We said nothing, just small noises, murmurs. I felt her small breasts under the thin shirt. She moved away quickly and went to the bed and lay down with her arms open for me. I plunged into her arms and held her, and just rocked her. The feel of a live, vital body pressing into mine. It was a feast, but not the time to feast and savor, but to devour. My hand went under her shirt. With a quick motion she stripped it off and unsnapped her bra and offered her breasts, at the same time reaching down to my erection. I thought I would come before I got near her. I wanted just to lie by this body and hold it and touch it and experience it, but I also wanted to be in it, moving strongly and unafraid. I reached for the buttons on her jeans, but she was there before me, and the whole awkward business of removing clothes was over in a second.

I reached down to fondle her, but she took my body and urged it on top of her. She was ready. She needed no more. With a cry that was half a groan I entered her. Her legs clasped around me. With her arms she clamped me to her. She would allow no control, no waiting, no technique. With a kind of purity she insisted, and gratefully I accepted and selfishly drove on to my own release.

TWENTY-FOUR

When I came, I didn't stop because I knew she had not come yet. But after a minute or so she stopped and put her hand on my head and murmured, "No . . . No . . . Just . . . No." And she stopped my movements.

I lay there, chagrined. She had seemed to want it this way, had wanted no caresses, had simply wanted me to go ahead. My feelings were confused, part enormous gratitude, and part resentment that she had almost forced me to use her like this. I had not always been successful with Fran after our marriage. It had been so great before. But after, I had sometimes found myself coming long before she was ready, and when I had tried to take a longer time before, with my hands or mouth, she had said, "No . . .

No . . . I want you in me." And sometimes when she hadn't come and I had tried to bring her around with my hands or mouth, she would say, "No . . . No. It was nice just having you in me." I had never believed her. I came to hate that phrase.

Now I reached down to try to do something for Marianne, and she stopped my hand and said, "No. No . . . Just stay close."

"I'm sorry."

"Why?"

"It's just . . ."

Her eyes were still closed, smiling. "I wanted it that way."

"It's just so selfish."

"No. I'll be selfish later on. Perhaps. If we feel like it. Just rest."

I reached down and pulled the sheet over us. I stroked her breast, but she said, "No . . . No. Not now." I raised myself on one elbow and looked at her, smiling. She smiled back, a smile of satisfaction. I shook my head.

"What?" I kissed her lightly. "Don't you want to rest?" I lowered my head next to her. "What?" she asked again.

What? Everything which one day I might tell her. How incredible it was to have everything all together again, love, desire, affection, sex, and richer still for the sadness that lay behind it. I would have been incredibly happy just to lie beside her and hold her cool body for a long while, but she had been eager and so pure in her eagerness, that I should be with her completely.

"Thank you."

"Oh, no, no. I wanted to come to the Inn back at college and be with you that night."

"I wanted to reach out and touch you at Miss A's."

"Why didn't you?"

"It would have seemed . . . incongruous. We'd been

talking about Fran and your feelings for her, and mine . . ."

She raised herself on her elbow and looked down at me with great seriousness. "Does this, our being here like this, upset you? I mean . . ." I smiled and frowned. "Because if it does, if this makes you feel in any way . . . I don't know . . . I'd rather die than do anything to your feelings for Fran."

I reached up and pulled her down and kissed her. She snuggled in my neck. I kissed the top of her head. I knew that in some odd way she was here with me because of my marriage, or what she felt about my marriage.

We lay there for a while, not saying anything. I was filled with the complexities of my feelings, the ironies. I was here because Fran was dead. Out of my deep sadness had come this great delight. Did Marianne, this child, feel anything for me, or was this just an act of mercy? Did she feel she was some surrogate come to take care of me in my grief? What grief? I felt no grief at the moment.

She began to stroke my chest. "Why don't you take your shirt off? You left your shirt on."

"I know."

"Do you always leave it on when you make love?"

"Years ago . . . years and years ago, some girl I was embracing said, 'My, you're thin.' I think I've always been self-conscious of that ever since."

"Let's see how thin you are." And she unbuttoned the last button and opened my shirt. "I don't think you're too thin." And she kissed my nipple. "I'm the one who should keep my top on with these little breasts. They're ridiculous, aren't they?"

I reached over and cupped one. "They're adorable." I started to kiss them, excited again, to my surprise. I looked down at myself. "Later is now."

She ran her hands over me, and addressing my rising cock, said, "Thank you." I started to caress her, leaning on one elbow, but she eased me down flat on my back and said, "I can only seem to manage if I'm on top. Does that bother you?"

I was delighted with her frankness. "Of course not." I was touched and aroused even more by her openness.

"Just lie back and I'll do all the work." She smiled.

While she arranged herself, I again had the fear that I would be too fast for her. I would have no control now, since she would be regulating the pace and the movements. Fran and I had tried this way a couple of times when we were first married, but she hadn't liked it.

She leaned down and kissed me. "Are you shocked?"

"No, delighted." I reached up and held her breasts, then ran my hand down her long arching back and stroked her bottom. I moved my hand to her clitoris.

"No. I don't need that."

And I went back to stroking her breasts. In a surprisingly few moments her pace quickened, her eyes closed, and driving herself upon me, she reached her climax and sank on my chest, her hips still moving sensuously against me. I hadn't come. I was delighted. What was this? It gave me an incredible feeling.

After a few moments she looked down at me through her dark hair falling over her face and smiled. "It wasn't good for you."

"Yes it was," and I hugged her.

"What a pair we are! You don't like it that way."

"I loved it."

"Come now!" And she started to move her hips.

"No." I stopped her. "Save it for later."

She laughed and rolled away. We lay spoon-fashion, and in a few moments she was dozing.

I had no desire to sleep now. I was too filled with paradox and pleasure. And gratitude. Why had I always felt gratitude, as though the woman were doing me a favor?

With Sarah, I had felt gratitude but also shame. I had

had no desire to hold her damp, fleshy body after sex. I had simply wanted to get out, embarrassed that I could not show tenderness with any conviction. I had held her and fondled her and smiled at her through half-open eyes, as though it were all real, but I sensed the hypocrisy.

Lying there with Marianne dozing in the angle of my neck, I couldn't believe it. That was the overriding feeling. Wonder. And again, gratitude. And the exhilaration of feeling my own sexual power, in a sense, returned to me. The beautiful simplicity, uncomplicated by tension and resentments.

I looked down at Marianne's lithe, tan body nestled against my white body. I had never felt particularly comfortable undressed, not thinking much of my rather thin body. "Women are not as conscious of bodies as men are." But I didn't believe it. Little-boy talk, little-boy thoughts. Obsessed with questions of virility. Yet I remembered the great judge who had confided in me in his last years when I had gone to sit with him in the afternoons that the one thing he would like would be to have an erection, and he had told me that the happiest times of his life had been spent in bed making love.

My arm was going to sleep. My hand twitched a little holding her small breast. I had lied about her breasts. I liked breasts, had always liked womanly breasts. But now I loved her breasts. My hand involuntarily started to move gently across her nipple. She murmured. My erection returned.

The telephone rang. She woke with a start and looked across my chest at the phone by the bedside. I looked at it and frowned. She looked up at me, questioning. I just let it ring, troubled by its implications, more complex than I could realize at the moment. Finally it stopped ringing, and Marianne dropped her head to my chest again.

"I'm not here. I don't want anyone to know I'm here."

"Didn't you tell anyone you were coming here?"

"No. I just told a few friends I was going away, to be alone, and that I'd be back."

She looked up and studied my face seriously. "Have I done something wrong, breaking in on your being alone?" I kissed her forehead.

"People will find out you're here, of course, sooner or later. I used to hear the phone ringing when I was on the beach."

"I hope they don't find me. I really want to be alone." She looked up again. "With you." And I put my other arm around her and held her. My erection, which had died when the phone rang, came back, and she smiled and leaned down and kissed it.

"We must do something about this."

I brought her head up to my chest again. "No. Not now."

"But doesn't it hurt you if you don't?"

"No, it's a lovely feeling. I want to keep it for a while. I can't tell you how lovely."

"You haven't had your breakfast."

"Man cannot live by bread alone." It was very weak. How long since I'd bantered with a girl.

"Just lie there, and I'll bring you breakfast."

"I hate breakfast in bed. My Puritan soul. My Calvinist soul."

"Are you a Calvinist?"

"No, but in many things I might as well be. Terribly disciplined."

"I like that."

"It gets the world's work done. It's not always easy to live with. I mean, for a person to live with his own Calvinist soul." She reached out and touched my cheek and looked at me a long, long time, then smiled and shook her head in a sense of disbelief.

She reached down by the side of the bed and pulled

on her T-shirt. "We made a terrible mess of things," indicating our clothes on the floor and chairs. "Look the other way till I get my jeans on," and she slid out of the bed. I understood her shyness. Her nakedness in bed was quite distinct and of a different quality from her nakedness walking around the room. "Which bathroom shall I use?"

"Use the one there. I'll use the one in our room." We both caught the "our." My friends at home had gently tried to get me to shift my pronouns from "our" to "my," from "we" to "I." But it was impossible. It was not my room. It was our room, Fran's and mine. I did not do this and that, travel here and there. We did. It was useless to try to censor a person out of your life by changing pronouns.

She ran water into the basin. I got out of bed quickly and grabbed my clothes from the floor and chair and went to our bedroom. I threw my clothes on the unmade bed and went into the bathroom. All Fran's lotions and creams and sickroom things were there. As I closed the door, I saw her nightgown hanging on the hook. But I did not respond. I looked at myself in the mirror. A mess, sunken-eyed, unshaven.

There had never been any pleasure for me to look at myself in full-length bathroom mirrors. But it was a shock now. Marianne's loving had somehow transformed my body in my mind's eye. Now I looked at it, long and poorly put together, and I wondered how she could have handled it so lovingly. There had not been any real change in my body since I was in my late teens, so I did not feel middle-aged or decrepit in that sense. I was just very white and not very prepossessing.

I shaved quickly but carefully. I had forgotten my razor and had to use one Fran had for her legs. Then I showered, and as I dried myself, I could still feel Marianne's body, and I began to get excited and exhilarated by the stirring in my cock.

[143]

In the bedroom I opened the bureau and found some underpants and a sweater. I didn't like the way I looked in the first and found another. In the closet I looked for the khaki slacks I liked. They were too big around the waist. I knew I had lost weight in the last year, but not that much. I slipped into sneakers. From the time I was a kid, there was always something about getting into sneakers for the first time each year. They meant summer, outdoors, games, running, sloshing in the water on the beach. I combed my hair carefully in front of the mirror. I was going out to play. It was a fantastic feeling. I didn't think about anything except that there was this extraordinary girl out there who had dropped into my life. She was life, not death, and for some reason I could not understand, I functioned beautifully with her.

TWENTY-FIVE

In the kitchen Marianne was opening and shutting cupboards.

"I can't find a squeezer." I got it for her. "Don't look in that corner. There's a dead mouse."

"I smelled it yesterday. I wondered where it was."

"Well, it's very dead. A long time."

I scraped it up in some cardboard and went outside and threw it into the brush and came back. Watching her cutting the oranges and getting the glasses did something to me. I came up behind her and put my arms around her and pressed myself against her. "You have an adorable bottom, do you know that?"

"Yes." She giggled.

"Good. That night at Miss A's, your blue jeans all worn pale over your bottom . . ." I pressed my hardness to her.

"You see, you should have let me take care of that."

"I want to preserve the feeling as long as possible. I haven't felt this way in . . . so long." My hands cupped her breasts. "Kitchens do something to me. A woman being womanly. I don't know. For other men it's black nightgowns. For me it's an apron and a frying pan."

"I'd see a doctor about that if I were you." And she wriggled her bottom against me.

"That's how it was with Fran the first time. She offered to cook me a dinner on our second date, and . . . we never ate the dinner." She turned and smiled with that look of concern in her eyes. I let her go and reached for the coffee cups. "My friends tell me I shouldn't talk so much about Fran."

"I want to hear about her, and you."

She stopped squeezing the oranges and came to me. "You came down here to be alone. Whenever you want me to clear out, just say so."

I looked at her a long time and shook my head. "I was going to clear out this morning. I came down here yesterday because I was desperately lonely, not for people, but for some meaningful human contact. And I knew, though it would be murderous, I could find it only with Fran. Here. Morbid, perhaps. But I was being driven crazy by the kind but essentially superficial contact with my friends. I wanted to find someone I could . . . let myself go with . . . and Fran was really the only one. Now . . ." I reached out and touched her cheek.

I felt tears come into my eyes. I had thought there were no more tears after last night. Marianne came to me quickly and put her arms around me. This is what I had wanted. Someone to say, "You've been hurt, you're suffer-

[146]

ing. It's awful. It isn't just awful what's happened to Fran. It's awful what's happened to you." I made no sound. I stood there imposing my needs on this girl. How seldom in my life I had told anyone what I needed, or asked for it. But there I was with no defense against the urgency of my need. My mind was ashamed, but there I was. It was not the way I had been alone the night before, convulsive, endless tears, but quiet tears in her hair punctuated with "I'm sorry" and her cooing "Shhhh."

Within an hour or so I had rendered myself up to this girl whom I hardly knew. I had smothered her with my physical needs, my emotional urgencies.

My tears were over in a few moments, and as I held her, I felt myself hardening against her. I shook my head at this contradiction. Something insists on living, on surviving, on seeking out its own interests and satisfactions.

Marianne was obviously aware of my excitement, but this time she made no move. As I pulled my head away, still saying "Sorry," she said, "Imagine loving anyone that much."

I was surprised at this. "Haven't you?"

"No. I wonder if I could. I envy you."

I needed to be honest, at least as honest as I could be at that moment. "I'm sure it's not all love. I can't tell you what it is. It just happens. But I think there must be some very unattractive motives, some very selfish ones."

"Well, that's all right too."

"Thanks."

"Please don't thank me again." She looked very stern about it, although she was smiling. "Do you still feel like eating?"

"Yes. By all means."

She finished squeezing the orange juice and handed it to me. She held my eyes for a moment. "Thank you for

[147]

that." She nodded towards the corner where we had just been.

"Why?"

"Just thank you." And she turned back to the counter.

TWENTY-SIX

All during breakfast I couldn't keep my hands off her. I would reach out and touch her face, stroke her hair. Suddenly I would get up and crouch by her chair, pressing my face into her breasts, or stand beside her and press my hardness against her shoulder. Ordinarily we would have moved from there back to bed, but we had time, and the prolongation of the feeling was exciting. As I stood beside her, she would cup me through my khakis and whisper, "How's my friend?"

"He's fine."

She was a very tidy girl, insisting on cleaning up after breakfast and wanting to go beyond that and clean the whole kitchen. I pulled her away from that.

We stood in the living room with our arms around each other. I didn't want to stay in the house. I wanted to get in the car on this shining day and drive through the countryside with this girl. I wanted to show her all the lovely spots, the beaches, the old houses, the moors and marshes. Strangely, I wanted to shop with her. I wanted to push a cart for her in a market. Amazing how quickly I revert to the domestic. I wanted this lovely girl, but I wanted it to be domestic. And yet I had hated so much of the domestic, but that was when I had had to do it alone, when Fran had been away.

"I would like to put you in the car and drive you to all my favorite places, faraway beaches, junk shops, hot-dog stands. But . . . I don't want to go out that gate. I have a feeling that once out there, I'll pass someone, meet someone . . ."

"There seem to be miles and miles of deserted beach right out there. Let's walk there."

We left the deck and headed down the beach, arms around each other, stopping every once in a while to clutch each other tightly and exchange looks of disbelief, or kiss lightly on the cheek. I realized there were hundreds of things I didn't know about her, but I wondered if I wanted to ask.

I felt that if I said, "Tell me something about yourself," there would suddenly be a gulf between us. We had leaped all formalities and clutched each other desperately in bed. It was now strange to go back and say, in effect, "Who are you?" There was a dimension between us, also a simplicity which might be spoiled with particulars. There would come a time when touching, grasping and stroking would not be enough, and we would want to know more.

We picked up shells and unusual-looking stones. I looked for delicate white shells, while she hunted out egg-sized stones she said would make good paperweights for me. Finally we were tired, and flopped in the sand. I immediately kissed her on the neck and started to nuzzle.

"You know, you're like a little puppy dog."

I thought of what Miss A had said. "Your puppy dog is waiting for you out there . . ." But I said, "I just can't stand not being in contact with you. Does it annoy you?"

She laughed. "No. It's lovely."

"I just can't get enough of touching you and holding you. I suppose there are all sorts of reasons why, which we could talk about. But I'd rather just enjoy the feeling without trying to analyze it."

Side by side was not close enough for me. I stretched out, and curling my legs up behind her as a back rest, I put my head in her lap facing her belly. I pulled up her T-shirt and kissed her stomach. I thought of Fran. "The important thing is to be able to see your ribs. As long as you can see your ribs, you're not fat." She loathed fat people.

"You know, you're a surprise." I looked up at this. Were we going to start to talk about us?

"In what way?"

"I don't know. Just a surprise."

"A disappointment?"

She pressed my head to her stomach. "No."

"What had you expected? Perhaps you'd better not tell me."

She looked at me, obviously trying to be careful. "I hadn't expected you to be so . . . physical."

I laughed. I'd heard this before. "I must give a very strange impression I'm not aware of. An ascetic?"

"No, it's not that. Maybe I don't have much experience in these things."

"No, it's been said before. Even when I was a kid, mothers would trust me with their daughters when they wouldn't let them out with other boys in our group. I always found it insulting, but in the end, rewarding." I smiled.

[151]

"It's a nice surprise." She leaned down and kissed me.

"It's had its advantages. I get away with murder because I seem so innocent."

"What kind of murder do you get away with?" She looked at me as though she had caught me.

I shrugged. "If people were to see us together, for example, they never would suspect anything. He's harmless. Besides, in this instance, he's an old man, and she's . . . How old are you?"

"Twenty-two." She lay back against my legs. "Were you ever unfaithful to Fran? That's a very little-girl question, I suppose. But in reading all the stories you write about marriage, and what other people have said, I wondered."

Without hesitation I answered "No." Because that's what she wanted to hear. And because, though she would have understood Sarah, I was so ashamed, I couldn't mention it. It hardly seemed an infidelity. Just something mechanical. And Jean . . . ?

"I thought not."

"Remember, you only know what I want you to know." It was a poor saving of face for my conscience.

She laughed in a kind of disbelief. "I'm sure."

I raised myself on an elbow and stared at her.

"Why do you stare at me so?"

"I just can't believe it."

"Am I a surprise?"

"I had no opinion of you. I knew from that night at Miss A's I wanted to touch you and hold you . . . But *we* are a surprise."

"Are you glad?"

I leaned down and kissed her, and holding my lips to hers, moved my body closer to her. I covered her face with kisses. There was a smile on her face which seemed to be saying "I'm glad you're enjoying me. Find every place on me that gives you joy."

I kissed her breast through the thin T-shirt and felt the nipples rise. Did we want to be together here, or did we want to wait? I stopped suddenly. She opened her eyes. "Let's go in the water and then back to the house."

She smiled, understanding that the water and the sun would only elevate us to another plateau of excitement. She half raised herself and looked up and down the beach.

"Nobody. Nobody ever comes around here this early in the season." She looked at me a moment. It was a new kind of nakedness in front of me. "Come on!"

I stood and kicked off my sneakers and took off my khaki pants. My cock was erect under my boxer shorts. She laughed. "I'm sorry. It just looks so funny like that." And she wriggled over on her knees to kiss it through my shorts, as though in apology.

"It does not like to be treated as laughable."

"Oh, it's not. It's just that in your shorts like that."

"Well, then, we'll take them off." I pulled them off rather awkwardly.

"Now, that's something different." She touched it, then started to laugh again. "You know, I once thought a man had three of these."

"Only pawnbrokers."

She rocked back, laughing.

"Where the hell did you get that idea?"

"I don't know."

"Come on. Let's go!"

"You've left your shirt on again." I stripped it off. "You go ahead."

Her modesty was strange, but to be respected, no matter. I backed away from her a few yards. I had my own feelings of modesty about my behind. I then ran towards the water and recklessly and uncharacteristically plunged in. Immediately I leaped high up into the air to escape the cold, then sank into it again to wait for it to become warm. I lay on my back and looked towards Marianne. She was bending over, taking off her jeans.

I was filled with an incredible joy. The expectations and the certainties of the next few hours were beyond belief. The sun, the water, this enchanting girl and my own feeling of power and vigor. Uncomplicated. Pure. Sensual.

Marianne came running down to the water. She had left on her T-shirt and her cotton panties. She was right. She had good instincts. There was something infinitely more erotic that way, though she probably hadn't thought of it. I stood up and came towards her, my cock now momentarily shriveled from the cold water. She shivered for a moment, but then taking long strides, she waded into the water and dived in and swam towards me with clean, strong strokes.

"You're quite a swimmer."

"I like it." She stood next to me. The dark nipples clear through her wet T-shirt. I reached over and cupped one breast. "Let's just swim for a few minutes. All right?" She flashed a smile.

"You go ahead." I felt it was something she enjoyed doing alone.

"Just for a few minutes. It's such a fantastic day." And she set off, moving swiftly and beautifully through the water. An exercise, a routine, a discipline. With slow, steady strokes, head down, head up, she kept going. It was indeed something she did well.

I swam, then turned over on my back and floated. The sun beating on my face and exposed body. I looked out towards Marianne. Beyond her were some boats. Damn it, I hope nobody takes it into his mind to come in. I hadn't thought about that. Friends with boats. We were quite far down from the house. They might not make the connection.

Marianne was coming back in now. I turned over and

swam towards her. There was something deliciously sensuous about the flow of the water on my naked body, the movement of the ripples through my legs, almost caressing as my body turned with the strokes. As she approached, I stood up. The sensations had excited me again.

She looked at me and laughed. "How can you swim with that like that?"

"As you can see, I don't swim much." I moved towards her. Shaking the water from her ears, she breathed deeply, still out of breath from her exercise.

"Oh, that was lovely. Did you mind?"

"Of course not."

"I don't like to just dunk in the water. I like to swim until I'm tired and then get out."

I kissed her lightly on the lips. "Don't go away yet." I started to run my hands over her body. "The texture's all different in the water." I pulled her down and we moved about in the shallow water for a few moments, just staying afloat by kicking our feet, or shoving against the bottom. "Doesn't it feel different?"

"Mmmm."

"You're very smart, keeping your things on."

"Why?"

"It's nice." My hand ran down between her legs. "Different."

"I was just suddenly embarrassed."

"I understand." I took one of her hands and guided it to my cock and balls. She immediately took the initiative. She looked at me. "Is that nice?" I just closed my eyes and smiled. "Will you tell me what you like?"

"With pleasure." Her fingers and the movement of the water were almost unendurable. I moved my body away and kissed her. Our heads went under water, and we separated, each struggling to gain balance. Coughing and laughing and choking, we headed for the beach. I suddenly grabbed her and kissed her. "I can't stop touching you."

"It's not something you have to apologize for." And she ran up to where we had left our clothes.

We had no towels. We stood looking down at our few clothes. I handed her my pullover to dry herself. We didn't want to sit wet in the sand. We looked at each other. "Let's go back to the house." She skinned her T-shirt over her head and pulled on my sweater, but not before I leaned over and kissed her breast. "Sorry. Now you can put it on." She shook her head.

We slogged back through the sand, arms around each other. We were in a hurry. The teasings and caresses and sensations of the morning had been building up. I made it difficult for her to walk as my hands roamed over her body. I touched her panties. "Aren't these uncomfortably wet? Don't you want to take them off?"

She laughed. "I will. In time."

When we reached the house, we went to my study, where we had been earlier. I slid open the windows so that now the room was part of the sun-drenched deck. I threw my clothes on the chair and turned to Marianne. She was already in the bathroom with the door closed. I went to the linen closet and brought two fresh bath towels. I heard the shower running, and I opened the door.

I moved to the shower stall and knocked on the glass door. She opened it and looked at me. "You've been away for two minutes." I stepped into the stall. She was glistening with soap. I held her to me, running my hands up and down over the slippery surface of her skin.

She looked at me and smiled. "Another texture."

"Yes. An infinite variety." I crushed her to me, my cock hard between our bellies. "I don't know how to express it. I feel I would like to press you right into me, to absorb you." My hands cupped her bottom and pressed it still harder to me. I held her like that for a moment, then the wave passed, and I stepped away. I took the soap from the dish and moved my hands between her legs.

"I've already done that."

"It needs doing again." And I ran my soapy hand up her legs. The sensation was almost too much. I reached my hand through with my strokes to her bottom.

"No. No." And she tightened and wriggled away. She took the soap and started to wash me. I winced with the sensation. "That's enough," and moved away from her. I turned on the cold water, and we both gasped. I turned it off, and opened the stall door and we stepped out.

She started drying herself, but I took her towel and insisted on helping. She tried to dry me at the same time, and as we got tangled up in arms and legs and towels, we both started laughing and she said, "I think it's simpler if we each do ourselves."

"Simpler, but not as much fun." I kissed her belly button. She backed away, and for a few moments we worked on ourselves. But then I moved to the toilet seat and started on her again.

"This needs special attention," and I gently started to dry between her legs. She just stood there looking down at me, smiling, enjoying the gentle rubbing. Suddenly I dropped to my knees and began kissing her belly, and then her hair down there, and then opening my mouth, I moved lower. She moved away slightly, and I looked up and saw her frowning. "Why not?"

"I don't know."

"You kissed me there."

"I know . . ." There was a pleading look of distaste on her face.

"It's very nice for me. You're lovely all over, you know."

Still the little frown. I wasn't going to force it. Obviously there was a story. I might hear it in time. I just pressed my lips to her hair again, my hands stroking her bottom, and then I stood up . . . and we moved out of the steamy bathroom to the sunlit bedroom.

TWENTY-SEVEN

I pulled the curtains partway closed so that the sun would not be in our eyes. When I turned back to the bed, she was lying face down, her head buried in the pillow. I crouched on the bed next to her and leaned down and lightly brushed my lips over her back. She shivered. I blew on her back, gently, as though I might be cooling something. She giggled. I ran my hand the full length of her back. It was so beautiful and strong, and even lying like this, proud in the arch at the base of the spine. A sudden double image of the indelible-ink crosses on Fran's spine. I shut my eyes and quickly kissed her bottom, seeking by some immediate strong sensation to blot out the crosses.

While I was kissing, I moved my hand up her legs and began to caress her.

Then I realized I didn't want to "do things" to Marianne. I had "done things" to Sarah in the messy, dingy apartment. We had "done things" to each other, to excite, stimulate, even humiliate to the point of excitement. I wanted to touch and kiss and feel Marianne, but it must not be "doing things," mechanical tricks.

I lay on my back next to her. She raised herself on her hands and slid over so that her breasts were above my face. It was a lovely invitation. I raised my head. "Sometimes it happens for me just from having my breasts kissed." It was a challenge I accepted, but after a minute or so, she swung her leg over and straddled me and guided me into her. Her face flushed from her position. Her eyes closed, she began. Again I experienced this strange sense of control and power. Though it was enormously exciting, I felt I could go on forever, that I could will almost whatever I wanted. This extreme control was something new to me and added pleasure in performance to pleasure in the act. Why was it happening? I thought of other times, sometimes with Fran, when I had been too fast, and I had flushed when I had heard that psychologists interpreted this as an expression of hostility, resentment, a desire to frustrate and disappoint. Disappoint Fran? Why?

Marianne started to murmur, and her breath came more sharply, and I thought, "Shall I hold on? I could." There was an impulse to exploit this new control, to revel in it. But I sensed we would not be together again that afternoon. It was not a time for sexual athletics. That was not the character of our relationship. I looked at her face, contorted in concentration, eyes tightly closed. Imagining what?

I lay there conscious of the power to give her pleasure. I almost smiled at her determination to press on to her own completion, aware all over again that sex is at once selfish, selfless, together but alone, impulsive, calculated, colored by all the hues of each personality. There was something demanding in Marianne. I wondered how she could say, "It's nice just to have you inside me." The pitch of her involvement was so intense that I imagined she would be half crazed with frustration if she didn't achieve orgasm, once she had been aroused.

She came in a series of short climaxes, separated by ten or fifteen seconds. And then I knew she was through, and though I had not come, I had pretended. I almost laughed. I, pretending!

She half turned over on her side, I still inside her. She hadn't opened her eyes. Her long dark lashes fluttered, and then there were tears. Why? I suddenly felt like an intruder. I did not think she wanted me to share the tears. I did not think she wanted to be comforted. I slowly withdrew and reached down for the sheet to cover us. Though we didn't need it in the bright sunlight, it seemed called for. She turned her back to me and drew herself up in a semi-fetal position. I turned on my side and put my arm around her. In a few moments she was asleep.

I stared blankly over her shoulder out the window at the water and the sky and the white clouds. It is a strange thing that I find impossible to explain, but often during the months and years when I knew Fran was dying, I would walk along the street and would say to myself, "How will I think of her when she is gone?" And for no reason that I can understand, I came to attach her to white, floating clouds.

As I looked at the clouds over Marianne's shoulder, I suddenly wanted to be alone. I wanted the mirage, the oasis to vanish, and I longed for the desert again. That was my life. Fran's death was my life. Though I had not been drained sexually by orgasm, still I sensed "the little death." The relationship of this day with Marianne was over. It had saved me, but now the rest of my life rushed in with a completely different kind of urgency and richness. I was sad, frowning. Wondering why, I finally sensed it was as though I had been listening to some overpoweringly beautiful music and thinking, "I wish this had been with Fran."

But it hadn't been like this with Fran for years.

The telephone rang. Marianne started out of her sleep, raised her head. I held her tighter. We listened to it ring till it stopped.

"I must go in a few minutes."

I didn't protest. I just kissed her shoulder. "I haven't asked you anything about how you like the theatre. What's happening?"

She turned and looked at me. "Are you going to stay down?"

I looked at her and then smiled. "Yes." I kissed her lightly.

"People will sooner or later find you're here."

"I suppose so."

"Where will you shop? How will you get food?"

"I'll go out under the cover of night. Some town far enough away from here. Where are you living?"

"Over Mrs. Grader's barn."

"Yes, I remember that." Fran had lived there as an apprentice.

"I could bring you things. Shop for you."

I didn't want her to move into the cottage with me. I wanted her, but I didn't want her there, living there.

"I'm involved at the theatre, of course, most of the time, and they like us to watch performances at least a few times a week, but there would be time."

"Why don't we see how I manage."

She perhaps sensed my feelings of withdrawal. She looked at me a long time. "May I come here . . . sometimes?"

I smiled at her and kissed her. "What a question!"

"Well . . ."

"Please come."

"I only want to come when you want me. How will I know? I can't call you."

I thought of Fran's signal, two calls in quick succession. But then, if I started answering the phone, someone might find the line busy, and the local operator . . . I touched her face. "Please come whenever you can."

I found myself excited by what I had said, by this kind of commitment to this girl. A moment ago I had wanted her to go away. And now I had said "come whenever you can" and had been moved by my saying it. And yet wondering if I really meant it.

"Why don't you tie a dishtowel on the doorknob when you want to be left alone?"

"All right." She sat up and moved to the edge of the bed. I reached over and touched her long, lovely back, and then moved to her quickly and kissed her and held her for a moment. She was sad, perhaps just the normal sadness after sex, and I wanted to hold her. I could never stand the abrupt change that sometimes came after making love, as though it were the end of something rather than just an episode in a continuing feeling.

Marianne slipped into her jeans while I watched. She turned and smiled. "I'm no longer embarrassed." Her T-shirt was still wet.

"Wear my sweater." She pondered this for a moment. I thought, There's a whole bureau full of things in "our" room, but it would offend Marianne if I had offered them to her. I watched her pull the sweater over her naked breasts, then turn to the mirror and brush her still-damp hair.

Watching Marianne perform these homey, feminine routines made me excited again, and I thought for a moment of pulling her back to bed, but I also wanted her to go. She went into the bathroom, and I quickly got out of bed and slipped into my trousers and sneakers. When she came out again, we just stood and looked at each other for a long moment. Then we smiled and shook our heads in acknowledgment of what had happened between us.

"We strike the set tonight, and tomorrow's setting up and dress rehearsal, and more rehearsing Monday . . ." It sounded as though she were outlining a schedule which would make it difficult for her to come back. I thought of David and his avenues of retreat. And my own.

"I know you're busy. Come when you can." That sounded very casual. What were we doing here, offering each other open doors?

"What will you do here?"

"Oh, lots of things." I smiled. "I find myself doing all the little things, repairs Fran wanted me to do which I never did." I shook my head. I kissed her. "I'll be here." With my arm around her, I walked her out of the bedroom onto the deck and around to the shed where she had left her bicycle. Now that she was about to go, I didn't want her to go.

We held each other without saying anything, then she kissed me quickly and walked her bike into the yard with her long, strong strides, mounted it, and rode off. Just before she entered the tree-lined road, she waved without looking back, and though she couldn't see me, I waved too.

TWENTY-EIGHT

I turned back to the cottage, walked around to the deck and went in by the door to my study.

As I lay on the bed and looked at the ceiling, I could still feel Marianne's body on my body. It had been that way in the beginning with Fran. We had just lain on her couch in her room for hours on end, just holding each other. And when I left in the early hours of the morning, I could feel the pressure of her body long after I had turned out the light in my own room fifteen miles away.

I felt very much at peace, as I had felt the first time with Fran when it had been for the most part an emergence from the grubby world of adolescence, with grabbed opportunities in dark and furtive places, morbid and solitary fantasies and practices. And then suddenly a sense of rightness and of focus.

But again I felt the sadness, not the sadness of Fran's death, but sadness for the loss we had suffered long before, long, long before.

Sadness and guilt in some ways more troubling than her death. I had tried. We had tried. Fran, I think, more to humor me, perhaps knowing that I would not accept what was supposed to be inevitable. It was too bleak. That was for other people who did not try hard enough. If only we tried, we could make it. Aging and habit and familiarity and resentments were for other people.

Had she been depressed at my periods of silent moodiness, periods when she must have known I was wondering "Why?"—periods which ended with another try, and still another. "Depressed people are very susceptible to diseases, even things like cancer." Once she had decided to leave me, because she felt she was making me sad. But she didn't leave. She had simply taken a position as an actress in residence for a semester, and then returned. Nobody had ever known of this, and she hadn't told me till long after.

"These things happen." But that's too simple. Why? How often affectionate impulses were stifled by some resentment or hurt or insensitivity! My longing, and her longing too, to hold, to press, to fondle and kiss and lie all over each other on the couch. But inherent in doing this was forgiveness for slights and hurts. "Everything is all right, then?" But it was not easy for either of us to give in, to imply forgiveness. And it is impossible to love freely and still hold resentments in reserve or abeyance. By your insensitivity you have hurt me or belittled me or been completely unaware of my feelings, but tonight I need you. I do not need *you* specifically, my wife, my husband. I need a body. And so it all becomes fragmented and so rarely all together. Tonight because I am lonely. Tonight because I

think I did a good job today. Tonight because you are depressed. Tonight because we both drank too much at the
party and we can overcome our resentments and defenses
and have at each other desperately and lie back exhausted
and wonder why it can't be like this always.

And for the next day, stay clear of differences, pretending that our free and urgent coming together proved
that basically we are good together. Intimacy which passed
for the real intimacy we had somehow lost, and then
found in the days of her dying and now had lost forever.

Marianne had said "I just want you in me." And Fran
had said that and I had not believed her. But Marianne
had gone on to her own release, and many times nothing
had happened for Fran, and I had suggested we go back to
ways we had known, things we had done before we were
married, but she had said "No. I just like the feel of you in
me. It doesn't matter that I don't come." And often I had
felt diminished, inadequate, and had sometimes for long
periods stayed away from her, avoiding contact or closeness which might lead to contact, unwilling to face again
this defeat, this feeling of inadequacy, yet troubled and
angry that she would not let me help her in other ways.

And then sometimes we would manage. That strange
night in Vienna when suddenly for no reason she was open
to everything, taking the initiative, possessed. And the
sense of relief for both of us. But in the end the relief only
telling me that "just you in me" was not enough . . . Or
was it, really? If it had been, how sad! The nights we could
have been close.

I turned my head and saw Fran in her white flannel
nightgown standing in my doorway, her face lit up with an
extraordinary wild smile. "Look, I'm walking. I made it
from our bedroom without my canes." I had smiled and
said, "That's marvelous," knowing she would soon be
dead.

I turned and buried my head in the pillow, trying to

block out all the compounding sorrows and guilts. "Man is in love and loves what vanishes." Loves it with a guilt for not having loved it more while he had it. I wanted Fran back so that we could play it all over again and have it different.

TWENTY-NINE

I looked at my watch. Ten o'clock. I had been asleep on the couch for almost an hour. I had slept for a couple of hours after Marianne had left, and now this hour after writing letters.

I looked across to the one spot of light in the living room, the large table I had cleared around four o'clock for Fran's letters. Seven letters written, long letters, interrupted by a supper of hash, a sliced tomato, half a head of lettuce, and coffee.

The letters had drained me. Letter by letter I had reinforced the image I would hold of Fran, the image I could live with, the image I wanted people to live with.

I reached for my drink on the floor beside the couch. What happens now? Only ten o'clock.

The phone rang. Nobody but Marianne would call at this hour. I wanted to hear from Marianne. There was at last somebody I wanted to call. But our being together was perhaps dependent on my not answering. When she came back, we would have to arrange something.

"When she came back." Would she come back? How had we left it? We'd left it that she couldn't reach me. I wouldn't answer the phone. No plan for a future meeting. Had I seemed disinterested in a future meeting? Ridiculous after our day together. Yet there had been caution, the usual almost compulsive caution, or why hadn't I made plans with her? Partly out of consideration for her. We had said practically nothing. What we had done had been spontaneous. I had wanted her to leave when she did, and she had sensed it, or had she sensed my need to be alone before I expressed it? Did I express it? No. I was just "that way."

How would we be at our next meeting? There would inevitably be some shyness, awkwardness as we went back to "introductions" and got to know each other. Who is she? What are her commitments? Does she have any? Is she thinking it all over now? What would she be doing now? I looked at my watch again. In a little while she'd be helping to strike the set and move in the new one for next week's show. They used to send the girls home at midnight.

I wanted desperately to see her.

I realized that we were not going to drift together again as we had the first time. Someone would have to make a move. She might come down again "for a swim," but she could hardly do that now. She knew what coming down would mean.

I could drive to the next town and call her from a

phone booth. Call her where? Nobody's answering phones at the theatre now. I doubted she had a phone in her room, and I couldn't wake Mrs. Grader.

I could drive out. It was late now. The village was asleep except for the town constable driving around. If she was through at the theatre, she might be in her room over Mrs. Grader's barn. Maybe she shared the room with another girl. Fran and I had lived in that room her first summer. I hadn't asked her if she lived alone. I hadn't asked her anything.

And if she did live alone. Barging in in the middle of the night. She may be thinking things out too, need time. But I wanted to be in touch with her! "Touch" was the word. I wanted to touch her, to hold her. I wanted to tell her everything this day had meant to me.

It was unthinkable to spend such a day with a girl and not reach her in some way. What kind of man is that? In town I would have rushed out for armsful of flowers. Much of the pleasure of being in love is to rush out and buy things, silly things, oddities with hidden meanings known only to the two of you. An orgy of trivia which would show up years later, treasured in the back of a bureau drawer. To overwhelm someone with significant small attentions. When Fran had not received an acting award she had deserved, I had learned of her itinerary for the following day and at each stop, hairdresser, fitter, luncheon, doctor, I had arranged to have her met with a small nosegay of flowers along with copies of the fantastic reviews she had received for that particular performance. My desk at home was practically awash with such mementos—a porcelain mouse nibbling on cheese, small paperweights, a china jar from Fortnum and Mason which had contained some caviar we had had on some special occasion.

Tomorrow I must go into the next village and get Marianne some silly things. But tonight. To be in touch.

Something! Some object I could get to her which would not embarrass her if she came home with a roommate. My eye fell on a few of the smooth stones we had found on the beach this morning.

THIRTY

The village was quiet. No lights in the houses. At the far end of the green was the town hall, converted to a theatre in the summer. Lights were on but there was no activity outside the building. A car passed, and I rubbed the side of my face as it went by. Would they recognize the car? Then I remembered that I had a new station wagon since I'd been here last. In a village like this, you are known by your car. Get a new car and it's months before you get that finger of recognition barely lifted from the steering wheel.

I drove slowly past the theatre. There were a few cars in the parking lot and a few bicycles in the rack at the side of the theatre. Was one of them Marianne's? I drove closer and saw her red bike with the basket. I could leave the stone in the basket. Would she see it? It was only as big as an egg. I could leave it on the seat of the bike. She might knock it off in the dark without seeing it.

I moved away from the theatre and down the street the few blocks to Mrs. Grader's house. I looked down the dark, shaded path to the barn. There was a light on at the top of the steps, just outside Marianne's door. If Mrs. Grader were awake, she would have already heard the car slow down. In the country a person can hear a car stop in front of his house even when he is asleep. I could be up and down the stairs before she could really be aware of anything, since she didn't have a view of the back of the barn and the stairs. Still, the bicycle was perhaps a better idea. I was right. In my rear-view mirror I could see the yard light go on.

I stopped a few blocks from the theatre and wrapped the stone in my handkerchief. Then I slowly approached the theatre, drove up as close as I could to the bicycles and hurried over to Marianne's and tied the ends of the handkerchief around her handlebar, got back in the car and drove away, my heart pounding.

It felt good to be out and away from the cottage, and I wanted to drive for a while. I wanted to drive in and out of the streets of the village and perhaps wait until Marianne came out of the theatre and watch her find the stone. But that was not a good idea. The village was in effect a mutual protection association, and soon someone would notice a car moving in and around the streets.

I took a chance and drove once more past the barn. The yard light was still on, and I didn't slow down. I just went right on and took the next turn that would lead me to the main road.

As I drove, I didn't want to go back to the cottage. I wanted to go back to the barn and up to Marianne's room, and get into that big bed and wait for her. I assumed that it was the same as when Fran and I had been there many, many years before. A great old room with a fireplace and window seats, exposed beams. I had an almost overwhelming desire to be absorbed into Marianne's life. "Take care of me." The image I had of myself in the bed was curled up, a child, a baby. I would just stay there curled up for days and days and wait for her to come home and care for me. I had an enormous longing to be cared for.

Finally I began to feel damp and chilly, and I turned back towards the cottage. Perhaps when she found the stone, Marianne might come down. This was ridiculous, a throo milo biko rido aftor midnight. But oho might.

No one saw me enter my drive. It was a couple of hundred yards before I could see the house and the lights. I felt a pang as I remembered how Fran and I had liked to go outside on a summer night and walk around the house saying how cozy it looked all lit up. We would look in the windows and say, "This is a nice house. I wonder who lives here?"

I drove the car into the shed and entered the house. I was about to turn off the outside light when I stopped. I knew it was ridiculous, but I left it on. An hour later I turned it off and went to bed and fell asleep immediately.

THIRTY-ONE

I awoke the next morning smelling burnt toast. I
lay back, smiling. My God! I listened to her tiptoeing
around in the kitchen, rattling a cup and saucer and
making a little sound of annoyance when she did. I just lay
there for a few moments, enjoying the prospect. Then I
called out, "I can hear you trying to be quiet."

She burst out laughing. "Are you awake?"

"Yes. I'll be there to help you in a moment."

"You stay right where you are. I'm getting you breakfast in bed."

"I hate breakfast in bed. You haven't read my books.
All my men hate breakfast in bed."

"Well, you'll have to put up with it for once, because

I've been planning this all night. Go to the bathroom and do whatever you have to do and get back into bed."

I went to the bathroom, then padded down through the living room to the kitchen. Her back was to me. She was wearing my red sweater, her jeans and sneakers. I came up behind her and put my arms around her and pressed myself to her.

"You were supposed to stay in bed."

"I'll get back in whenever you're ready." My hand was on her breast. She looked back at me and kissed me. We looked at each other for a serious moment. "I missed you."

"I missed you too. Thank you for the stone."

"Crazy. I wanted to be in touch with you so badly. I thought of writing you a letter, but then I figured if I left that on your steps and you had a roommate, it might embarrass you. Do you have a roommate?"

"No." She went on with the breakfast.

"All that ingenuity for nothing then."

"I loved the stone. It was just right. Just enough. I slept with it under my pillow." She turned and looked at me. My erection was bulging in my pajamas.

She laughed. "Is that a permanent state with you?"

"I wish it were. You forget it's been a long time."

She put the bacon on paper toweling. "I snuck down to your bedroom when I arrived, and there you were all sprawled out, the covers off you, and just like that." She pointed at my pajamas. "Only it was all out in the open. It was very funny. You sound asleep but our friend very much awake."

"Most men wake up with erections. Didn't you know?"

She looked at me quickly. I shouldn't have asked that question. "No." And she put the things on the tray. "Now run back and get in bed and be surprised and grateful like a normal man should be. Go on!"

I went through the living room and into my room and jumped into bed and pulled the covers up and sat there grinning, as she followed, carrying the tray with the orange juice, bacon and eggs, toast (scraped) and coffee. Also a glass with a rose in it, one she had been tending, Fran's birthday rose.

She held the tray and hovered over me for a moment, looking at my lap. "Is it safe to put the tray down?" We both laughed, and she put the tray on my lap and sat on the bed next to me. My laugh faded to a smile and then to a look of complete adoration. I reached out quickly and drew her to me, just holding her. Then I drew back and looked at her, and shook my head. She kissed me lightly. "You need a shave."

"You didn't complain yesterday."

"I know you better now. I feel I can be frank with you." She smiled and reached out and touched my face. "You have a button off your pajamas. I'll see if I can find one to match."

I was infinitely touched by this small domestic gesture. I kissed her. "I keep wanting to kiss you."

"Eat your breakfast."

"Have you any idea how lovely you are?"

"Tell me after breakfast."

"Have you had your breakfast?"

"Hours ago. I only take juice and coffee anyway. I'll have a second cup with you."

"You cycled down here in this fog?"

"It isn't bad until you get right down here."

She watched each mouthful. I couldn't keep my hands off her, or my eyes off her eyes, large, intent. I touched her face and looked at her for a moment, seriously. "How are you?"

"I'm fine." She smiled. "How are you?"

"Fine. I worried about you."

"I worried about you."

[178]

"Why?"

"You tell me first."

I nibbled a piece of toast. "I don't know. It was all so marvelous, so perfectly right. But then being out of touch with you, I began to worry that you might be having second thoughts."

She shook her head. "I felt terribly lonely for you. You know, all the time I was working at the theatre last night, I could still feel you here." She put her hand on her breast.

"I could feel you too. That's nice, isn't it?"

"I'd never had that lingering feeling before." She broke into a broad smile. "I guess nobody ever held me so hard before."

"Nobody ever needed you as much before." I put the tray aside. I had to hold her.

"You haven't finished."

"I just want to hold you." I quickly drew her to me. "You're so incredibly dear."

"I like that word. I don't think anyone has ever called me that before. I mean, they've never said 'You're dear.' "

I just groaned and held her, feeling the young resilience of her body. I began to put my hand under her sweater. I could feel her draw into herself.

"We're out of luck today."

"What do you mean?"

"I've got the curse." Instinctively I drew her closer and rubbed my face against her hair. She went on. "Bad timing."

"I'd say perfect timing. You didn't have it yesterday."

"That's right."

I just held her for a few moments. She reached over to the tray and snitched a piece of toast. I hesitated before I went on. I didn't want her to misunderstand. "You know, it doesn't bother me, your having . . . if it doesn't bother you."

She looked at me. "It bothers me."

"Okay. I just wanted you to know that there is absolutely nothing about you that I could possibly find . . . distasteful."

"I should think it would be awful."

"No."

She shrugged her feeling of discomfort about it, then abruptly changed the subject. "Did you like my breakfast?"

"Fantastic."

"Liar." She snuggled down next to me. "I have the most terrible desire to have you hold me. But if it's going to make it difficult for you and our friend . . ."

I drew her down close to me and eased myself to a prone position. "He loves it."

"I always thought it was painful like that, if nothing happened."

"It's a totally bearable pain." Then I intruded on her world again. "That's an old line with boys, to tell you how painful it is and you've got to do something about it."

She nestled her head in the crook of my neck for a long moment while I stroked her hair. "Do you want me to . . . do something about it?"

"No . . . No." I kissed her hair.

"I will. I'd like to, if you want me to."

"No." And I slid down to face her and kiss her "thank you" and just look at her.

"Are you sure?"

"Yes." As I held her, I wondered. It would have been very exciting to have her "do something for me" but, in another way, it was almost more exciting to say "No." One day we might do this together, or something else. Her willingness to "oblige," to "service" was very touching and a little sad. And it told me something of whatever relations she'd had with boys. But at that moment it was important to my feelings about myself to say "No," to say, in effect, that man does not always have to be served. He is capable of an unselfish act. Perhaps I was being sentimental. I knew that there were times when a woman enjoyed being regarded simply as a sex object, enjoyed being used, even degraded.

I held her tight. She was indeed "dear," the most open girl I had ever known. (Was that really true? Fran had been an open girl.) She grappled me to her. "Hold me hard! I want to feel you there the rest of the day." I held her hard. "I suppose this is not so good on a full stomach."

"It's delightful any time." I relaxed my grip on her. Her hand stole down my belly and to my erection. She began to fondle me. I reached down and took her hand and moved it away.

"Are you sure?"

"Sure."

"But what if I want to?"

"Then I would know it." I kissed her and sat up. "Let's get up and start a fire and lie on the couch, and neck like a couple of kids." I realized suddenly that, of course, she was a kid. I leaned back and kissed her. "Do kids still neck, or is it all . . . ?"

She looked at me, a small mock reprimand on her face. "We neck."

As I started to get dressed, she looked the other way. "Missing a good deal if they don't neck. I used to say to Fran . . ." I stopped. "I'm sorry. I don't mean to go on talking about what Fran and I did."

She smiled. "I hope to hear a lot more . . . if you'll tell me."

She left for the kitchen with the tray, and I finished dressing, shaved quickly, and went to the living room to make a fire. It occurred to me that my apology was to the wrong person. It should have been to Fran for discussing us with someone else. She had always hated this. "You've been talking about us to friends."

Listening to Marianne in the kitchen, I wanted to join her and watch her and hold her. For me the need was still very much to hold, to be close, to touch. In the normal course of the relationship we would have spent the next days touching, holding, cuddling, romping, swimming, walking, shopping, laughing, eating, fucking. Affectionate animals. On safe, mutually pleasurable ground.

Now with Marianne's period, we would be possibly defining ourselves, expressing attitudes, opinions. There had been a girl I had slept with early on in college, and we had had a great time until we had gone to the college art museum one day and argued violently over styles of painting. We had both apologized later, but it had never been the same and we drifted apart.

Marianne brought in a tray with two cups of coffee, napkins, cream and sugar. A very neat girl. I took the tray from her and kissed her. "When you become bored with my compulsion to touch and kiss you, please don't say so."

She laughed as we sat on the couch. "I'm the one who asked to be held." And she curled up against me. "How did you get the idea of the stone?"

"I just wanted desperately to be in contact with you. It seemed all wrong after the day we'd had, for us to be apart. It just seemed cold." She kissed my hand, which was on her shoulder. "I didn't know the setup at Mrs. Grader's. Sometimes two people have that room over the barn."

"When I found the stone, I almost laughed out loud. It was so dear. Then I went to the phone booth by the post office, and I was going to call you, the double ring that you and Fran used as a signal, but then I didn't. For a lot of reasons. First, your hearing that signal ring in this house. Then I thought you might feel you had to answer, and I knew you didn't want to answer the phone. Then I thought I'd ride down here."

"I wish you had."

"Do you? I wasn't sure, just barging in, assuming, intruding. The stone was charming but a touch ambiguous. It said 'I'm thinking of you.' It didn't seem to say 'Hurry down!' "

She had caught every nuance of what I myself hadn't really known I had meant. "I left the outside light on till I went to bed."

"Did you?"

"I didn't really expect you to come all that way at night on your bike."

"That's one thing that kept me from coming." She didn't mention the other reasons. "How are we going to keep in touch?"

"I'll just be here whenever you feel like coming down."

"I want it the other way around. Not you waiting for me, but for me to come whenever you want me." I hugged her. "That's impossible, your just sitting here. There may be times when you don't want me to come down. How will I know?"

"I can't imagine any such times." I knew there might be, but at that moment I didn't want to think about reservations.

She squeezed my hand, acknowledging the commitment but too wise to believe it. "There are times when *I* have to be alone."

"Of course."

"Do you mind being alone?" She turned to look at me as though it were a question that concerned her more than me.

"I have always said I don't, because I've had to be alone a lot. Fran's work, and for that matter, my own work. I love solitude. I hate being lonely. I not only hate it, it frightens me."

"I'd rather be by myself than have a lot of chattering."

"Did you read that in one of my books?"

[183]

She looked at me, surprised. "No. Did you write that someplace?"

"I must have, because it's the way I feel. It's a very selfish feeling, you know. Very undemocratic. Life, people, can't always be that meaningful, significant. It's nice when it is." I tightened my grip on her and kissed her hair.

"When I say to boys, people, that I don't think I want to get married, they say I'll be lonely. I think I'd rather put up with that than the loneliness I sense in most of the marriages I've seen."

I smiled. "That's an enormous subject. In a way it's a choice of which loneliness you can stand."

She looked at me, puzzled. "Your marriage is the only one I know about that seems to have been what marriage should be." I tightened my hold on her shoulder. "I'm sorry. Do you want me to shut up?"

"No."

"I told you that when I knew I was winning the award, I read everything I could about Fran and you, everything you had written about her after she died. Also, I've read some of your stories, which I took to be at least somewhat autobiographical, and . . . I don't know . . . the way you worked together, appreciated each other's talents, encouraged them, respected each other, maybe that kind of marriage . . ."

I didn't say anything. I felt uncomfortable listening to her, yet it was what I wanted to hear. I curled in closer around her, wishing really that I could change positions with her and that she could hold me. Odd quick changes of feeling, sometimes to want to be with her as a man, flaunt the pleasure of my reawakened virility, sometimes to want to be held and comforted.

After a long silence, she asked, "Do I make you happy?"

"Don't you know you do?"

"I also make you a little sad. A little."

"No." I kissed her cheek.

"If I ever make you sad . . ." I shook my head. She insisted. "No, I know from what you write that you're a fiercely moral person."

"Oh, come on."

"Maybe that's not the right word. But if what we do troubles you, makes you have any troubled feelings, then I'd hate myself." She looked at me seriously. "Do you understand what I mean?"

"Yes." I kissed the end of her nose. "Do you think I should have troubled feelings, being such a moral person?"

She smiled, but also frowned. "Don't tease about it. It's a part of you that's very important to me. I feel very right about it all, but if you didn't . . ."

"I, too, feel that it's all very right. But I have a very selfish interest in thinking that. Does that change your feelings about me?"

She snuggled against my chest. "I have a feeling I've committed a kind of adultery."

I looked at her a long time. "Then you do feel I should feel troubled."

"No, I don't want you to. Oh, I'm saying it all very badly. I shouldn't have said that."

"My mother, who lives in England, is having a very hard time getting over Fran's death. She's gone into some kind of deep mourning, has canceled all her engagements, and so on. I wrote her that I didn't think she should do this. I said that nothing any of us did now could make any difference to Fran."

She took my hand and kissed it. "That's nice." She was comforted but not convinced. Nor was I.

We just lay there for a few moments, feeling the pressure of each other. "You know, I haven't asked you anything about how you're getting on here at the theatre, if you're enjoying it."

"Oh, yes, I am. It's a fabulous opportunity. I can't tell

you how grateful I am." She turned and beamed at me.

"Are you going to get a chance to act?"

"I think so. I'll know soon, but just being around, watching actors develop parts. I've always played a little small, a little tight. Miss A's been trying to get me to open up, vocally, physically. I always listened to her, but I could never quite grasp the idea. Well, the first week of rehearsals, watching some of the pros, I knew immediately what Miss A was talking about."

"So now you have opened up physically and vocally?"

She swept her arm out in a grand gesture and boomed out, "How now, brown cow!" and laughed.

"Tremendous!" I looked at her mouth, smiling. Her whole face lit up when she smiled, the big dark intense eyes shone. I shook my head.

"What?"

For years I had written of and believed in married people crawling to each other over the shards of their broken romantic illusions, loving more desperately, more really. Did I believe it? Compared to this? Yes, I believed it, had done it. But this. I longed to be ignorantly drunk with this girl and the possibilities. For a time not to know what I knew. In so many areas of my life I had learned to hold back because I knew too much. Commitments to causes which faded away, to ideals which were compromised. "I adore you."

It was too much. She parried, smiling, "I'd rather you found me dear."

"I do. Dear and adorable . . . and funny."

"I'm not funny. Nobody has ever found me funny."

"I do. Funny and witty."

"What have I said that's witty?"

"You just are."

"I'll believe you because it makes me feel good. I do feel good with you." She pressed her face into my chest. "That's important, isn't it?"

[186]

I stroked her cheek. "I wish we could get in a car and take off and drive all over New England, do whatever we wanted to do, picnic, antiquing, country inns with big feather beds. I have a tremendous desire to go shopping with you."

"Shopping?"

"I'd like to buy you things, clothes, trinkets. I miss not having someone to buy things for."

"I don't want you to buy things for me."

"If I want to, you must let me. I would get great pleasure in browsing through stores looking for things you might like. It will please me seeing you wear things I've picked out. It will keep me close to you when we have to be apart."

She looked at me—at this unconscious projection of our life together.

A car door slammed outside. I sat bolt upright, almost pushing Marianne away from me. I rose from the couch and moved to the kitchen, where I could look out the window. It was Frank in his pickup truck. He hadn't been there to take care of the place all spring. What instinct brought him here today? He was one of the last of the originals. Way back when Fran and I had first bought the place, he had showed up the second morning and just lingered around out on the lawn until we came out to ask him what he wanted.

"You bought this place?"

"Yes."

"Well, I come with the place." And he laughed. He must have been about fifty or so then, and ever since he had taken care of the grounds and the cottage. The last time I had seen Frank had been at his wife's funeral, last September, just before we had left.

I quickly opened the kitchen door and went out to meet him before he could reach the house. He was at the side of the house where Marianne had used the lawn-mower and cultivated the roses.

"Hello, Frank."

"I didn't come down to take care of the place. Wasn't sure what you wanted." We shook hands. He was looking over the grounds. "You want me to, I can come down to-morrow with my rig, get the place in shape."

"No, thanks, Frank. Maybe later. I don't know how long I'm going to be here, and just now I'd like to leave it. Just want to hole up."

He looked at me. "Don't blame you. I wanted to do that when Helen passed away. But I had the girl." The girl was his mentally deficient daughter, now probably in her thirties. "I used to come down here evenings last winter, light a fire and smoke a pipe. Hope you don't mind."

"I'm glad you did, Frank."

"I filled up the wood box again."

"You didn't have to do that."

"Read one of your books."

"My books? One I'd written?"

"Sitting there night after night looking at that wall of books, I got up one night and looked closer and came across one of yours. Can't say I understood it all, but I liked it."

"I'm very pleased. How are you? How are you making out?"

"Just came down to take a look. Someone said they saw some kids coming through the gate. Thought I'd better check it out."

"Thanks, Frank. Probably some kids from the theatre. I don't mind if they use the beach."

He broke a dead stalk from a plant. "Got myself married again, did you hear?"

"No. Congratulations!" I patted his back.

"Nothing to be congratulated about. Wouldn't have

[188]

done it except for the girl, you know. Someone to look after her."

"Who is it, Frank? Do I know her?"

"Girl friend of mine from when I was a kid. Used to play piano when I played fiddle at the dances. She don't play piano no more and hates for me to fiddle. I go out and fiddle in the silo."

"Well, when I leave, Frank, come over here and fiddle."

"Fiddle makes a pretty sound in the silo." He moved off, looking at the roof of the house. "I patched a couple of places on the roof, the wind blew off. Earn my keep." He smiled at me.

"Thanks. The place seems in good shape."

I turned and saw Marianne's bicycle leaning against the shed, her scarf tied to the handlebar. Frank couldn't have missed it. He walked around a few moments, feeling the paint, checking on repair jobs he'd done over the years. "Thought you might bring Mrs. Larsen up here. I pass Helen's grave every day on the way to town."

"I thought of it, Frank, but we decided on back there." What could I say about the bicycle?

"Wonderful woman. Nice woman." He poked around the windows. "Looks like the shutters could stand some touching up."

"Maybe when I leave." I looked through the window, wondering if Marianne could be seen.

"Lots of junk mail in your box. Didn't think you were here when I saw it."

"I thought I'd fool people, Frank. If Bessie saw the box empty next time she delivered the mail, the cat would be out of the bag."

"People gonna see you around."

"I'm not going to be around, if I can help it. I'd appreciate it, Frank, if you didn't tell anyone, even your wife."

"Lettie?" He snorted. "Hardly speak to her as it is. But she looks after the girl, kind of. Never would have done it except for the girl. People around here thought I showed disrespect for Helen, marrying five or six months after. What was I gonna do? The girl. Anyway, I don't consider myself really married to her. Helen's still my wife. Don't tell Lettie that, not that she don't know it. She's forbidden me to mention Helen's name in the house. Helen's house! How do you like that! She even gets mad as hell when we go into town and I look over at Helen's grave."

"Couldn't you have found someone else?"

"An old goat like me? Now in your case it's different. Hell, if I'd been your age, you think I'd have settled for Lettie? And if I hadn't had the girl . . ." He considered the house for a moment. "My great-grandfather came over on a boat, and his wife died on the trip, and by the time he landed in New York, he was married again. 'Course, the trip took longer then . . . You don't want I should cut any of this down?" He indicated the tall grass.

"Not until I go, Frank."

"Yup. Well, all right then. I know how you feel. After Helen passed away, everyone was baking me cakes, bringing in stews and things. I had to let them do it because of the girl. But I just wanted to sit and talk to Helen."

"Yeah, I guess that's about it."

"That's what I come down here for nights. Well, I'll call you to see how you're doing."

"I'm not going to answer the phone, Frank."

"Well, then give a holler if you want me." The telephone rang inside. We looked at each other and smiled. "I could never do that, sit listening to a phone ringing. Might be some feller wanted to give me some money."

"As a writer I've done it all my life."

"When you decide to get out, take a drive over to the cemetery and look at Helen's grave. It's fixed up nice."

"I will, Frank."

He walked to his truck and opened the door, then called back, "I appreciated you coming to the funeral." He got in the truck, pulled into the road and disappeared in the trees.

I moved Marianne's bicycle into the shed. A futile gesture. I was angry with Frank and ashamed at the same time. I rationalized that I was angry because he had intruded on my widower's right to privacy, and yet I knew that what really bothered me, and made me ashamed to be bothered, was that he might have found Marianne, might even now have put two and two together. I felt a quick flash of hatred for Marianne, and then a feeling of shame for that hatred.

In the house, Marianne hadn't moved. She was still lying on the couch, scrunched up, hiding. I was embarrassed at my dash out the door to prevent him from discovering her, and embarrassed that Marianne had felt she had had to hide.

"Is he gone?"

"Yes. Frank. Old man who takes care of the place."

She made a place for me on the couch, but I was too upset to sit down.

"I'm sorry. I suppose now it will be all over town that you're here."

"I don't think so. Frank's a kind man."

I suddenly flushed at having hidden Marianne's bicycle. It had been a reflex action. When she found it moved, she would know my real feelings, that in addition to not wanting to be disturbed, I did not want people to know she was here.

She smiled a little-girl smile at me. "I was pretty good, wasn't I?"

"What do you mean?"

"Hiding."

"Yes." I sat down and touched her face. It was obvious that we were both upset at this feeling we had to hide, but she was carrying it off with humor and style.

"Did he see my bicycle?"

I was relieved. "He may have seen it. I moved it into the shed after he left." I shook my head.

After a few moments she looked very serious. "Maybe I'd better stop coming down."

"No." I drew her close to me.

"It would be awful if I ended up hurting you, making you hate me."

"How could you?" But she knew how she could. She couldn't help but sense my preoccupation with this man and what he might mean. Something had been lost.

She kissed me, as though to reassure me. Then, "I have to go."

"What time's your call?"

"Ten-thirty." I got up. "I'm afraid I won't be able to get back today, or tonight for supper. It's opening, you know, and there's the inevitable beach party after with the apprentices, and . . ." She finished with a gesture. Again she sounded like David, as though she were giving me an inventory of her obligations to cover her retreat.

"I understand. I'll be here."

She shook her head, frowning at the idea.

"I have my letters to write, and it's clearing, so I'll swim, and I'll sleep. I'm tired. I'll be all right."

"May I call you? I could use two rings . . . no, three rings, and you'd know it was me." I hesitated. She retreated. "We'll think about it."

We kissed good-bye in the shed. She looked into my eyes intently, worried, as though she were trying to fathom what was going on inside me. She held me more tightly than I had ever been held; there was a sense of desperation in it, as though this might be the last time we kissed.

I looked down at her. "Have a good day. I hope the

show goes well tonight, and the beach party. Where do they have them? Down at the cove?"

"Yes." The eyes still searching.

"Have a good time. They're fun." They were fun because Fran and I were together. Was Marianne together with someone? I didn't ask.

"I can't stand the thought of you here alone."

"It's the only way I can see you."

She took a step towards me and hugged me again, pressing her head against my chest. "If you hear your phone ring three times . . ."

"If you find a stone on your stairway."

She leaned away and looked at me, smiling. "You're a funny man, Christopher Larsen . . ." And she turned and mounted her bike and headed up the road, her graceful long back straight as she stood to get more power.

THIRTY-TWO

As I turned back into the cottage, I was frightened by that sudden gut feeling of resentment towards Marianne. To resent someone I adored because she threatened my love for Fran. Not my love, the image of my love, the public image. And somehow it all reflected not just on me but on Fran.

I thought of an entry I had made in my notebooks some years ago, an idea for a story. A man alone, suffering a heart attack, a mild one from which he would have recovered, but sensing death, he had struggled up the stairs to his study to destroy some embarrassing or incriminating material, and was found dead with his desk drawer open and the material half torn in his hands. No wonder I had made that note. I was capable of doing that if an image was threatened. What was the moment in my own life which had made me think of that idea? I couldn't remember. I did remember. A letter from Jean which was perfectly innocent except that it mentioned Fran's illness, so that if she had found it, she would have known.

Another entry. A man whose wife had died at home under questionable circumstances trying to prove to a court of law that he loved his wife. And the proofs which would be most conventionally acceptable would be no proof at all. No sins of commission, only of omission. And why that entry?

I went into the living room. It should have all happened in Paris or Rome or London. The legend and the idyll could have been kept separate, and I not so aware of my hypocrisy.

I looked at the letters on the table. If I wrote those now, there would be nothing for the afternoon. Besides, I somehow felt cheap, not the husband who could sit down and write feelingly about his wife and his marriage.

There was so much to be done, but I didn't seem to want to do any of it. I looked at myself in the mirror. Pale, still pale . . . I could do that, lie in the sun on the beach. Get some color. Look a little less old. One minute Fran, the next, Marianne. I shook my head.

I entered "our" room and sat on the bed and started taking off my shoes. And I began to notice things. The small antique silver candlestick, our "fucking light." Very daring for Fran, who did not use words like that. Another version of the reading stand I had built so that she could read lying flat. I was comforted by the love I had put into that. It was as if I had imagined that if I made that just right, everything would be good again. The sense of triumph when she found she could use it and could stand being left alone. Small pathetic victories on the road to inevitable defeat.

None of this had registered with me yesterday when I had dashed in to shower and change before going back to Marianne.

Another of Fran's "Should" lists on the table by her side of the bed. Strong, beautiful handwriting. She drew the same way. Costume sketches as suggestions for a designer. Stroke! Stroke! The same way she walked. I could always tell her firm step on the pavement. My sketches were a series of short, hesitant lines. And I ambled. And again, the shoes where I had thrown them in anger that last day.

I couldn't go through all these things. "When I go to the village finally, I must get boxes for them and store them away in the attic back home, for some later quieter time."

I put on my bathing trunks, still sandy from last summer, threw a sweater around my shoulders, and started down the beach.

Perhaps I should be with people, talk to them. This constant introspection! Had I thrown away the crutch of their consideration too soon? I remembered when I had had an operation on my knee, and I had used crutches and then a cane, and people had been so helpful in getting taxis and holding open doors. The first day without the cane had been a shock, and I had gone back to the cane for a couple of days, and had finally kept it in the closet, saying to Fran, "I'll keep it and use it on days when I need a little extra kindness."

I scuffed through the sand, the sun warming my back.

Marianne and I could be together in a motel up the coast. We could meet someplace on the road, and I could put her bike in the station wagon, and . . . It would never work. I felt a certain shame in even thinking about it. It was not that kind of relationship. Why had she hugged me so desperately just now?

What did other men do? How often I had asked that

question in my life! And what did it matter? It did. I knew nothing about my friends, how they managed the deeply personal parts of their lives, the really important parts. I had learned most of what I knew about men from women. Men talk to women, some women, some men, in the depths of intimacy or loneliness. And then women talk to men and tell them how other men feel, and that's how we learn.

Without thinking, I stooped to pick up a stone. Marianne would like this one. Then a few yards further on, another one. Then when I saw a third, I discarded the first one, and suddenly I found myself zigzagging down and along the beach, bending over, examining, comparing, eager to show my cache to Marianne. "Look what I found for you!" "Look what I brought you!" "Look what I wrote you!" "Look what I made for you, did for you!"

I found a sheltered spot and lay down. I was going to strip off my trunks, but then I remembered Fran's saying it was "sexy" to have that part white and the rest tan. "Focused attention, like long black silk stockings on a woman are sexier than bare legs." Thinking of our two small triangles of white flesh and dark hair made me excited, and I shook my head. Doesn't a person still live if the thought of her body can excite you?

The excitement passed, and I reached over and started examining Marianne's stones. The smooth and rounded stones were warm and oddly sensuous in my hand. I put one against my chest. I would rest it on her belly. I put it on my belly, then slipped it inside my trunks and felt its smooth warmth against me and was excited again with thoughts of Marianne. The warm, smooth stone was Marianne, and I enjoyed the sensation, and smiled at my easy and spontaneous reaction. "I want. I want." This part of me was going to lead me back to life, was going to insist on living.

[197]

I lay there drowsy in the sun, when I thought, "What if she should call? I won't hear the phone." I sat upright. "But what difference does it make? I'm not going to answer it." But not to hear it! It suddenly seemed terribly important for me to hear the phone.

I ran down to the water and dashed in and floundered around for a few moments, then ran back to my sweater and the stones and hurried back to the cottage, listening as I got closer.

When I reached the deck and stretched out in the sun, the phone rang, but it was not Marianne's signal. Who was trying to reach me? David? I suppose I should not be cut off from my son. But he was not alone. But in case he needs me, I must let someone know I am here. Roger, my lawyer.

After a late lunch, I napped again, giving up the hope that Marianne would call. Why should she call? Hadn't I given the impression that her presence here troubled me?

Later I drew the curtains in the living room, lighted the lamps on my desk, and was able to write some more letters, stressing perhaps more than usual how important Fran had been in my life, how dear she had been.

The phone rang. I stopped in the middle of a word to count. One, two, three. It stopped. I waited. It rang again, one, two, three. Without thinking, I reached out and picked it up, just raised it from the bar and held it there, listening to hear if Marianne would say anything. Nothing. I hung up.

I wondered where she was. At the theatre? A phone booth near the post office? Eight o'clock. Probably at the theatre. I hadn't asked her if she was on the crew or if she was just going to watch the opening.

The mood of the letters was broken. I got up and went into the kitchen and poured myself a drink, suddenly feeling trapped in my cottage. What was there for dinner? My old stand-bys—hash, tuna fish, frankfurters, soups, lettuce, tomatoes, bread, jelly, milk. I'd lived on these for weeks sometimes when Fran had been away.

I started to open the hash, then stopped. I wanted to get out. I could drive twenty miles or so up the shore to some joint where I wasn't known, walk through some of the shops in a shopping center where I'd never shopped, and call Roger. Just get out!

THIRTY-THREE

For a while I just drove around, enjoying the evening afterglow and the exhilaration of being out. When it was dark, I returned to the Coast Road and stopped at a place that was new since last summer. BAR AND GRILL, CLAMS, LOBSTERS.

There was no counter. The owner, in shirt sleeves, showed me to a booth. "Are you alone?"

"Yes." They hate wasting a booth on loners, but it was late and the place was almost empty.

I looked around. In the coldly lighted room the few people looked like corpses. I was the only person alone.

I ordered my drink from a beefy waitress and sat there looking around. I should have brought a newspaper or magazine. I was an old enough hand at eating alone to know that. "Do you by any chance have a newspaper?"

"You can get one over in the shopping center when you leave."

"Yes. I wanted one now. But thank you." As she turned away I remembered I was going to call Roger. "Is there a public phone?"

"By the rest room."

"Roger, this is Chris. Sorry to call you at home."

"Where the hell are you?"

"I'm at the cottage on the Cape."

"I've been trying you there."

"I know you have."

"How do you know I have?"

"I've heard the phone ringing."

"Why didn't you answer?"

"I didn't want to. I came up here to be alone. I have a lot of friends up here and I didn't want to be in touch with them all, yet."

"I understand. How are you feeling?"

"Pretty good."

"How long you going to stay there?"

"I don't know."

"I'm not sure it's the smartest thing, up there alone."

"I'm okay. Don't tell anyone I'm here, please, except David, if he calls. Has he called?"

"No. Some people have called, wanting to start some kind of fund in Fran's memory. But listen, all that can wait. The important thing is, how are you?"

"I'm okay." What would Roger think about Marianne? It was almost unfair to accept his concern based on the assumption that I was up here going through "cold turkey." We had all been at college together and he had been very fond of Fran.

"Look, we've got to get together with the Revenue

man and open Fran's safety-deposit box. It's holding things up."

"There's the one in Boston too. Can't I send you the New York key with authorization? You're co-executor, and you and he can go down and see what's there."

"I'd rather you be there. You never know."

"Roger, you're an honest man. I don't know about the Revenue man, but you'll keep him honest too."

As I returned to my booth, the waitress put the sea-food salad in front of me. I ordered a beer and picked up my fork. "Music I heard with you was more than music." Conrad Aiken's line. Food I ate with you was more than food, and food I now eat alone is almost disgusting.

I took out my wallet, and while I picked at my food, started going through my cards and receipts and licenses and all the bits and pieces of paper I had stuck in there over the last months.

The waitress brought the beer and looked at me as I sorted things out. "We don't accept credit cards here."

"No. No. I understand."

I spent a few minutes trying to figure out what a sales-girl had written on a charge slip at Bloomingdale's. Whatever it was, it had cost $25.67. I couldn't read the date either. I tore it in two. Bonwit charge card. Bergdorf's. All Fran's which I had had to use the last year, shopping for her. I'd keep these cards. A cleaning ticket. What was that? God, I hadn't been through this stuff in months. The safety-deposit-box key wrapped in tissue paper, which I would send Roger. Another one for Boston.

I scooped up the scraps and put them in my pocket to discard in a more private place. I felt the small stone I had found for Marianne and cradled it, warming it, missing her.

I took another mouthful and a swig of beer and looked across at the shopping center. Lots of jalopies over there, with boys leaning against them, smoking, talking.

Then I saw a boy and his girl standing in the shadow of a car. He had her pressed up against the car with his hips, and he was kissing her and rubbing against her, and she was laughing.

I almost retched. I closed my eyes and I felt an enormous pang of loneliness, to hold and be held. My God, didn't this ever stop? The instinct to touch, to hold. Broken and exhausted men during the war . . . my blind old grandmother when I was young, reaching out and groping, "Chrissie, where are you?" and just holding my hand and nodding and smiling . . . in my own loneliness, as a boy, holding myself, my hands clutched between my legs

"Is there something wrong with the salad?"

I opened my eyes. "No." I looked out at the boy and girl again. From somewhere I remembered "To live alone a man has to be more than human or less than human." I looked at my watch. Ten-thirty. There was no way I could see Marianne tonight. The play would be over in a few minutes. Then the beach party and all the young people, sitting on blankets, lying on blankets, wrapped in blankets.

I had a terrible need to be in touch with Marianne. To tell her what she meant to me. Each desolate moment of loneliness was making her meaning more clear and urgent. If I couldn't be with her, I could write to her, achieve a closeness by writing of my need, and love, and devotion.

On a couple of pieces of paper which the waitress reluctantly found for me, I started to write in a frenzy of longing. "Dear Marianne . . ." And I said everything I was feeling, all the words, reckless, impassioned, tumbling on top of each other, "saved" . . . "never before" . . . "adore" . . . "never so needful, never so happy." I finished the letter, deeply and passionately in love with Marianne. I was exhilarated, feeling a very pure and direct and honest feeling which I had expressed without reservation. There was something joyous in just doing that.

I sat back, excited, anxious to deliver the letter, to

have her read it. I read it over several times, charged each time with the wholeheartedness of it, the absence of checks and balances.

I paid my bill, left much too large a tip, which I hoped would embarrass the waitress (but I knew it wouldn't), and walked across to the shopping center and bought a package of envelopes in the news and stationery store and got in my car. The lovers pressed against the car did not make me feel lonely this time. I smiled at them, and the girl waved and smiled.

I sat in the car for a moment. I couldn't be with Marianne even if she wanted me. Which I wasn't sure. She would be at the beach party. How close could I get to her? As a young man I had sat in front of girls' houses just to be close to them when they weren't able to be with me. I had watched lighted windows far into the night. What was the good of it? The good of it was that it was obeying an instinct. It was somehow being close. I would be able to tell her next time I saw her that I had . . . What? Oddly enough it was Fran's voice I heard saying "If you have an impulse to do something, do it."

Eleven o'clock. I started the car and headed for the cove and the beach party.

THIRTY-FOUR

As I neared the bluff overlooking the cove and the beach, I looked down to see the fire and the shadowy figures huddled together in pairs or scampering in and out of the light. I had said that I wanted to see Marianne function in her world, but now I did not want to.

I turned back away from the coast road. Quarter to one. The town usually insisted these parties break up at one. They broke up officially, then couples wandered off down the beach or into cars. Who had brought Marianne? It was impossible that there wasn't some boy, or many boys. Usually by this time in the summer there had been pairing-off. Also, young leading men with the touring companies, away from whatever homes they had and irresponsible, would dabble among the younger and prettier apprentices who might be flattered by the attentions of a professional actor. I suddenly felt like a father. I knew all the pitfalls my daughter must avoid, all the ruses of young men.

I drove back towards the village. I would leave the letter and the stone on her stairs.

As I approached the barn, I visualized Marianne's room and had an overwhelming impulse to be there, not just to leave the stone and the letter on the steps, but to be in that room, in her world, taken care of by her.

There was no light in her room. Her bicycle was not in the rack. Not allowing myself to think, I drove two houses beyond the barn and turned into a long driveway and drove behind the house and pulled into a parking area in front of garage doors. I turned off the lights and sat quietly, listening. Dorothy and Ben were abroad. They had written that if I wanted to use their house to stay in while I was cleaning out the cottage, nobody would be there in July. The key was behind the deserted wasp's nest on the back porch. I didn't want their house. I just wanted someplace dark to park the car off the street.

I opened the car door, but didn't close it completely, and started off across the back lawns and gardens like a burglar. I shut off my mind. I knew what I was going to do, what I must do, and if I were discovered, well, I still had to do it.

With my heart pounding, I climbed the stairs two at a time. Only as I reached the top step and looked at the door did it occur to me that it might be locked. People were beginning to lock doors now, even in a village like this.

It wasn't locked. I opened it quickly and went inside and closed the door and listened. No sounds. I turned and looked at the room in the glow cast by the streetlight. I knew this room very well. Fran had had it as an apprentice while she was still in college, and we had had it our only year down here as a married couple. She had been a regular member of the company then, and I commuted to Boston twice a week to teach in summer school.

A car drove by slowly, and I felt like a thief. I looked out the window but I couldn't see who it was. I moved away from the window and approached the double bed and sat on it.

One o'clock. She should be getting back soon. Shouldn't I give her some warning? How? What if she did have a boy and he did come up here with her? I couldn't possibly get out if they started up the steps. What the hell was I doing here? I'd only wanted to come to her, to be with her, to make a committing gesture, but it might cause her embarrassment, and if not embarrassment, it was forcing the situation. What was her mood after this morning? She had made the phone call.

I heard a car come down the street and I rose so that I could see it as it passed. It was the constable's car. Sad old man. Nothing ever happened in the town, but some years ago his wife had run off and left him, and since then he had taken to patrolling the streets late into the night.

I felt Marianne's stone in my pocket. I went to the table and there was the stone I had left the night before. I could put these on the steps. That wouldn't tell her I was inside. I could leave a note under one of them. But what kind of note that wouldn't cause trouble if the boy were to pick it up first? I sat at the table and thought about it. Finally I found some note paper and wrote in large letters which she could read by the light from the streetlight. I AM INSIDE!! In looking for an envelope, I saw some letters addressed to her from Ohio. No return address or name. I had not even asked her where she lived. Were these from home, or someone else?

I put my note in an envelope, sealed it, and wrote in block print (which might be Mrs. Grader's writing), IM-

PORTANT MESSAGE FOR YOU . . . OPEN AT ONCE! I opened the door and put one stone on one step, and the new stone on the next to top one with the envelope under it, and quickly withdrew into the room. The whole thing was becoming complicated.

I lay on the bed and waited. I had surprised Fran once, and it had turned into a fiasco. Coming back from a shakedown cruise during the war, the day before the ship was due in Philadelphia for repair and overhaul, it had put in at Annapolis so that the midshipmen could take a look at it. I left the ship at Annapolis with the idea of getting up to Philadelphia by train, surprising Fran and spending a few hours in bed with her, and getting back to the ship before it sailed for Philadelphia in the morning.

I started trying to reach her the moment I left the ship, but all I could find out from my parents, with whom she had been visiting, was that she had left the house and was presumably on her way to Philadelphia.

I arrived in Philadelphia full of the excitement of my own effort, found out she had not arrived at the apartment hotel where we were going to stay, and proceeded to sit in the station and meet every train from New York. It was madness. By the time she finally arrived at one o'clock in the morning, I loathed her, and the whole reunion was a shambles, and at four o'clock I had headed for Annapolis and the ship with very little desire to sail back up to Philadelphia. Ridiculous! We had laughed over it many times.

I looked across at the single bed near the window, where Fran's roommate had been the first few weeks of that first year. She had conveniently left in a huff when she wasn't promised any parts, only scene painting, costumes and props, and I had been able to come up and spend some nights. (There was a Mr. Grader in those days, and Mrs. Grader had slept more soundly.)

And later, the summer we lived here legitimately, the single bed had been a kind of escape when I'd feel stifled sometimes by Fran's closeness. How long it had taken me to get used to this closeness, to cherish it and crave it! It had almost been as though I had had to preserve some privacy, some secret part of myself that preferred to be alone. How long, in our courting days, before Fran had been able to coax me into spending the whole night. I had loved being with her, sleeping that lovely "afterwards sleep." But then I sometimes had wanted to go back to my room in the middle of the night. There was some final commitment involved in spending the night. Possibly some hint of domesticity that frightened the young lover. Or maybe just that instinct for detachment that lurked in me always.

I suddenly remembered the letter I had written in the restaurant. I jumped up and took it from my shirt pocket and propped it up on her desk and lay down again.

And began to have misgivings. I was coming on pretty strong in the letter. It could easily frighten her, scare her away. In a sense, I was laying my life at her feet. It had excited me to write the words, to feel so committed. But did I really mean it, or did I just long to mean it?

A car came down the street. I held my breath and listened. It stopped in front of the barn. The motor was idling. If it was switched off . . . It was switched off. I broke into a cold sweat waiting for the next sound, the sound of doors opening and closing. It didn't come. They were sitting there.

I lay there looking at the ceiling, and suddenly I got a picture of myself, and I was ashamed and felt ridiculous. If there had been a back way, I would have escaped. I was not a romantic young apprentice having a lark lying there waiting for my girl, I was a middle-aged man, a recent widower, waiting for a girl half my age to whom I had awarded a prize which I had established to memorialize a wife whom I presumably adored.

I got up and took the letter from the table and shoved it in my pocket.

The car door opened. A mumble of voices. A "Shhhh." Then a moment. A last kiss? The door closed, the car started and after a moment pulled away quietly.

I started breathing again. I went to the window and watched her pick up the first stone and then the second stone and open the envelope. She looked up quickly towards the door. Instinctively she glanced around as she came up the last two steps.

She opened the screen door and I opened the inside door. She stepped in quickly and closed the door and then in an intense whisper, said, "You're crazy. Do you know that?" But she was smiling.

"I know. I just had to be near you." And I put my arms around her. She was still holding the stones and the note.

"My God!" She let me kiss her, then moved her mouth away. "How did you get up here without anyone seeing you?"

"Sheer genius."

"Shhhh. Where's your car?"

"I parked it back of a friend's house down the street. He's away. I snuck through gardens and hedges."

She moved away to put the stones down, looked at me, shaking her head, and then came to me and put her arms around my neck and hugged me.

"I was suddenly so lonely for you."

"Then it's good you came." And she kissed me. "But I get so nervous." She looked out towards the street.

I had a sudden wild thought that perhaps the boy in the car was going to park it in some hiding place and return. But I said, "This day and age, is anybody shocked at a man in a girl's room?"

"In this town they are. It's fantastic. It's causing a lot of trouble with the apprentices. They're used to pairing up in college, but down here . . . boys in one house, girls in another."

"I hate to disillusion you, but even back in my day, boys managed to find their ways into girls' rooms. It's been going on for centuries."

"Well, you'll never believe it, but a boy and a girl were sent home."

"I believe it. Mackenzie has always had to be careful not to outrage the locals. I think it's mostly that it's in their houses that it's going on that bothers them." All the time I was pressing her to me, moving my hands over her body. I moved us towards the bed and sat down. She stiffened.

"Don't get upset, I'll go in a minute."

She pressed my head to her cheek. "It's absolutely silly. But somehow I'm nervous, worried. For you, too, you know?" She moved away and looked at me, reminding me of my reaction to Frank.

"I thought of all that, but I was having dinner in some dreary joint up the beach, and I saw a boy and girl kissing and holding each other, and I just forgot everything and had to come to you."

She leaned over and kissed me. "I sound so selfish." But there was no easing of her tension. Her lips were on mine, but her eyes were "listening."

I was tense too. We had managed to get together, to make the statement after the chill of the morning, and now both of us were more concerned with my getting out unnoticed than with anything else. I got up. "I'll go."

A small protest. "Oh?" and she pressed against me.

"I wanted to bring you this stone. It was warm from the sun when I picked it up. Knowing that I was going to bring it to you, that it had already become yours, you, I kept it warm down here."

"Oh, my poor friend."

A car passed slowly. She stood up. We both looked towards the window. "I'll go."

"All right. I'm sorry."

"I just had to come. Selfish."

"No." She held me. "Did you hear my phone call?" She smiled like a delighted child.

"Yes. Thanks. I picked up the phone."

"You did? I didn't hear you. Did you say anything?"

"It was after the third ring."

"I must have hung up."

"I didn't say anything. I just wanted you to know I had heard it."

She moved away and went to her bureau. "I almost forgot something. I bought you a present. I was shopping for props this afternoon, and look!" She held out a false nose with a big mustache attached.

"What's this?"

"A disguise for you. So you can wander around town and nobody will know you. Put it on." I slipped it on. She was tickled. "Wonderful." She kissed me again. "I never kissed a man with a mustache before. Shall I come down tomorrow?"

"Please!"

"But not in the morning. I've got a part, a very nice part. I just found out this afternoon. I've been planning how I'd tell you, and with all this, it just went out of my head."

"Congratulations." I hugged her.

"We rehearse in the morning, but I'll be down later, and since I'm in the show, I don't have to come to the theatre at night." She smiled and looked at me wisely. "So . . ."

"Lovely." I took off the nose and mustache and held her one last time tightly, in anticipation of those nights, pressing into her. "Good night."

"Good night," she whispered in my ear.

I released her and moved towards the door. "You know, this part of it, the escape, is all rather undignified. To preserve the romantic atmosphere, perhaps you should go into the bathroom and only come out when I've made my departure."

She giggled and put her hands over her mouth. "I'm going to watch."

"Very awkward for a middle-aged man."

"Why do you keep saying that?"

"Because it's true." I put my hand on the doorknob. "Stand back in case there's shooting."

She doubled over in silent laughter. I opened the inside door and listened. Then the screen door. It used to squeak. Someone had oiled it in the twenty years since I'd used it last. Now there was nothing to do but just to go and trust to luck. I went quickly down the stairs, and back to my car through the lawns and gardens. As I opened the car door, I looked back at Marianne's room and saw the light go on.

I did not close the car door, but started the car, and holding the door with one hand, went out the drive and into the street. At the end of the block I slammed the door and drove off, feeling giddy, daring, and very much alive.

THIRTY-FIVE

The next afternoon David and Gretchen arrived from Boston.

I had been having a fine day. I had gone to sleep the night before, still shaking my head over my impulsive adolescent "occupation" of Marianne's room. When I had graduated from prep school, the headmaster had said to us all, "My fondest wish is that while you develop the minds of men, you will retain the hearts of boys." In my case, at least, he had his wish, sometimes.

I had slept late, awakened around nine-thirty by Marianne's ring (she must be about to go to rehearsals). I had done everything with the knowledge that Marianne would be there later.

I cleaned up the kitchen, removed the winter's mouse droppings from the backs of cupboards, scrubbed them with ammonia, and made a marketing list for a party dinner. I ran a mop around the floors and put fresh linen on the bed in my study, after airing it in the sun.

Early afternoon I sunned myself, swam naked in the ocean, now enjoying the play of water over my body, "our" body, "our" friend. My body had taken on a whole new meaning now that it was shared with someone, alive to another person. I noted the slight color which had started everywhere but the pubic triangle.

I found a few new stones for Marianne, and around two thirty I dressed and drove away with my shopping list to a distant town. Joy infused every purchase. "I wonder if she likes red wine or white? What kind of vegetables? Cheeses?" At the fruit section I saw oranges. Would she be there for breakfast? Did I want her there for breakfast? I bought the oranges, not quite sure.

On the way back to the cottage, with the rear of the station wagon loaded with provisions, I picked up some geraniums.

Then I found the gate open. I entered the drive and got out and closed the gate. As I reached the end of the wooded drive, I couldn't see a car. Then David came around the side of the house.

I froze. My mind rushed ahead to Marianne's arrival. All the things in the car. I stopped far short of the house to avoid his looking in the car, and got out. "David!"

He came towards me, and Gretchen appeared from around the house. As I approached him, I saw his MG pulled up alongside the shed. "David, this is great." My hand outstretched, my voice too hearty.

"Hi, Dad." We shook hands. I had always kissed my father. I don't think David had ever kissed me, or at least, I couldn't remember.

"Gretchen." I kissed her cheek. She was wearing a T-shirt and jeans, no shoes. I was suddenly aware that my girl was the same age as my son's girl.

"We tried to call down here to see if anyone was here, but we never got an answer."

"I've been hiding out." I moved them towards the house. "How long have you been here?"

"About fifteen minutes. We couldn't be sure if you were here. It looked that way, but we weren't sure."

"Well, this is very nice. Have you shown Gretchen the house?"

"Yes, but mostly the beach."

I must have had a glassy look on my face, completely phony. My mind was racing, trying to figure out some way I could reach Marianne. While I was talking, I was trying to think what I'd say if I reached her. What kind of message could I leave? How would she feel about being asked not to come down? I suddenly felt angry that she was coming. Angry with David for busting in. Angry with myself for being angry. "Why don't you and Gretchen go in for a swim?" If I could get them away from the house, I could call the theatre.

"Actually, Dad, we're on our way further down the Cape . . . to visit friends."

I was relieved but also annoyed at what I was sure was a lie. They had taken a chance to come down here for the night, but finding me, David had gone through that instant withdrawal. My feelings were corroborated by Gretchen's quick look at David.

"We could take a quick dip."

David was firm. "We promised them we'd get there to swim with them before dinner."

Gretchen obviously disapproved of David's brusque treatment of me. She and I had always gotten on very well. "Well, at least I'd like to look around a little more. I've heard so much about this place."

I could excuse myself to go to the bathroom and shut

the bedroom door and try to call. The phone rang. It was not Marianne's ring.

"I could never stand not answering a phone," Gretchen said.

"I've wanted to be alone for a while. Get caught up with myself. I was pretty much overwhelmed by friends back home. Nobody knows I'm here. I haven't been to the theatre, and I go to great lengths to stay out of the village, shop several towns down, where I'm not known." I almost broke into a sweat at what I was saying. How would it all sound if Marianne were to arrive? "Would you excuse me for a second while I go to the john, and then I'll show you around?" Oh, Jesus, those phony exit lines, but it all just kept coming, and each thing I said sounded worse than the last. "David, show Gretchen the shed, where you used to camp out. David established his independence very early." I tried to smile, and went into our bedroom as David and Gretchen sauntered around the side of the house.

I called the theatre. Who would answer? It was the girl at the box office. Disguising my voice very little, I asked for Marianne. She would send someone to see if she was still rehearsing. Before she came back on the phone, I heard Marianne's bicycle bell announcing her arrival.

I hung up. I didn't want to go out there. I didn't know what to say. I was tired of the little half-truths, all self-serving. What would Marianne say? Let her say it before I came out. But how would I know what she had said, to match stories?

I couldn't stand the picture of myself hiding in the bedroom. I went out into the living room and towards the back door. As I went, I could see Marianne standing there, still holding her bicycle, shaking hands with David and Gretchen and saying something. The first thing I noticed was that she had my sweater knotted around her neck. It was a fairly common sweater. David probably wouldn't recognize it.

[217]

I tried to learn something from watching David's reaction. Gretchen was smiling and chatting with a girl her own age. David wasn't smiling. He was just standing there looking at Marianne.

I went out the back door, calling a hearty but ambiguous "Hello."

Marianne sang out, "The others can't come swimming today. Mac's got them scrubbing flats and doing all sorts of dirty chores. I think he suddenly got the idea the apprentices are having it too easy. I'm privileged, since I'm rehearsing." She said the last like a grand lady. How beautifully she'd brought it off!

"You've met, then?" I asked as I approached.

"Yes."

Relieved, I babbled on. "I've been trying to persuade them to stay for a swim," now actually eager that they should stay to normalize the situation.

"We've got to be getting on." David was unrelenting.

I wondered if Marianne had had time to say that she had Fran's scholarship, and if this would make things worse. I decided not to mention it.

I became overeager. "Why don't you reconsider and stay on overnight? You know it's going to be too late to swim when you get wherever you're going. Where did you say it was?" There was something small in my "calling" what I considered David's lie.

"Truro," David said, and I could tell he was annoyed that Gretchen had looked at him with a frown, as though I had caught him out.

Marianne said, "I'll go get my swim, because I've got to get back." She moved her bike to lean it against the shed. "If I don't see you again, it's nice to have met you." David mumbled something, but Gretchen called out "Yes!" and fluttered her hand in a wave.

"There are plenty of beds, you know. I've been sleeping in the study, but you and Gretchen could . . ."

[218]

"No. We're expected down there. I just wanted to drop in and show Gretchen the cottage." His awkward, somewhat spastic jerking motions with his arms and body always let me know when David was under tension. As a boy it had been a certain repeated hunching of the shoulders before he said something difficult.

"Well, how about stopping on the way back, tomorrow or whenever you're coming back?"

"We'll be getting right back. Gretchen's got classes . . ."

"I could cut that one."

David was again annoyed with her for not playing the game. "Well, I want to get back. We'll come down later in the summer."

"I may not stay here very long. But you know where the key is and how to turn things on."

David's hands were jammed into the back pockets of his jeans. "Yeah. Thanks."

I looked at him a moment. "How are you?"

He ducked and dodged. "I'm fine."

"Good." I smiled at Gretchen and put my arm around her. "Taking good care of him?" I could see that David was uncomfortable at my touching her, and somehow it was different for me this time too. I had not been a father who had secret longings for my son's girls. There was a natural barrier which I understood and accepted. Was it because my mother had once said about a forty-five-year-old man in our town who was chasing a girl of twenty, "What does he think a young girl would see in an old goat like him?" I had accepted this attitude as valid and had not allowed my yearnings to go in directions where I had understood they would not be acceptable.

David had turned away from the spectacle of my touching Gretchen and was moving towards the car. Out of consideration for his feelings, I omitted kissing

Gretchen good-bye, but she reached up and kissed me and put her arm around my waist.

"How are *you?*"

"I'm okay."

"I can't see how you stand it down here."

"Well . . ." I looked at David. I thought I saw a trace of a smile as he stood with the car door open.

"You know David and I could clean this place out for you, pack things away . . ."

"Thanks. It's really something only I can do."

"Come see us in Boston if it gets too grim." She gave me a last peck on the cheek and got in the car.

David and I looked at each other across the top of the car.

"Thanks for dropping by. I still wish you'd stay."

"Another time." He reached over the top of the car, and we shook hands. He was in a hurry to get out of the situation.

He started the car, wheeled it around expertly, and headed for the drive. Gretchen waved out the window, but I noticed as they drove past my station wagon, David cast a long look at the boxes and bags and pots of flowers.

"Close the gate!" I called. But they didn't hear.

THIRTY-SIX

When they had disappeared into the trees, I drove the station wagon nearer to the house and just sat there for a moment. I could imagine the conversation in the car. Gretchen: "Why didn't we stay?" David: "Oh, come on, Gretchen, couldn't you tell what was going on?"

How did Marianne feel? I hadn't denied her, just not acknowledged her.

I left the provisions in the kitchen and went down the beach to where she was sitting, hugging her knees and staring at the water. As she sensed someone's approach, she looked up with her "public" face, but then seeing me alone, she smiled wanly. I moved quickly to her and held her tightly, wishing that this gesture could handle all the words that should be said. An essentially verbal man, but always so eager to communicate by simpler and more ambiguous touching.

She looked at me with a little bright smile. "Were you proud of me?" I hugged her. "I did well, didn't I?"

"Yes. And I did very poorly."

"How?"

"I should have said, 'I'd like you to meet Marianne, whom I love.'"

She looked quickly at me, a small frown. I had not known what I was going to say. I kissed her.

"That would have been very silly, even if true. Anyway, I had already said my little piece about the others."

"You're a very good actress. I was a complete coward, more so than you know. I was inside the house when I heard your bicycle bell. I saw you coming towards them, and I just stood there and said, 'Let her handle it.'"

She looked at me. "Do you think he knew?"

"I don't know."

"It's all very confusing. I've been trying to project myself outside the situation. But I can't. I'm *in* the situation, and it all seems so right."

"My father used to say, 'Whenever you wonder whether or not you should do something, always imagine what it would look like in headlines on page three of the *Daily News.'*"

"Good Lord!" She stroked my hand for a moment. "How are things between you and him? I mean David."

"As complex, I suppose, as they are between most fathers and sons. He adored his mother. He didn't see much of her because she was often away, on tour, making films. But he adored her. Understandably. I did most of the bringing up, with a Nanny, of course, after we could afford one. Fran was more like some lovely indulgent aunt who floated in with love and presents. She used to say, 'It's not the quantity of time you spend with a person, it's the qual-

[222]

ity of the time.' And Fran gave full quality to every second
. . . I'm sure he finds me guilty of many wrongs, some I'm
not even remotely aware of. I don't know. We've just
never been very close. Nothing specific. I accept my part
of the blame, whatever it is." I kissed her cheek and
rubbed my face against hers.

I returned to the more immediate issue. "Of course,
when I was his age, I couldn't imagine a man of forty-three
being in love. Men of forty-three were businessmen, heads
of families, golfers, poker players, drinkers. And as for a
young girl having anything to do with one of them . . ."

She just smiled and touched my face. "It bothers you
a lot what he thinks."

"Yes, I suppose so. One always wants to be understood."

"If you could make him understand, what would you
want him to understand?" She looked at me.

I thought for a few moments, then smiled. "I don't
know."

"Sometimes I would be horrified if people understood me." She shook her head. "It bothers you what
other people think too, doesn't it?"

"Doesn't it bother you?"

"Oh, very much. But in this, with Fran, you *know*
how it was, don't you? At the theatre they talk to me a lot
about Fran and you, because they think having the scholarship I should know. And my God, it's . . . well, you
know."

"I told you the survivor is always the sinner. Death
puts a person beyond reproach. *De mortuis nihil nisi
bonum.* Which leaves the survivor with some almost mas-
ochistic compulsion to take the blame for everything."

"What was 'everything'?"

"Oh . . . petty, trivial cruelties."

"Oh, well . . ." She shrugged.

I was being forgiven, which is what I wanted, but I

felt dishonest. I felt there was some more major charge I wasn't mentioning, didn't know myself, wanted to discover.

"It sounds very ruthless, I mean, you with yourself. I somehow have a feeling that God is more forgiving than you are."

I smiled. "Perhaps He doesn't know as much about me as I know about myself."

"You want to know definitely, finally, without question that you loved Fran and that you were a good husband."

"Yes, I guess that's it." It was too simple, but it was as far as we were going to get.

She looked at me, took my hand, and then said very formally, "Then I tell you just that. Go and sin no more" —then she smiled—"except with me." And she kissed me, laughing.

We lay there in each other's arms for a while, kissing, nibbling. The sun was going down behind us. "You know, I don't know anything about you. I know some of your attitudes and opinions, but nothing about where they came from."

"There's not a great deal to know that I want to talk about. My ideas on marriage were formed very early, specifically, at birth. I never saw my father. Oh, I've seen pictures of him, all I could get my hands on. Very handsome. Good family, whatever that is. My mother was just a pretty girl in the town, poor family. My mother tells me that there was a marriage and a quick divorce, and some money changed hands. She never married again. She has a very low opinion of men. She's a physical-culture nut. Used to hail me into her room periodically to show me how well she was keeping her figure. Almost like a boy's body. A rather dull woman, I'm sorry to say. Her interests don't seem to extend beyond her body, a neat house and television. Sometimes I'm very sympathetic to my father."

[224]

"Did she come for graduation?"

"No. She came once to see me act, and she felt so uncomfortable with the other mothers and fathers, she's always made up some excuse since then. Miss A has been more of a mother to me."

"Do you know where your father is?"

"No. He turned into a bit of a hermit, I understand. Strangely, I don't feel much bitterness towards him. My mother used to go on and on about how horrible he was, but since I couldn't stand her, I instinctively got very defensive about him. His image has been very important to me. A man who couldn't stand the mediocrity of my mother's mind and attitudes . . . I fantasize that he's somewhere in Europe, living alone, writing day and night on a great body of important work, and one day . . . one day he'll show up at a stage door where I'm playing, and . . ."

"And what will you do?"

She didn't answer. I looked down and saw that she was pressing her lips together very tightly and she was frowning to hold back tears. Then suddenly she turned her face into my neck and cried. I just held her and stroked her head.

"I'm sorry. It's very sloppy. I can't stand sloppy people." She dug in my trousers' pocket for a handkerchief. "You don't need my troubles." She blew her nose. "I'll wash it and bring it back." She sat away from me, looking at me, her eyes blinking with tears and trying to smile. "I don't cry very often. I really don't feel that strongly about my father. It was just . . . today . . . and I'm always more susceptible when I have the damned curse."

I reached out and brushed back her hair. "I like girls who cry."

"Why?"

"It's very trusting."

She smiled. "I'm feeling a little cold. Can we go inside?"

THIRTY-SEVEN

We had dinner in the kitchen—candles, checkered tablecloth, wine. "I'm afraid I'm not a very good cook." She wasn't. I kept reaching over to touch her face, getting up to crouch beside her and rub my head against her. She kept eating and enjoying her food and laughing at my need to be close to her. "Do you do this all the time when you're married?" She fed me a mouthful.

I smiled. "No. I come from a very affectionate family. Though you might not think it from what I've said about him, my father was a tender man. He didn't want us to have animals in the family. He said that if there was to be any petting or cuddling, it should be done with another member of the family."

She laughed. "But what if you wanted cuddling and petting but at that particular moment loathed all the other members of the family?"

"My father's theory was, I think, that if you needed the affection badly enough, the hunger would make you overcome your loathing. I think he was afraid that if no effort were made towards each other, we'd all sooner or later just turn to the dog for easy and ready affection."

After dinner she wanted to tidy up, but I wouldn't let her. "It spoils the whole feeling dinner gives you. Come on, let's lie down."

I headed towards the couch and the fire, but she guided me along to the bedroom we'd used. "I feel this is more ours, all right?"

We didn't light a light. There was a half-moon over the water. We just lay down and held each other, saying nothing, kissing, nipping, fondling. Then she lay back. "I've never spent a whole night with . . . anyone." I kissed her neck, waiting, oddly enough still not sure if I wanted her to stay. "I feel more like it with you than I have with anyone else . . . but I'm not going to."

Perhaps she expected me to try to persuade her. I only said, "I understand," and kissed her chin. She didn't ask me what I understood, and I didn't ask her why she hadn't spent the night before and wouldn't this time. Perhaps there was something too married about it, too committed. She kissed me for "understanding," and seemed somehow relieved.

She went back to the subject of marriage. Miss A had told me, "This one isn't going to get married." Her family history gave some reasons. She gave others.

"I sense that I'm too impulsive for marriage." Her face hovered over mine as she absent-mindedly traced the outline of my lips with her finger. "For instance, if I'd been married, I couldn't have come here to you. And think what I would have missed!" She kissed my forehead.

[227]

"Because if I marry, which I won't, I'd want to play by the rules . . . You did." She rubbed her cheek against mine. "If you don't want to play by the rules, don't get married."

"The rules seem to change constantly."

"But I don't think people can love each other very much if they don't care if the other person sleeps around . . . if they're married. It would seem to me to mean it was time to get out if I didn't care."

"I keep hearing that sex has been removed from the moral hierarchy . . . that it just 'is' now, neither moral nor immoral."

She looked at me a moment. She snorted and lay her head on my chest.

After a few moments there was a new note in her voice. "What I want in this world is to devote my life to some one or some thing. Complete, whole. Dedication. When I was a girl, I thought of becoming a nun. Their concentration and dedication excited me. I get the same feeling about some dancers, musicians, artists. To give up everything to do one thing well, and not make anyone else pay for that dedication."

I recognized the feeling, the intoxicating words. I stroked her hair. "You're so loving and giving. You'd miss that."

She raised herself and looked at me. "I could still love and give . . . but only as long as I wanted to." She laughed at her selfishness, and then she looked serious. "And only as long as I was wanted and needed."

"I once started a poem with the line 'Some must leave and some be left.' It's not good being left, and if the leaver is sensitive, knowing this kills the exhilaration of his leaving, and he stays."

She shuddered, then lay her head on my chest again and was quiet. After a while her hand slid down to my erection, and she just left it there. Neither of us said anything. Then she brought her hand up to the tab and started to draw down the zipper. I put my hand down to stop her. "Hey!"

"What?" She didn't move her hand.

"I told you."

"Don't you like it?"

"Yes, but not when I can't do anything for you."

"I would like to do something when you can't do anything for me. Consider it a gift."

"I just like holding you, touching you. There's a different quality to it."

"I like doing something for you when you can't do anything for me. There's a quality to that too." I could feel my cock suddenly become stiffer at this idea. She felt it too. "Our friend down here would like to be selfish. What have you got against being selfish?"

"I just want you to know that it doesn't always have to be . . . I enjoy just the tenderness and the feeling of your closeness."

"I understand that."

"I think you have some feeling that a man . . . that I have to be satisfied down there all the time."

"You've made it clear that you don't have to . . . last night . . . that you're not demanding. I think you should be demanding. I would like it if you were. It would mean I could feel I could demand back. Does that scare you?" Then I could tell that she was smiling. "If you won't demand, I will. I demand that you let me give you a gift . . . without obligation." And she finished unzipping my trousers.

THIRTY-EIGHT

Afterwards, as we lay holding each other, my mind was awash with confusing crosscurrents. I had loved what she had done. Had always loved it. Didn't this tell me something about myself? Why this extra rush of excitement when someone started doing that? Did I really prefer to be wholly selfish?

Fran had once done exactly what Marianne had done just now. It had been my birthday, and we had been to the North Shore for a lobster dinner (before we were married), and we had come back and almost before she had her coat off, she had pushed me on the bed. "I want to. I just want to." I had wondered at her insistence. Was it something that she had had to prove to herself that she could do? She seemed so compulsive about it and a little awkward. In later months we had explored and experimented and made suggestions and discoveries. "I want my mouth on every part of you."

Marianne snuggled up to me, very pleased with herself. She had forced me to accept a gift and had fought off all efforts on my part to reciprocate. "You owe me." She laughed. "Or don't you like to owe?" She looked at me.

"I already owe you so much."

She snuggled. "Oh, no. I was only teasing. I would like to do so much for you, get you deep in my debt, and then tear it all up in front of you and let you know you are free." She nuzzled me. "I love your body."

"Very ordinary. It can be very disappointing on occasion."

"I don't believe it."

I wanted to ask her about the boys, the men she'd been with. Hadn't any of them ever disappointed her. But I couldn't ask.

I ventured one question. "I was wondering . . . you did that so freely, with seeming enjoyment, yet when I wanted to . . ." I drifted off.

"I know." She hesitated a long time. Obviously it was difficult to talk about. I shouldn't have asked the question, because though she was still holding me, she had gone away. I ran my hand through her hair. "You have such beautiful—"

"—There was this boy once." She stopped, then went on. "And, I don't know, but he'd read everything, and he used me to . . . experiment on, and . . ." She turned and hid her face in the pillow.

I turned and half covered her with my body and put my head down next to hers. I didn't want to know any more about it. I suddenly felt very protective, very angry at the insensitivity of the boy performing his mechanical experiments on this girl's modest flesh. I suddenly felt very possessive, almost sick to my stomach imagining anyone else touching her, being inside her.

My mind went back to the evening with Fran, soon after we had started making love, when she had told me she had been with another boy before I came along. I had lain on the bed in the twilight of that Boston spring day and felt sick, an instinctive feeling welling from God knows what conditioning. I had the same feeling now, and though rationally I knew that Marianne would not have been there with me if she hadn't had other lovers, I couldn't reason away the primitive feeling. Whatever it was, it told me something more about my feelings for Marianne. With Sarah it had been amusing, even erotic, to hear her go on about her other men. With Marianne, I didn't want to know.

She raised her head. "I'm sorry. It's really stupid of me. After all, it's not the Middle Ages. A girl knows about these things."

"There's a difference between knowing about . . . and knowing . . . It's always the Middle Ages first times. And there are ways and ways." I disliked myself for sounding so sententious, so understanding. It made me sound as though I not only knew all the answers, but also was always gentle and considerate and effective in my "ways."

Later that night I heard Marianne do her lines. She was a little shy at first, assuring me that she would just be saying the lines, not acting. "After all, you've never seen me act. You may be wasting your money, you know."

But I could tell just from her mumbled readings that I wasn't wasting my money. There was an intensity, a quality, a style. It made me stop the reading at the end of the scene and kiss her and look into her eyes with a new sense of who she was. This girl was going to be great. It was exciting. I have always been excited sexually and every other way by this kind of emerging greatness. There is something pure and beautiful about it. A person who knows what she can do and is going to go through hell to see that she does it.

I have perhaps always been too oversensitive to this kind of "rightness" and completely intolerant of its absence. An insensitive reading of a part can destroy whatever other feeling I might have for a beautiful actress. It had happened so often. A first reading of a new play which I might be privileged to attend. I settle down and begin falling in love with the young actress sitting near Fran, but then three minutes after she has jumped into the reading with a complete lack of comprehension and sensitivity, I not only am not in love with her, I can't stand sitting in the same theatre with her.

With Marianne the readings were all true. She had a great deal to learn, but her instincts were absolutely right. She grew more confident and asked me for suggestions. I raised both my hands in protest and said, "Never!" She seemed surprised and wondered if Fran and I hadn't talked over her parts. "Never! Oh, we might have discussed them generally when she was offered a play, the character, but I never opened my mouth about a performance except to praise it. That is something for you and your director to work out. Beware of listening to anyone else. He learns to speak your particular language, and you learn to understand his."

Watching this girl perched on Fran's slipper chair by the fire, drilling herself on a scene she felt she had missed, I was tempted into all kind of fantasies, most of which involved my protecting her. A few hours ago, even just a few minutes ago, before she had started muttering the lines, she had been essentially what *I* had needed, a loving, comforting, responsive, beautiful presence. I had completely forgotten that other part of her, the reason she was here, the actress. It reminded me of one night with Fran, when she had happened to sit in on a talk I was having with a young writer about his work. She had sat in the corner sewing while we were talking, and when he had gone, she had looked at me with a new awareness and said, "You know, I'd completely forgotten about that part of you, how your mind functions in your work." And she had kissed me.

Now here was a new and tremendously exciting part of Marianne's life. She was very special. Some instinct in me made me want to protect and nurture very special people. To serve. Was it some awareness of a kind of second-rate quality in myself and my work? I suddenly wanted to be part of her life as I had wanted to be part of Fran's.

"I think I know it now." And she thrust the script at me.

THIRTY-NINE

I knew that returning to Boston for the first time would be difficult. Boston had been beginnings for Fran and me—meeting, courtship, marriage, first apartment, first book. But Roger had set up an appointment for me with a local lawyer so that we could go into Fran's safety-deposit box with the Internal Revenue man.

Marianne had said I shouldn't go so soon, but in a sense I was eager to finish touching all the painful spots and move on. Marianne would be opening Monday, and, and . . .

I had to smile at all the fuss and concern over going into these boxes. It had been a matter of principle for Fran to have deposit boxes of her own. A very private person. When we had moved from Boston years before, she had kept her box there, for sentimental reasons, and she always paid it a ceremonial visit on our trips back. I remembered how she had walked into the Chase Bank in New York when we arrived there, had taken one look around and said, "They don't look like bankers to me." Boston bankers looked like bankers.

It was ridiculous, of course, to stay at the Ritz, where she had always stayed when she was on tour in Boston, and where we had earlier, as students and young marrieds, managed one or two meals a year. But it was "home" and to have avoided it would have defeated one of the purposes of the trip. I almost changed my mind when I smelled the perfume in the elevator and remembered how we had hunted high and low to discover where they hid it, finally locating it under the corner seat.

At the bank I met the lawyer and the Revenue man, who didn't think my jokes about what we might find in Fran's deposit box very funny. "Husbands and wives don't always know the affairs of the others. I mean, of course, financial affairs."

As we went down to the vaults, I felt a certain eeriness about it. Fran was the most private person I had ever known, and now these two strangers were going to examine some things which she had considered so private that she put them in a safety-deposit box. I secretly hoped there would be nothing. And yet, there might be something. I remembered a month or so after our marriage, while rummaging through a drawer looking for something Fran had phoned and asked me to find, I had come across a recently mailed letter with a return address from her father. I had been shocked, because she had always told me that her father was dead, killed some years before in an accident. When I had asked her about the letter, she had been angry that I had come across it, but finally told me that she had had a fierce fight with him, and that at the end of it he had said, "You may consider me dead." And she had done just that.

I signed the forms, handed over the key, and the three of us went into a small room, the Revenue man carrying the box almost as though he were shielding it from me. My hands and feet were cold. I realized I was nervous and angry at this invasion of privacy.

The Revenue man opened the box with great ceremony. It was not empty. He lifted out an envelope. I recognized it at once, the letter I had written Fran on our wedding day. Before he could take it from the envelope, I reached for it, clearing my throat to say, "That's . . . uh . . . very personal. A letter I wrote on our wedding day."

He proceeded to take out the few sheets of paper. "I'm sorry, but we have to look at everything."

"Why? It's obviously just a letter."

He shrugged. "Sometimes there's information in letters about financial matters." He proceeded to read the letter rather carefully.

"Surely you can see, you can tell from the first page . . ." He read on. I looked at the lawyer for help. "I'm sorry, but it's regulations. However, these gentlemen are discreet."

I could damn well imagine how discreet they were. "You should have seen the letter I had today, this guy telling his bride how she excites him . . ." I couldn't look at the man. He finished and handed it to the lawyer, looking at me with what I interpreted as slight distaste. I reached out and intercepted the letter.

The lawyer smiled understandingly. "I really don't have to look at anything, unless you want me to, or unless it concerns any property or any wish she might have expressed as to the distribution of her estate."

My head throbbed with anger and checked emotion. This small fluorescent room was suddenly a torture chamber. It all seemed an outrage. The things that one wants to be most private become most public. I looked at the envelope and my handwriting and started to remember, but there was no time.

The Revenue man plucked out a pin and turned it over. The first pin I had given her, the first of many during our courtship. Small, silver. He examined it. I got angry.

"Eight dollars and fifty cents. Silver."

He looked at me and set it next to the letter, and reached in again. Ah, a bankbook, small, blue. His interest perked up.

"Our first savings account." He riffled the pages, saw it marked "canceled" and with some disappointment set it in front of me. I began to look at the book, to remember, but there was no time to remember, to make contact with my feelings, and this wasn't the place.

The Revenue man was studying a filled-in form I couldn't recognize. I frowned in concentration trying to remember it, annoyed that he was paying so much attention to something I couldn't identify. He passed it over.

It was the report of Fran's fertility checkup years ago, when we had been unsuccessful in having a child, before David. The lawyer looked at me, curious, but I didn't say anything, just nodded my head. Starting to remember that sad-funny period of our life when—

Now he was looking at what seemed to be Fran's "Numbers," and I smiled. Fran had been a great believer in numerology. Incredible! A bright woman like that.

Why should he study those scribbled pages so carefully? Did people hide codes with directions to find secret treasures in such documents? Finally he handed it over to me with no expression on his face. "That's all."

"Then we have no problems." The lawyer smiled. "We can have our release of all this." The Revenue man was already filling in and signing the forms.

I looked at the last sheet of paper. The heading, CHART FOR CHRISTOPHER LARSEN. The date was several months before we had been married. Fran had had me worked up by the numerologist to see what kind of husband I would make. I smiled and shook my head. I wonder what kind of man she thought she was marrying.

I put the papers in my jacket pocket and stood up.

My head splitting, I thanked the lawyer and the Revenue man, signed some papers, and in a daze walked up the stairs and out of the bank.

I walked down Boylston Street, past the bookshop where I had wasted far too many afternoons browsing after my writing or teaching while Fran was rehearsing. Past Shreves, where long before we were married we had come night after night to look at the silverware patterns displayed in the windows. Should it be Francis I or absolutely plain Contemporary? Past Bickford's, the all-night cafeteria where after rehearsals we had eaten late and had looked across at the Ritz and said, "Someday." And that day had come.

And I walked on, touching all bases. The Garden and the swan boats. A rainy winter day and a bitter fight in which each had wanted to run away from the other but we had only one umbrella, and Fran, refusing to take it, had dashed towards Boylston Street in tears . . . The Commons, skipping across the path in imitation of some dance step we'd just seen in the new musical at the Shubert . . . Park Street station entrance where she had given me the signet ring I had wanted ("I'm embarrassed it's only twelve carats") . . . The church where we were married, Fran chattering away nervously with the minister about the state of the world, perhaps trying not to think of what she was about to do.

Scollay Square that wasn't Scollay Square any more. ("I want to see a burlesque show, a tassel-tosser. I just don't believe a woman can make her breasts go like that.")

And I had prowled here too, after our marriage, lonely while Fran was rehearsing at night or teaching in the afternoon—had walked past the church where we had married and come here to prowl among the sleazy sailors' bars, the burlesque houses and cheap hotels. Had only prowled.

I walked on, up and over the back of Beacon Hill, down towards the river, and finally stopped in front of our first home, an old brick town house converted long ago into apartments. I looked at our windows. Just behind the glass curtains, an old lady was sitting holding a cat. It suddenly struck me as odd that she had no idea of what used to go on there.

It had been Fran's small, cheerful apartment, and after we were married, I had simply moved in, had been absorbed into her life. But the difference. Whereas before I had been one of the acting groups invading her apartment (the one who always stayed on), now writing, working, earning a living, I was no longer part of the group and they were in *our* apartment, and they wouldn't go home. Fran had never wanted anyone to go home. I smiled as I remembered before we were married when after lovemaking I would finally put on my big overcoat. "Don't go!" And she would snuggle inside my coat, and I could almost button it around both of us. Then finally for the tenth time, "I must go."

Our happiest days, and also the first sadness and tears, and Fran so forthright, almost eager. "Have we made a mistake? If we've made a mistake, let's admit it and break up." The Valentine's dinner, uneaten . . .

Then suddenly I was tired. I had walked for hours, saying "Good-bye" to places, times, good and bad. I wanted to go back to my room now.

I bought a bottle of gin in the liquor store on the corner of our street, and looked across at the flower shop where I had bought all those camellias, the only flower Fran would wear. White on the long black-velvet dress which moved so beautifully when we danced at the Copley Plaza on Friday nights.

We didn't really drink in those days, except to use up our minimum at the Copley, and an occasional highball. We drank later, but not really until after the first operation when someone had sent us a case of Dubonnet, and then it became Dubonnet and gin, and then, for me, just gin.

As I passed, I smiled and nodded at the lady who ran the flower shop, but she didn't recognize me. I was usually not recognized out of context, without Fran.

I entered my room and thought I should call David, I should call friends. But I knew I wouldn't. I was too much with Fran and she too much with me. And I wanted it that way.

I took off my coat and tie and opened the bottle of gin and propped myself up on the bed and stared at the things from the safety-deposit box. I sensed the danger of this, but I could not help myself. I had a feeling of being whole again, connected, of being back in the condition of my life, which was Fran, her death and my surviving.

I had tried to shut her out too soon.

Fran would not have approved of this. She never looked back. She would say "Good-bye" and turn and not look back, while I would be standing there waving, take a few steps and wave again. That's what I was doing, of course, standing there waving, in the European way, with the palm up beckoning the departing person to come back.

I looked at Fran's fertility checkup and shook my head, smiling. Her tests. My tests, charts, temperatures, our efforts till we got to hate making love because it was all so calculated. But it became a point of pride. Our continuing efforts until we had conceived David lost sight of the question of whether or not we still really wanted a child. Our lives had changed. But somehow our egos had been wounded by our inability to conceive, to be the complete man and the complete woman, and we were flushed with a sense of satisfaction but not necessarily of happiness when we knew that Fran was pregnant at last.

And as one does with a friend whose name one can't remember, we had greeted him with unreal and unfelt but extraordinary enthusiasm, and guilty with our not quite understood feelings about him, we had showered him with attentions and care and concern.

Fran's numbers. "You're in a Seven year, Chris, and you must not expect . . ." One day in anger at having our life or our living influenced even slightly by such nonsense, I had ordered her not to get her weekly or monthly chart any more.

But when she was sick, I had relented, and again they arrived at the house. I hoped it had given her comfort to read in her chart, "You will have some poor days at the beginning of the week, but by the end of the week you will feel some marked improvement." I had reached the numerology woman and had told her the truth about Fran's dying, and I had said I didn't want her fed any horseshit, but that if the woman could be supportive, all right.

The first savings book. I looked at the deposits. Five dollars, ten dollars. How proudly we had watched it grow. What misers young marrieds can be! "If we can get together five thousand, that will be enough security for the rest of our lives, and we can spend all we earn from then on." What innocence! How little we knew about anything.

And finally . . .

Dearest Fran:
This is the most wonderful day of my life . . .

And I knew all the rest but couldn't read it, couldn't face it. "I am so proud of you and want to protect you and help you grow. And I want to grow along with you, to make you proud of me too. We know it's going to be difficult, but how exciting! I know you are afraid. You said over and over you never wanted to marry. I promise you you will only know you are married because you will feel my love now constantly. Don't be afraid! I love you. I love everything about you. I love holding you and . . ."

I suddenly didn't want to be in that hotel room. I wanted to be back home sitting by the grave. Were the pine boughs still there or had they seeded it? Had they been careful? From the catch-all of poetry remembered from college, I thought of

> The grave's a fine and quiet place,
> But none, I think, do there embrace

As I turned my head into the pillow I thought "Wrong, wrong!" All over the world at all hours of the day and night the dead are reached for, clutched and embraced.

FORTY

I awoke the next morning eager to get back to
Marianne.

Sex after months of starvation had made me hungry
for sex. The hunger during Fran's illness had been of a
different kind, release, oblivion. There was vigor and ongoing life in this feeling for Marianne. And there was caring.
I lay on my back, thinking of her, seeing her strong presence in my bed back at the cottage. Such an active, loving,
playful solicitous presence! Some women were content to
lie back and be "served," as it were. Marianne seemed always to be serving, "doing all the work" as she smilingly
put it as she looked down on me through her tumbling
dark hair. But it was more than that.

I got out of bed, moved the gin bottle from the bedside table and looked at Fran's mementos with no emotion.

I brushed my teeth, shaved, showered, all the time turning over in my mind how I might reach Marianne. Telegraphing was useless, since in the village all telegrams were phoned or sent by mail. "Arrive home noon . . . Unsigned." And what message would I leave if I called Mrs. Grader or the theatre?

As I entered the Ritz Coffee Shop, I saw Jack Gresham, an old college friend and now a successful businessman. Jack had liked me and adored Fran, and though we had seen him and his wife only rarely since the early days, we were always able to take up where we had left off. He was a burly, attractive red-cheeked Irishman, an "operator" but also deeply interested in things like philosophy, Japanese art, and "What the hell's life all about anyway?"

He was deep in his paper as I stood in front of him. "May I share this table?"

He looked up, annoyed, then roared with laughter and pushed back the table and jumped up. "Chris, you son of a bitch. How are you?" He grabbed my hand and gave me half a bear hug, trapped as he was behind the table. "Why didn't you tell me you were coming to town? Sit down, for God's sake. This is wonderful!" He laughed with genuine delight. "Waiter, some breakfast for Mr. Larsen here!"

And for ten minutes he enveloped me with gusty affection and warmth. "God, what a great girl she was! I never laughed so much as when we three used to be together. She was a very funny woman. Not jokes, just funny because she was Fran. Some incredible innocence and naïveté that came out funny . . . oh, Christ, what a shame! . . . How we all hated you! Do you remember Paul Rafferty, with all his damned charm? He told me once he

[245]

took Fran for a long walk along the Charles to ask her very seriously what she saw in you. What a prick he was!"

Finally Jack talked about himself.

"I guess you haven't heard. Nancy and I have been separated for some months. Nothing bitter about it . . . I don't know, Chris . . . complex. The kids are gone. There just, well . . . there just doesn't seem to be anything there any more for either of us. I know it sounds cool. But it never was anything like you and Fran. I mean, you had it made." And he chuckled with appreciation. "The way it all finally happened was funny. We made all sorts of plans to build a new house, I guess something that would hold us together, and then one day when we were trying to decide whether or not to have a porch or a terrace, we both realized almost simultaneously we didn't want a new house. We didn't want each other. Nancy's still very attractive, lots of tennis and swimming and riding, you know. She'll be married again in a flash, if she wants it."

"And you?"

He looked at me a long while. "I don't think I want it. Oh, if I could have something like you and Fran. But I don't know. All during my marriage I was too conscious of missing a great deal. So now I'm going to see. I have my little black book." He patted his breast pocket.

"You had a little black book back then, if I remember rightly."

"With about three names in it. Mostly bluff." He smiled.

"I was always pretty much a one-name person."

"Well, you had the best name. How long are you going to be in Boston?"

"I'm leaving almost immediately."

"Oh, why don't you stay over and have dinner with me tonight?"

"No." I shook my head, smiling.

"Jesus, we haven't talked in years. I've got a dinner

date with a girl, someone I see once in a while." He
smiled. "Very attractive, very obliging. But I can put her
off, or . . ." He paused for a moment. "She has a friend, if
you'd be interested."

"Thanks, Jack, but . . ."

"Look, don't think me an insensitive horse's ass for
suggesting it. I just didn't know how you feel. I understand
your feelings. As a matter of fact, I envy you your feelings."

I wished he would keep still about my feelings. He
made me feel the most complete hypocrite, assuming that
in my grief I would find it distasteful and impossible to be
with a girl. I thought of a conversation he and I had had in
college, and for some reason out of it had come his statement, "Well, sex is probably not as important to you as it
is to me." I had smiled but not said anything, because at
that time Fran and I were spending a good deal of time in
bed, but it was a period when you didn't advertise it. He
probably thought now, "Well, old Chris hasn't changed."

Back in my room I packed my overnight bag and then
decided I should call David. He might wonder why I
didn't call last night. Well . . .

"David, how are you? It's Dad."

"Oh. Where are you?"

"I had to come up to Boston on business yesterday.
I'm at the Ritz."

"Oh. Well, you caught me on the way to a class."

"I won't keep you. I just wanted to check in before I
left."

"Did Mackenzie reach you?"

"No. Why?"

"He's been trying to reach you to tell you that that
girl who won the fellowship is going to make her first appearance Monday and he wondered if you'd come see her.
There's going to be quite a thing in honor of Mom."

I was confused and said nothing.

"I didn't tell him you were down there, but I wondered why he didn't know, since the kids used your beach for swimming." He just let it hang there.

"Well, only a few of them use it, and I asked them not to tell anyone around." Oh, shit!

"There was a picture of her in the paper this morning on the entertainment page."

"Oh, I haven't seen it."

"She's much prettier in person."

"Why don't you and Gretchen come down to the opening?"

"I've got this class that meets in the evenings, and . . ."

"I think it would be nice if you were there."

"Are you going?"

"I think I should."

"Well, we might make it sometime during the week. I don't know. I've got to run now. Do you want to speak to Gretchen?"

"No, thanks. Just give her my love."

On my way out I bought the paper at the hotel newsstand, and looked at Marianne's picture. David was right. It was not very good, but she was smiling, and unconsciously I smiled back at her.

I was about to give the doorman the order for my car, when I suddenly wanted to bring something back to Marianne. I asked him to watch my suitcase, told him I'd be back in a few minutes, and headed for Shreves a block away.

I was a notorious bearer of gifts, trinkets, trifles. It was one of my pleasures, one of my needs. It kept me in contact while I was away, looking for things to bring back. Carlyle had written that if we had no heroes, we would invent them, make them. I wondered if there were no one I loved, if I wouldn't invent her to satisfy my need to give. The pleasure of going through a magazine and saying

"That would be nice for Fran." Now "for Marianne." Though still I found myself looking at a dress or a blouse and saying "Nice for Fran."

I had given Fran a charm bracelet soon after our marriage, with one charm. After that, each charm had to be significant. You could practically read our lives by "telling" the fifty or sixty small gold charms. It would be nice to start something like that for Marianne, for her opening, her professional debut.

I looked at the bracelets in the case. Then I felt strange about it. I should find something else for Marianne. What to get for her that would be hers? I had brought Fran almost everything I could think of, brooches, scarfs, leather-bound scrapbooks for her reviews, Battersea boxes with little messages, "From a Friend" . . . "Love the Giver." Each one had had to show some knowing idea behind the gift, some nudge to a common joke or feeling.

As I walked through the floors, I became aware of a certain irony in all this. I had been here before, playing this part before. Was it possible to play it all over again?

I was becoming tense with the impossibility of finding anything for Marianne which I had not thought of for Fran or actually given her. It seemed impossible to be original. I knew her so little, her likes and dislikes, colors, shapes, her passions and loathings. I smiled, remembering one Christmas when I had almost come to hate Fran because after weeks of desperate shopping and looking, I couldn't come up with anything special and unusual and "just right" for her.

I was about to give up looking when I turned a corner and came upon a case full of rocks and stones, jade, quartz and crystal.

FORTY-ONE

As I drove out of Boston with my silly but very personal gift for Marianne tucked in my suitcase, I was eager to see her, to be with her, to ask how rehearsals were going, hear her lines, be swept up in the activity of her life.

I wanted to rush in on her, arrive at her room with an armful of flowers, crawl into bed with her and simply say, "Here I am." That seemed to be all that needed to be said.

But of course I couldn't do that. She would be at rehearsals, and I wasn't going to walk into rehearsals and put my arm around her and kiss her and say, "Here I am! And incidentally, this is my girl."

No.

I felt she wouldn't want that either. I kept thinking that her feelings were prompted not so much by me as by the situation and her feelings about Fran and our marriage. Part of it was her way of being close to this whole experience of our life together. This was her way of sharing something she felt was beautiful and sad and romantic. But was I right? What was her real world?

I would not worry it. I wanted to be close to her, to help her, to love her. The relationship would define itself eventually.

· It was ridiculous to think beyond. Yet I could not resist thinking about her. I adored her. I was in awe of her talent and her dedication to her talent, as I had been with Fran. But the whole thing would be different this time around. Now I was secure in my work and career. I had money. There need be no meanness, no cheapness. (I winced as I remembered that Fran and I had found that we could not afford to eat in the hotel where we were honeymooning, but had to go for most of our meals to a bean-wagon.)

There would be no grubbiness with Marianne. No five-flight roach-infested walk-up. The Christmas in those two rooms with the skylight when we decided we couldn't afford a tree, but I couldn't stand a Christmas without a tree and late Christmas Eve bought a small one for "nothing" and decorated it with red, gold and green snips of metallic wrapping paper left over from gifts.

With Marianne, it would all be the same, but it would all be different.

Coming around the last curve of the beach road, I saw Bessie, the mail carrier, putting something in my mailbox. Not wanting to talk to anyone yet, I kept on going, down along the shore road, and then I came around again a half mile down the way.

I had done this by instinct, the instinct developed in the last week, to hide, to be alone with Marianne. Just as I came around back, I had a revulsion at this secrecy, a desire to throw open the gate and leave it open, to live publicly whatever that might involve. The complex hypocrisies and dishonesties were beginning to depress me. I wanted to feel the exhilaration of coming to a clean decision, in spite of knowing somewhere that I had felt such exhilarations before and that most of them had dissolved later in compromise.

I stopped the car, went to the mailbox, and hefted out the pile of junk mail accumulated there and tossed it in the car. As I had grown older, I had actually come to hate the mail and used to put off looking at it as long as possible. Except for the rare personal letter, mail was a series of small clutching hands eager to choke off one's time. Bills, requests, "Will you read?" "Will you speak?" "Will you judge?" "We are forming a committee . . ."

In spite of my resolve, I found myself shutting the gate after I had driven through.

As I came out of the drive and the woods and saw the cottage, I noticed the doors and windows were open, the curtains moving in the breeze. I had not expected Marianne to be there. I had thought she would be rehearsing. I got out of the car, excited. The sound of the car door brought Marianne to the back entry.

"This place is not for sale. How many times do we have to tell you?" And she opened her arms.

"I'm so glad you're here."

"I'm so glad *you're* here."

"I thought you'd be rehearsing."

"I will be this afternoon."

I stood there, holding her. "I missed you."

"I missed you. It's awful." And she looked at me as though she hated missing me and wondered why she did.

We walked into the house, arms around each other. "How was Boston?"

"All right."

"All right doesn't mean anything."

I stopped and held her again, savoring her, looking at her, shaking my head in wonder.

"What's the matter?"

"Nothing." And I rubbed my face against her hair.

"Nothing doesn't mean anything either. Is there something wrong with me?"

"Nothing . . . absolutely nothing. Can't a man shake his head in wonder?" She moved to the counter to prepare coffee, and I moved behind her, cupping her breasts.

She giggled. "You'll make me spill."

I moved my hands away, but stood there pinning her against the counter as she measured out the coffee. I had been thinking about her the last miles, visualizing her body, working up a hunger for it. And there she was. And there I was. How many times in my life I had done that. Ready before I entered the door, assuming always that the girl would be ready, that she had been fantasizing along the same lines, was ready. I always assumed the woman would be complimented. Sometimes she was. Sometimes she wasn't. The time I had awakened at college and wanted to get to Fran and took a taxi into Boston at seven-thirty and slid into bed with her and made love and left in time for my nine o'clock class. She had been pleased that time.

I stepped back. "I'm sorry. I forgot. You have rehearsals."

"Not until two."

It was an exciting time, the separation heightening it, the realization of how much I had missed her, just being away one day. I blurted out, "We mustn't be apart again." She drew back and looked at me with a questioning frown, then nestled her head against my shoulder.

She was loving and passionate but, I thought, a little reserved. I had the feeling that she was doing something for me, enjoyable but a little accommodating, as though it

[253]

were a prelude to something more important. As we lay afterwards in each other's arms, I said, "I'm sorry. You didn't really feel like that."

"Yes, I did."

"That's the first time you lied to me."

"I'm not lying."

"I don't like being obliged."

She looked down at me, serious. "I wanted to. I really did."

I smiled. "Okay. But just remember that. Unless you want to, I'm not interested."

"A person enjoys doing something for someone else once in a while."

"All right. Once in a while." I kissed her lightly.

She smiled. "You funny man." She kissed me. "I once heard a friend of Mother's, a very sophisticated French woman. I have no idea how my mother knew her, but I was in the next room, and she was talking about husbands and wives, and after my mother said something about what a nuisance men could be, she said that as far as she was concerned she felt an enormous sexual responsibility towards her husband. She said she maintained a policy always of 'la bouche ouverte.'"

I laughed. "And that has influenced you. Right?"

"Not really. But I think about it sometimes."

I absent-mindedly traced a pattern on her shoulder. "But I should have known. You're in rehearsals. You have other things on your mind. Insensitive of me. I don't like being insensitive, in spite of the fact that I am all the time." She smiled and touched my face. "You'll find when I'm working, writing, I don't have too much interest in sex unless the work is going very well or very poorly. Celebration or anxiety. How's it going with you?"

"Very well. Mac's a darling. Says all kinds of extravagant things about me." She smiled shyly.

"Like what? Come on. Word for word." She turned

her head into the pillow and giggled. I tried to pry up her face. She was blushing. "Like what? Extraordinary? Brilliant? Genius?"

She giggled until she laughed. "He thinks I'm good."

"I told you that."

"Yes, I know. But you're suspect because of . . . well . . ." She moved her finger back and forth across my lips. "But he has me doing some phony things which bother me."

"Did you tell him?"

"No." Her tone was *of course not*. "He's got me . . . look . . ." and she sat up in bed.

I stopped her. "Don't tell me. Remember, no advice from me."

"But look . . ."

"No, period! You're going to have to work with dozens of directors in your life, you've got to get used to getting along with them."

"But I don't feel comfortable."

"You're not supposed to feel comfortable. That *is* something I'll say to you. General statement, not coaching. Fran always loathed actors who wanted everything— lines, movements, emotions—'comfortable' for them. You're not playing you."

"But I feel awkward."

"Maybe the character's supposed to feel awkward at that moment. Look, I've already said too much. Mac probably doesn't have the time to go over these things with you, help you into them. He has to be satisfied with rather broad effects in the time he has. He's a nice guy, not a great director, but good for what he has to do here, get a show on every week."

"But if I feel phony onstage, I'm not going to do anyone any good."

I drew her down to me. "You are going to be adorable."

"Adorable is one thing. Good is another. The one has nothing to do with me. The other does." She frowned.

"Adorable has a great deal to do with being you. I didn't say beautiful or pretty. You have a quality . . ." I let it hang in the air. She raised herself up and looked at me, waiting. I smiled. "You want more?"

She slapped me playfully and clinched. "I just don't want you to be disappointed."

"I won't be."

We lay there for a few moments, enjoying the sun coming through the window.

"You looked terrible when you came in this morning. What happened in Boston?"

"Oh, a lot of booby traps, land mines. It was inevitable."

She hugged me a little in sympathy. "Was there a fortune in the safety-deposit box?"

"No. Just mementos."

"Was the tax man crushed?"

"A wasted day."

"I hope you saw friends last night and didn't just sit alone."

I lied to her. "I had drinks and dinner with an old friend. He's separated from his wife, which I hadn't known, and he was going out to a late, late date with a girl who could find a friend . . . both very obliging. And he asked me if I wanted to come along."

It was strange. I had just been going through this story lightly, archly, building up to my "gift" to her of not having gone along, but suddenly there was tension building around this silly story. What would she say next? What did I want her to say? What would her attitude be? I was suddenly afraid that she might be casual about it. I didn't want her to be casual. I wanted her to care. Because if she cared, it might help define our relationship, define her feelings. She would be telling me something without really telling me.

She avoided the issue by not saying anything. She assumed I would go on. I did. "I didn't go." I kissed the top of her head, indicating in a way the reason I hadn't gone. She kissed my shoulder in reply.

"My friend apologized for suggesting it. Realized that it was inappropriate so soon after Fran's death." We both just lay there for a few moments. "That's the reason he credited me with. And I suppose it was part of the reason, but I think the real reason was you." I could see her face tighten in a frown. "Hypocrisies within hypocrisies. I don't like getting false credit, but I didn't say anything."

After a moment. "I'd kill myself if I made you feel . . . awful . . . about . . ." She raised her face and looked at me, frowning.

I looked at her and those large worried eyes. "You've saved my life." And I held her face and kissed her. I was diving deep again, longing to be enveloped in the pure waters of all-out commitment.

She smiled. "You like to say things like that, don't you?"

"I mean it."

She waited a few moments. I could see her eyes darting around. This was her particular signal that she was building up to something important to say. "I was lonely for you yesterday, lonely for 'us,' and I came down here. I ate my dinner alone here. I browsed around, made the bed. You know you're something of a slob."

"Only about making beds."

"And I sat for a long time in that room." She nodded towards Fran's and my bedroom. "I didn't touch it, or move anything. I just tried to absorb. Then I moseyed around the living room, looked at the scrapbooks, the things you'd left around. I also read your copy for the brochure you're doing on Fran . . . and I cried myself silly, of course." I kissed her hair. "And then I guess I did a crummy thing. I was just looking at your desk, all those letters you're answering, and I saw propped up there this envelope with my name in it . . . *Marianne.* And I wondered if I should read it. You hadn't given it to me, and yet there it was, as though I were supposed to come across it. Anyway, I read it." She looked up at me to see my reaction. I kissed her brow. "Was I supposed to read it?"

"I didn't leave it there for you to read, but it was written to you."

"When?"

"Before I came to your room that night. I was going to leave it for you."

"You didn't leave it."

"No. I was afraid it might scare you."

"It did. It's a beautiful letter. I never had a . . . letter from a writer before."

"That's not 'writing.' It was just the way I felt." I held her a little closer and rubbed my cheek against the top of her head.

"Felt."

"Feel."

She moved away and looked into my eyes, questioning. "You can't feel all that. You don't know me."

"I can feel it. I do feel it." My words, my declaration, moved me. I reached for her, but she kept a distance.

"You may think you feel it because of the situation, but I don't think it has anything to do with me. I mean, to adore, to want to put one's life in someone's hands . . ." I was embarrassed to be quoted. She went on. "I'm sorry. It's not fair to take things from the letter." She quickly leaned over and kissed me. "Your situation is so . . . unusual. You're so very susceptible. Your feelings are lovely, but . . . I don't think the letter was addressed to me but to some terrible need in you to . . . to fill the void, the emptiness. To belong to someone again." She looked at me apologetically. "I'm sorry. I'm sure the last thing in the world you want is to be analyzed. I'm so touched by your feelings, and grateful that you expressed them to me, but . . ." She nestled in the crook of my neck. "I've never felt that way about anyone. To want to surrender myself to them, to be completely at their mercy."

"It's not necessarily an admirable feeling. I'm just stuck with it."

She took my hand and kissed it and was quiet for a moment. "I've often wondered if that's why it's best for me when I'm on top. If that means, just that, that I won't surrender my satisfaction completely to anyone . . . I'm to a great extent in control. Silly, isn't it, to think about things like that, but I do."

"I don't think it's silly. Everything we do tells us something. But I don't think your liking to be on top means . . . well, I don't know what it means. I just know it's lovely." I kissed her shiny hair.

"You don't have to worry about it because it isn't you it's part of."

"Well, I could start wondering why it is that I have never been as satisfying to a girl or to myself too as when I've been with you the way you like it."

She turned and looked at me. "Is that true?"

"Yes. Now shall we puzzle that out together? The obvious answer is too obvious. I like to put myself in another person's hands, or body, and you like to keep control. Our neuroses mesh beautifully. Made for each other. A computer couldn't have done better."

She giggled and kissed me lightly, and we lay there. "I don't write very good letters. I don't seem to want to put my feelings into words, to define them that clearly. I don't really verbalize at all while things are happening. I don't think 'I adore this man.' If I do adore, I just adore. Do it."

"Well, you see, you're an actress. I have a great need

[259]

to verbalize. Way back, when I used to go to see Fran . . .
Sorry."

"No, please. Tell me."

"When I used to come to see her, I'd bring along a
letter and slip it into her hand and say, 'Read this when
I've gone tonight.' I am a letter writer. So often I find it
much easier for me to express myself in letters. Again, not
necessarily a good thing, but again I'm stuck with it." I remembered also the times when we had had problems and
instead of talking them out, I had waited till one of us was
away and then written about them in a letter.

"I think I'd be nervous writing you a letter."

"Why?"

"Oh, punctuation and all that."

"You have the feeling that I read my love letters with
a blue pencil in hand?"

"No," and she hit me playfully. "I'm just self-conscious about it." Then more seriously, "And it does involve knowing what you think and feel and putting it into
words."

I hugged her closer to me.

She lay there nestled for a long moment. "There's
something I've wanted to share with you, but I can't do it
without making comparisons, and I'm sure you're not interested in hearing about other people I've been with."
She looked up at me. "Obviously, of course, there have
been others."

"I'm interested, if the comparison is favorable."

"It's just that . . . there's never been a married man
before."

It was interesting that she thought of me as married.

She looked at me with a sad little smile. "It's just that
it's different. Something more . . . something, well, I can
only say 'sad,' but you must understand how I mean it.
You know that it has been exciting, and everything . . ."
She kissed me to reassure me. "But there's something, so

many more overtones, touching, beautiful, unexpected
. . . sad. You always seem to be groping for something
beyond just making love." She gave up with a smile. "You
see why I don't try to verbalize."

I kissed her and held her and rocked her gently. How
wise she was! We lay like that for a long time.

The telephone rang. She moved away. "Which re-
minds me, I'm a working girl." And she got up.

"I'm going to start answering the phone." She
stopped and looked around at me, knowing what this
meant. "With the next call." I smiled. "I'm coming to
your opening. Everyone will know. It's only a matter of a
couple of days." She looked at me as though to ask "How
will we manage?"

"We'll manage." She was slipping on her jeans and
T-shirt. "I wish the hell that when the play is over I could
whisk you away someplace. Rome. Paris. Someplace where
nobody knows us, and we could be alone." What a strange
thing to say when we had been nothing but alone.

I put on my chinos and a polo shirt and walked
through the living room with her, my arm around her
shoulders. I stopped and kissed her passionately. "I have
never had such longing for anyone."

She frowned. "You mustn't say that. It's not true."

She was right. It wasn't true. But it was what I felt at
the moment.

We passed my desk. I reached for the letter. "Don't
forget your letter."

She looked at it but didn't take it. "It still scares me. I
don't really feel it belongs to me."

I tossed it back on the desk. "It will keep until you
do."

As she wheeled out her bicycle, I said, "You know,
I'm going to have to buy a jalopy you can use, so we can
meet out in the country someplace."

"People are beginning to suspect something. The

boys. They've threatened to set a watch on me, a 'tail.' "

I wanted to ask her if it would bother her if they found out. I didn't ask.

"You know, I don't want to scare you, but Monday could be a momentous night for you. Suddenly, everything different."

"I'm not even thinking about that. I'm just scared. Anyway, I doubt it. It's not New York, and it's a small part."

"I know, but . . ."

"I just hope I don't disgrace you."

She rose on the pedals and started up the road, waving that quick risky wave without looking back, as she disappeared into the woods.

FORTY-TWO

I arrived at the theatre as late as possible before
the curtain. Mac was waiting for me on the lawn with my
ticket. I was to sit with him and his wife, Martha.

"It's good of you to come, Chris. I know how rough
it's going to be on you. Some of the Press are down from
Boston, knowing you'd be here. You know, Fran was always a great favorite of theirs."

We walked towards the theatre. "You're going to be
impressed with this girl, Chris."

"She seemed very attractive when I met her at the college."

"Style, dedication. Real excitement. I've got some

agents here to look at her and a couple of people from New York who are doing shows next year."

"I'm looking forward to seeing her."

"She's got all the boys around here bugged. But she keeps to herself more or less. The general feeling is there must be someone serious somewhere else."

Many old friends and the merely curious were loitering in the lobby, looking at the dozens of old pictures of Fran's shows which Mac had assembled. There is a certain morbid interest in looking at survivors. How are they managing? Perhaps it is just that we all know that in one way or another we are all slated to play the role one day, and we are curious and unconsciously eager for instruction.

There were many kisses and some tears, and heartfelt handshakes. It was difficult to stay in neutral. I had a sudden fantasy of Fran moving through this gathering saying something like "Yes, it's very sad that I am dead, but you mustn't grieve. Nothing is lost. Nothing is ever lost." She would be so selfless as to ignore the fact that she was dead and bend all her efforts to comforting her friends. "You were so kind to her."   "She was so fond of you both." "You helped us so much that first year."

These people clustered in the lobby had not always been so fond of me. I had so often been the one clutching at Fran's elbow, trying to take her home, to have her to myself. But now I was the symbol of Fran and the recipient of the kindness they would have liked to have shown her. I felt sure that to most of them I had never been good enough for her. A rather detached man married to this wonderfully generous and loving woman. But many of them had been around during the last invalid summer, and somehow my care of Fran had made them feel a bit more warmly towards me.

There were flashbulbs and pictures, posing with Mac next to the new portrait of Fran, shaking hands with members of the Board and old friends. Just below Fran's picture was a large photograph of Marianne, "The First Frances Larsen Fellowship Award."

Finally we got to our seats, though my progress up the aisle resembled a grand right and left. I could have ducked it all and simply hurried to my seat, but again, Fran would not have liked that, would not have done that herself.

I had a few moments to look at my program, more pictures of Fran and a picture of Marianne. I was relieved to be in my seat. I could regain my composure. I had not meant to be moved, but I had been, and I had a hard knot in my stomach from emotion denied.

Mac leaned over as the lights went out. "I know that was rough for you, but I can't tell you how much it meant to us all." I nodded my head and watched the curtains part.

Marianne had only two scenes in the play, but they were good scenes and she played them beautifully. Ruth Campbell, the star of the show, a one-time famous and glamorous actress now doing mostly television, was enormously generous to Marianne and let her have her scenes. It would have been difficult to have taken them from her. From the moment she made her entrance, I sensed that rare excitement that sometimes happens in the theatre when someone new suddenly is "there," very much "there," and you know she is going to be "there" for a very long time. When Fran and I would happen on an occasion like this at some summer or regional theatre, we would instinctively reach for each other's hand while tears of excitement came to our eyes. It didn't happen often.

I felt again that same thing I had felt earlier in the week when Marianne had first read her scenes. It was now heightened by other people's awareness. The excitement of the theatre, which is to share, to affirm one's excitement and have it reaffirmed by the excitement of those around you. As she finished her scene and made her exit, there was a burst of applause, encouraged, in a sense, by Ruth Campbell's generosity, holding her downstage position, watching for a long time the door through which Marianne had left.

I could sense that Mac was looking at me for my reaction. Without looking at him, I nodded my head, my eyes filled with tears, all the emotion which I had felt before now finding an acceptable outlet in the purity and excitement of Marianne's performance and the audience's appreciation.

During the intermission, more pictures, more greetings, and the lobby was alive with excited talk about Marianne. I received congratulations as I used to receive them for Fran's performances. "Fran would have been so proud." "It's happening all over again." "Had you ever seen her act before?" I wanted to rush backstage and tell her what everyone was saying, to share it with her, but I knew better than to do that.

"Remember when Fran first appeared here?" Mac was asking me with a smile.

"Yes."

"Of course, she's got a long ways to go, but there's something about her. It's not very flattering, but she's like a beautiful race horse who knows what she was sent on earth to do. Fantastic style. Quite different from Fran, of course. Fran had her own special quality too."

I finally escaped onto the lawn for a breath of air, to be alone, to hear my own thoughts. This girl was infinitely greater than Fran. At once I disliked her for it, and myself for thinking it. This girl had a fire that was undeniable. She might never be the actor's actor that Fran had been, highly respected, often consulted, a great teacher. This girl was an audience's actress, and she would be envied and hated by more skillful but less magnetic actors. "Fran, you would be very happy, very proud. You would be generous as Ruth was generous tonight. You had your niche, and you envied nobody else theirs. I wish you could have been here to have seen it. We would have grabbed each other's hand."

At the curtain calls, Ruth brought Marianne out to share her final call, and the audience responded with tremendous applause both for Marianne and for Ruth's kind gesture. The curtain finally closed on Marianne weeping in Ruth's arms. It was amateurish but deeply moving, a play within a play. Marianne had struggled to leave the stage after Ruth had almost literally dragged her on, but Ruth had an iron grip on her hand, and Marianne could do nothing but to go to pieces in Ruth's arms.

Tears were streaming down Mac's face as the house lights came up. "Well, that's what theatre's all about, right?" Unable to speak, I nodded my head.

On the way out, many pats on the shoulder. "Come over any time." "Someone I'd like you to meet" from the village matchmaker. "Playing any golf?" "I'm sailing Saturday, and I need a crew." "You and Fran have given us a great night. A privilege."

As we went backstage, Mac was receiving congratulations, and I was receiving congratulations and sympathies at the same time. "It must be a very difficult time for you, but this was exciting, wasn't it?" And the opinion expressed over and over again—"Fran would have been so proud. Another one of Fran's children."

It was easy to find Marianne's dressing room: there was a mob of people in the hallway outside her door, local photographers, and two or three girl apprentices jumping up and down because one of theirs had made it. Mac took my elbow and started leading me down the hall.

I stopped him. "I want to see Ruth first."

"Oh, yes."

"She was damned good, and also damned generous. This can't have been the easiest night of her life."

"She's been great about it right along. I think she sensed this would happen."

"That's why I want to see her first." I knocked on her door. "Are you decent? It's Chris Larsen."

"Come in."

I opened the door. Ruth was just fastening a dressing gown around her still very attractive body. "Chris!" And she opened her arms. "They said you were going to be here." And I kissed her cheek, and hugged her, transferring to her some of the emotion I was feeling for Fran.

"Good show, Ruth. Lovely job."

"But what about that girl!"

"Very promising."

"Promising, hell. She's fantastic."

"Yes, she's exciting." I smiled. "But you were terrific."

She kissed me, and I hugged her again. "You sat at Fran's feet too long. Always the nice thing. I gave my performance. It was okay. But this is a great girl you've got there."

For a moment I was confused. "I'd never seen her act before. The college chose her and I just handed her the award. This is the first time I've seen her act."

Ruth took a drink of Scotch. "Fran would have been pleased. Do you want a drink?"

It was strange and yet comforting to be back in a dressing room again. All the time I had spent in dressing rooms, Fran's, Jean's! Dinner brought in between matinee and evening performances. Drinks after the show. I wanted to get on down to Marianne, but she was all right. Ruth's feelings were the ones that needed consideration at this moment, and somehow I identified her with Fran. She was only a little older than Fran. "Just a short one. No water." I poured myself a "finger" and held up my glass. "You were a damned nice lady tonight." And I drank it off.

She kidded it. "What the hell else was there to do? When rape is inevitable . . ."

"Still, nice going."

She put her arms around me and kissed my cheek. "You're a nice man." And when she drew away, there were tears in her eyes. "How are you doing, Chris? Rough, huh?"

"Yes."

"When they said you were coming down for this, I said, 'He must be out of his mind.' "

"Well . . . I wanted to be here."

"That's how you and Fran were. The right thing. I was never good at that." She looked at me with a kind of sad tenderness, as though she were trying to read something in my eyes. Then impulsively she embraced me again, kissing my cheek and holding me for a moment, pressing her soft, voluptuous body against mine, then drawing back and looking at me. I had a feeling it was an offer, a compassionate suggestion. Not wanting to leave her kind gesture embarrassingly hanging there, I kissed her cheek with what she would understand as a thank-you kiss, held her for a moment, then said, "Well, I better let you get dressed."

"And you'd better run down and congratulate your little girl."

There was a knock at the door, some friends had arrived for Ruth, and I felt I could leave her.

"Are you going to the party, Chris?"

"I'm not sure."

"I understand. Well, if I don't see you there, I'm staying at the Whaler Inn, if you should want to have a drink sometime and talk."

"Thanks. I'm not sure how long I'm going to stay around, but if I do . . ." I blew her a kiss from the door and left as the others entered.

There were still people standing around outside Marianne's dressing room, but as I looked in, Mac saw me and beckoned over the heads of the others. As I squeezed by, Mac turned Marianne around. "You remember Mr. Larsen, don't you?"

She took one look at me, and her eyes started to fill with tears, and she rushed towards me and threw her arms around me. Everyone smiled and "ahed" at this spontaneous show of appreciation. As I patted her back, I was instantly aware of the dangers of the situation. Love is impossible to hide. Once in a play of Fran's a young couple seemed very stiff in early rehearsals. When I visited the show on its tryout tour, the first moment they looked at each other onstage, I turned to the director and whispered, "When did they start sleeping together?"

Marianne drew back and looked at me. "I'm sorry. It's just that kind of night."

I tried to look at her as the donor of the Frances Larsen Award should look, slightly paternal, kindly. "You were wonderful. Very exciting." I wanted to grab her and hold her.

"I'm so grateful." She dabbed at her eyes.

I said what was called for from the donor, and yet in a way I said it reluctantly because this was Marianne's night. "Fran would have been terribly pleased."

Marianne looked at me again and her big dark eyes filled with tears. "Thank you."

Mac rescued the moment from its emotion by introducing me to the other people in the room, the actresses who shared the room, and the apprentices, who were all smiles. "How do you do, sir?" It had been a long time since I had been "sirred," and I was promptly reminded that I was old enough to be the father of these "children," including Marianne.

"Thank you for the flowers. They're my favorites . . .

It was wonderful of you to come. It must have been very hard for you."

"I'm very glad I did come." We were both trying to read between the lines, saying things that were in the area of what we would have said alone, but with slightly different emphasis.

The girls kept coming up to Marianne and kissing her and squealing. Some of her college classmates who lived nearby had come. Several boys, too, stayed near her. They formed a kind of inner circle, a bodyguard. Mac and I were tolerated because we were tangentially involved, and my reaction to their star's performance was important. Marianne tried to steal me a look from time to time, but it was dangerous, so I busied myself talking to Mac.

"It turns out the kids are giving Marianne a party and we are specifically not invited, but I've told her she has to come to my party first because there are a lot of important people there she must meet. Helen Madigan is up in my office now telephoning in her review to Boston between gulps of gin, but she wants to meet Marianne. And there are a lot of others."

Marianne and I hadn't made any plans. I knew that openings and afterwards got very chaotic, but I had foolishly hoped that we would have a chance to be alone for a minute to settle where we could meet later. The cottage seemed impossible. She had said that the boys had begun to follow her, tail her. She had been able to shake them before, but tonight when they wanted her to be with them exclusively, she'd never be able to make it.

Mac was saying to Marianne, "Do you have a way to get to my house?"

Too quickly I said, "I have my car."

A very attractive young man standing next to her cut in quickly. "I'll bring her, and then take her down to our party." The two other boys were taken aback by this and started to pummel him playfully. "We've got our cars. How come you think you're going to take her?" And so on. I remembered back to dances and what maneuvering went on to be the one to take "the" girl home. Well, I was back in the maneuvering again, only I wasn't very quick on my feet any more.

Marianne was obviously in better training for this sort of thing. She came to me and said so that everyone could hear, "I hope we can get some time to talk alone at the party. I'd so much like to tell you what all this means to me, and to talk about Fran . . . if you wouldn't mind."

Again I smiled at her like an uncle. "I'd like to very much." I omitted the "my dear." I couldn't carry this off much longer without sounding ridiculous to myself.

A couple of the girls were trying to change down at the other end of the room. They thought they were covered because they had on their dressing gowns and their backs were to us. They didn't realize that they could be seen in the wall of mirrors. Mac sang out, "Wait! Wait! There are old men here. We'll get out and let you all get changed. Good show, everyone. Thank you very much."

The glimpse of the two other girls half naked in the mirror made me more eager to be alone with Marianne, to tell her how fantastic she had been, to share her euphoria. I knew from long experience that it was a very rare "high," the feeling after achieving something creative, and I wanted to be there to watch her savor it. She would probably never have any more love in her heart than she had tonight. Selfishly I wanted to be the person loved. Her love tonight would be a euphoric self-love. She would be loving herself and life through me.

FORTY-THREE

Though the party was large, it was an informal country affair with neighbor women in to help with the serving and the town postmaster officiating at the bar. He did this at most of the local functions and was on a first-name basis with most of the men and knew exactly what each drank (and approximately how much).

As the "stranger in town" I was the center of attention, and it was tiring. We went over Marianne's performance, how I was feeling, was I going to keep the cottage? Helen Madigan, her review safely filed in Boston, wanted an interview with me, a follow-up piece to the occasion.

But fortunately Marianne and her young man made their entrance, he extraordinarily handsome in very colorful "threads" and haughty and attractively contemptuous of this gathering, she in a long skirt and evening sweater. It was the first time I had seen her in a skirt, except for prize night at college. She was aglow with success and was parrying all the compliments with compliments of her own for Ruth and Mac. "But wasn't Miss Campbell great!" . . . "Mac really did it all." . . . "What a great audience!"

I had been right. Her life would never be the same again.

Her young man never left her side, his eyes shifting around the room as though he were a secret service man. He refused a drink when he found there was no wine. Marianne had a Coke though Mac tried to convince her she should have champagne. Ruth said, "Look at those eyes. Really turned on. There's nothing like it. I can remember when I first hit it. So aroused, I was ready to come if anyone touched me. I take it that's the lucky boy who's going to get it tonight." Involuntarily I frowned. "Oh, come off it, Chris."

Marianne made her way through the crowd to Ruth, again to express her gratitude. She was too young, too inexperienced, to realize that Ruth would like her to stay far away. Marianne meant it sincerely, of course, but the evening had been so undeniably hers that there had to be something almost patronizing in her thanks. She laughed with Ruth over a couple of small mistakes she had made, telling people in the group what a ninny she had been and how Ruth had rescued her. Ruth was pleasant but uncomfortable. Marianne was ready to play her grateful handservant, to fetch her a drink or a plate of food and then settle at her feet by the couch. But Ruth rose and said she wanted to look over the food and make her own choice, and she moved off with Harry, her leading man. Which left Marianne and me and her glaring young escort, who kept checking the time.

The young man did not bother me specifically. I knew

that Marianne wanted to be with me. But he bothered me generically. A confident, extremely physical and attractive "boy" of perhaps twenty-one. The right type and age for Marianne. Insensitive perhaps, but you can never tell. Maybe before I had arrived in the village, there had been something between them. In my mind I automatically cut his hair and dressed him in clothes I had been familiar with at his age. It helped me to place him, to size him up. It was almost like handling foreign currency. I always had to convert it before I could deal with it.

Marianne turned to the boy. "I want to speak to Mr. Larsen alone." He frowned and glanced at his watch. She turned to me. "Is this a good time for us to have a few minutes?"

"Yes." I looked around for where. The boy consented to leave us, and I guided Marianne towards the terrace, noticing as I did that Ruth was watching us over Harry's shoulder.

While we were moving, Marianne said, "This has been an absolutely glorious evening."

I smiled at her like an uncle. "It must have been very exciting for you, and I'm delighted." As we reached the shadows of the terrace, I spoke quickly, still keeping my avuncular smile. "You've got to be careful with your eyes. There are a lot of very smart people around here, sensitive to every demi-semi-quaver. Listen, you were fantastic. I can hardly keep from grabbing you and hugging you as though we were a couple of kids who have just won the school sack race. More of that later. Now you say something." And I leaned towards her with elderly concern.

"I just want to be with you. You know that. That's all I want."

"Careful with your eyes. You're telling me how touched you are that you've got the scholarship. Let's see some acting."

"But I've got to go to this party. They're all angry

[275]

with me for not running more with the group, dear Mr. Larsen, and they're going to watch me like hounds."

"If I may criticize your acting just this once, I think you should smile with a little more sympathy as you talk about your award."

"How can we get together?" The urgency in her brow could be interpreted as concern for me. "They're going to hang on to me like leeches."

"I'll be at your place, in your room when you come home. I'll manage it. Just don't let anyone come up with you. What time?" I touched her upper arm as though she had just said something extremely kind and thoughtful.

"I won't be able to get away before . . . what time is it now?"

"I don't want to look at my watch, but I'd assume it's around midnight."

"One-thirty, then. Or two. That's awfully late."

"I'll be there."

"They're talking about an all-night party, driving to Boston . . ."

"Tell them you have a performance to give tomorrow and you have to get to bed." I had all I could do to keep from smiling on the word "bed." "I'll be there no matter what time you get there."

"I wish it could be the cottage."

"I know, but there's no way if they tail you."

"Was it a terrible night for you? Terribly hard?"

She took me by surprise. My look was as genuine as her question. She shouldn't have asked it. I looked around and saw the young man hovering. It was clear that he would brook this no longer. Marianne "performed" a quick kiss on my cheek, impulsive, grateful, to be forgiven in an excited child. And she left the party.

I didn't want to stay any longer, but I couldn't think what to do with the two hours before Marianne would be free. I didn't want to go back to the cottage alone. I wanted to stay on the high of the performance and the evening. The cottage alone would be all wrong. An awkward pause. I decided my mood would be best preserved by staying at the party and at least talking about Marianne.

A half-hour later Mac approached me saying, "Chris, Ruth wants to go home. She's staying out beyond you at the Whaler." Ruth was pleasantly high. "Harry was supposed to take me home, but he's disappeared into the bushes somewhere."

"Of course. Glad to." I hadn't the slightest desire to drive Ruth home. I didn't relish being seen leaving the party with her. But I had spoken up with my little-gentleman manners. I was still feeling sorry for her, grateful to her.

FORTY-FOUR

Mac helped Ruth into the car, as several couples on the terrace watched. After all my evasions with
Marianne, here I was driving off into the night with someone who had the reputation of being one of the more
available women of her generation. To try to save the situation I called out, "Can I drive anyone else out towards
the Whaler?"

As we pulled away, Ruth lit a cigarette. "One can take
that sort of thing for only so long. Thanks for rescuing me.
Harry was supposed to drive me back to the Inn. I hope he
gets the clap." She roared with laughter. "They say these
kids who sleep around like greedy little rabbits are loaded
with it."

She scrunched down in her seat. "I don't know why the hell I do this sort of thing. I don't need the money. I have plenty of bread from TV and an occasional movie. I sometimes think I'm just trying to find my lost youth, when theatre was fun, no risks, beach parties after opening. It's all the same. It's just that I'm not. I want to be that damned girl, your protégée, down at that party. But I suppose we would be persona non grata . . ." She paused. "Oh, occasionally at some of the theatres it's different, almost like old times. An old heartthrob discovered temporarily on the outs with his wife, or some star-struck handsome apprentice. I keep moving. It gives me the illusion that something's happening." She looked at me for a long time. I became embarrassed at her attention. I looked at her for a moment and smiled. "You writing anything, Chris?"

"No."

"Too soon. Well, give yourself a break. It'll come. You should be in Europe, getting away from it all, meeting new people, new girls." She said the last a little tentatively. "God, if I'd died, Al would have been in bed with ten chicks before my body was cold . . . I'm sorry, I always was crude. That's my charm." She laughed. "If I were a man, I'd never marry again. Well, look, I'm a woman and I'm not marrying again. But a man, like you . . . I don't know whether you know it or not, but you're at a very attractive age. You're attractive at a very attractive age, and the world's full of women and girls. It's a whole new ballgame at your age. More fun and games. Not so deadly serious . . . It's indelicate as hell to say, but I'm sure a number of your friends envy you." She must have somehow been aware that I was frowning. "All right. Perhaps I'm out of line. Too soon. Whatever. I know with you and Fran it was . . . different. I read all the stories. I'm sorry. Just jealous. But life goes on. Oh, shit, I'm saying all the wrong things. Forgive me." She put her hand on my hand and kissed me quickly on the cheek.

She sat back and looked out the window at the moon. "Christ, a full moon. All the props and no play." She laughed. "Do you remember how many years ago it was, and if you do don't tell me, when Fran and I played down here in something? I can't remember what, and the kid pulled the curtain five minutes before the end of the first act. I was pissed off and mad as hell, but Fran was sweet and understanding."

"She may have been sweet and understanding, but I remember she had the stage manager and that boy up there for an hour the next afternoon practicing that cue."

"I didn't know that."

"Fran was kind, but she insisted on nothing short of perfection."

"I remember someone told me that on the last day of some tour she was doing she called a rehearsal to sharpen some moment or other. Too much! I mean, that's great, but I couldn't do it." She mused for a moment, then giggled. "Funny girl, too. Why do I always think of her as a girl? Because she kept her figure, I suppose. She was always after me not to wear a bra. Said it weakened the muscles. Did she keep that up?"

"Yes. And the ribs. Do you remember?"

"Christ, yes. You should be able to see your ribs." She laughed. I suddenly thought of Fran lying there with no breast, and the skin from her ribs grafted over her chest.

Ruth was quiet for a moment, then, "I'll bet that little girl can see her ribs. And she doesn't need a bra and never will. Funny, women are self-conscious about having too much or too little . . . Terrifyingly insecure gender, aren't we?" She turned to look at me, and put her hand on my thigh.

"Gives us something to do, to reassure you." We had pulled up in front of the Whaler Inn.

[280]

She just sat there for a moment and then said very quietly, "Chris, will you do me a big favor and come in for a nightcap? The bar's still open."

I still had an hour before getting back to Marianne. Ruth's appeal was so naked. She was a terribly pathetic woman and she was crying "Help!" Something masculine and vain in me responded to such appeals.

We were the only people in the dimly lit bar, and we sat in what had apparently become her corner. The bartender knew her drink, and I ordered a gin and tonic, which I could nurse "Double for me," she called after him.

We were sitting side by side, and as she made her points, or laughed at some memory, she put her hand on my hand, or my arm or thigh, casually in passing. It was obvious that Ruth was one of the "girls" she had told me the world was full of. And as far as she was concerned, I was being stupidly unresponsive.

She was on her second double and staring into it as she turned the glass around in her fingers. "I can remember the night that it happened to me. I mean, what happened to that girl tonight. When suddenly it is obvious that you are somebody. And I did it to someone the same way she did it to me." She turned to me suddenly. "Why the hell did she keep coming up to me, thanking me for being so kind. 'I've just destroyed you, and I want to thank you for being so kind about it.'"

"I don't think that was in her mind at all."

"Do you know what's in her mind?"

"No, but I think she felt genuine gratitude. I know what you mean, but I don't think that entered her mind."

"There was something pitying and patronizing in her gratitude."

"Come on now, Ruth. You were great to her. Don't

spoil it. You're just tired. The show was still your show. You're the star. She was just unexpectedly good."

"Good? Brilliant, for Christ's sake."

"In a very good part."

She put her hand on my thigh. "You're sweet. I played the play two weeks ago with another child in Bucks County, and there wasn't a murmur about her." She left her hand on my thigh and kept looking at me. "I used to be so damned jealous of Fran. When you'd pick her up at the theatre and take her and her accumulated friends for drinks."

I was tempted to tell her that I had often hated it, to make her feel better about it. "You should have come along."

"Huh . . . come along." She looked at me a long time with a slightly pained frown, studying me. "Can we see something of each other while I'm here? As I remember, your cottage had a lovely beach."

I felt very sorry for her, but I didn't want to see her again, alone. I stammered something to the effect that if I stayed around, we'd arrange something. She got the point. She removed her hand and stared at her glass. I just sat and watched her growing bitter self-pity.

"Have you heard from Jean recently?" She looked at me and smiled knowingly.

I frowned. "Jean?"

"Jean Hamilton."

"No." I shook my head. Why was she bringing up Jean?

"She's in New York on the way to the Coast to do a picture."

"Oh?"

"She and Perry are splitting up." She kept looking at me.

"It's been coming a long time." Then quickly, "I haven't seen or heard from Jean in maybe three years."

A Cheshire-cat smile. "You were very fond of her, weren't you?" How did she know that? I shrugged my shoulders. She went on. "Oh, more than that."

"Everyone who ever met Jean was in love with her."

"I wasn't." She smiled. Though my face was hot, I tried to look at her as blandly as possible. "I've seen quite a lot of Perry since they've been separated." She was drawing it out. Torture. "Perry says that you were very much in love with Jean a few years back when she was doing that play in New York."

My face was hot. My hands were cold. She knew she had a strike. "What did he say?"

She seemed to relish my discomfort. "He just said that . . . that you had been very much in love with Jean. He said 'passionately in love.' " She raised her eyebrows.

My mind raced around like a squirrel in a cage. How did he know that? How the hell did he know that? He hadn't been around. How many people was he talking to, and what did he know?

"I was very fond of her. It was a complex time."

"It always is." She smiled, enjoying it all.

I squirmed on with lies, cheating in the worst possible way, confusing, confounding. "It was when I first knew about Fran . . . I was keeping it to myself, that she was going to die, and then one day at lunch with Jean, she was trying to get someone to make an adaptation of a book of mine . . . it was too much, and I just blurted it all out . . . and she was very sympathetic, and I was touched . . . and for a while she was the only one who knew about it . . . and we'd meet . . . I wanted to talk to someone. But 'passionately in love.' I don't know where he got that idea."

I felt I might be sick to my stomach from the lies, from using Fran's illness to justify my feelings for Jean, for denying my passionate yearning for Jean . . . sick with loathing for Ruth for being so bitchy because I wouldn't go to bed with her because she had had a rough night in the theatre and wanted to strike out at something, somebody.

Very quietly she said, "He has the idea very definitely that you had a 'thing' with her."

"Well, I can't help what he thinks. Maybe Jean . . ." Oh, shut up! "It was a very mixed-up time. I . . ." I looked at her watching me coolly. I stopped.

"What do you care what he says? If it's not true, it's not true. If it is true, you were a lucky man . . . and the piper must be paid, you know. The rumor will make you more attractive. You know you have always had a rather forbidding image." I tried to smile. "He refers to you as 'That prick Larsen . . . the loving husband . . .'"

Then she suddenly became warm and sympathetic. "I'm sorry for being so bitchy. Forgive me. He's mad as hell at her now. He may be just thrashing around, talking irresponsibly, guessing. Maybe Jean got mad at him and blurted out something about you which he misinterpreted. Anyway, forget it. Have another drink."

It was now my move to be nice to her, to placate and silence her. You don't spread ugly rumors about a man who is going to bed with you. But I said, "I've got to go, Ruth. It's been a rough day." Without thinking, I looked at my watch.

She turned bitchy again. "Mustn't be late."

"Come on, Ruth. Don't talk like that."

"Why not?" She was drunk and angry now, her eyes flashing. "Why the hell not? I always say, 'Bury the dead and fuck the living!'" She burst into tears and rushed out of the bar.

I sat there for a moment with my eyes closed, angry at her but sorry for her, and sick at what she had told me.

FORTY-FIVE

I got in my car and just sat there for a few moments. What the hell was Perry saying? How had he found out anything? There was nothing really to find out.

The lights went out at the entrance to the bar. I looked at my watch. Fifteen minutes to get back to town and up to Marianne's. Two hours ago I couldn't wait to be with her, to share, to move on.

My pre-programmed body started the car and drove it back towards town while my thoughts were with Perry. The son-of-a-bitch! No, I didn't think that. Oddly, I had always liked him, had felt great sympathy for him. What had Jean said to him? What could he say? That I had been in love with his wife. Dozens of men were publicly "in love" with her, one of the most beautiful women . . . But that wouldn't be something he'd gossip about. It had been a bitter joke with him for years. "Oh, everyone is in love with Jean. I get used to it." Public lovers. But I had not been a public lover. I had been . . . what? Pathetic! Jesus!

The fog was drifting in patches now, and I almost missed a curve in the road. I must concentrate. I had said I would go. It was her night. When I saw her, everything would be all right. But then unconsciously I had the fleeting hope that she had already arrived home and the boys would be standing guard, and I wouldn't be able to get to her room, and I could go home and be alone with my confused thoughts and feelings.

But there were no cars in front of the barn. I drove into my friends' driveway. There was a low light burning in Marianne's room. Was she already there? I made my way over the back lawns and gardens and up the stairs. I knocked lightly and opened the door and went in. Nobody there.

I looked at my watch. Two o'clock. I glanced around the room. Christ, what was I doing here? It hadn't been right the first time I was here. Too public. And now . . . But with the boys tailing her, the cottage was impossible, and . . .

I lay on the bed and stared at the ceiling, my mind racing. What the hell did Perry know?

I felt sick.

I had not felt guilty when I was with Jean, pouring out my love, my disappointments, never specifically about Fran, never so petty. Just about marriage and its loneliness and . . . Oh, Jesus! that's not so. I turned abruptly on the bed—I had once written to Jean, "If Fran weren't dying, we'd be divorced." Oh, Christ! Had I really said that? Yes. Yes. Had I really meant it, or was I just trying to impress Jean, heap on misery, like dragging her to see Fran in the

hospital and then begging? I burrowed my head in the pillow, not wanting to believe any of it. How had I blocked it
all out? I had blocked it because I couldn't live with it.

But, God, it had been so lonely. (Oh, for Christ's
sake, don't make excuses!) Never so lonely as when Fran
joined new "families" with each play or film, and in their
creating, bringing something to life, achieving an intimacy
and urgency which we were losing.

"Shall I give it up? Is that what you want?"

"No, of course not. I just want some sense of
priorities, shifting priorities, if you will, but something."

I could never say right out, "I need you." Because she
would have given it up and that would have been unfair,
not part of our unwritten, unsaid contract and understanding. Not a mean and spelled-out understanding, but a
joyous understanding that we would grow along together
and always have interest and excitement in the home.

Demand? A ridiculous word in intimate relationships.
And demanding involved being arrogant enough and sure
enough of oneself to be able to say, "I can fulfill your life.
We can fulfill our lives together." But how? All the dull-
eyed couples, how had they fulfilled their lives? My
mother: "I regret that you will never know the joys of a
real home life." She had known "the joys" with my father,
and I had thought it a miserable marriage.

But it wasn't just the being apart. That's too simple.
How did we lose all the intimacy and sharing and accessi
bility to each other? I adore you and I will serve you, but
in so doing I make you responsible for fulfilling my life (of
course, never said). How stifling and suffocating my need
and adoration!

Clashing temperaments on almost every level except
that we loved each other and kept on trying. How many
times we started all over again . . .

Except when I met Jean and everything finally spilled

over, and I was infatuated, in love with love all over again, and in the process, only able to express it by writing of my misery and loneliness.

And I suddenly wanted to deny Jean and the beautiful-sad time it had been.

Fran must have been as lonely as I was, as disappointed. But she never spewed out her misery in letters. So private! So proud! Once, in tears, "Chris, I hear you've been talking about us" when I had dribbled out some petty resentments one night with friends. The night before that I had been so crazed with loneliness I had wanted to die . . . in the empty house, with the realization it was not just empty, but even with Fran in it, empty of all we had had. Even preferring the actual emptiness to the sadder emptiness of her almost meaningless presence.

But there had been no one else before Jean! Oh, Jesus, shut up! It was not just that there was Jean, it was what I had said, written. Why couldn't I have loved Jean just wordlessly, for herself, without running down marriage. But that was our sad bond, her marriage, my marriage. God, did I really write, "If Fran weren't dying . . ." I broke out in sweat.

A car stopped outside.

I held my breath, listening. The motor was turned off. I listened for the car door. Nothing. I just lay there for a few moments, then carefully approached the window, wiping my face with my handkerchief. In the car I could see Marianne's guardian, sitting in the driver's seat, looking straight ahead, sulking. Then he turned and made a quick move towards her and was obviously kissing her, though I could see only his back and their knees. She seemed to be protesting, but not violently, and finally she stopped. After a few moments he sat straight, and he was smiling. He said something to Marianne and then she opened the door on her side, leaned back in and whispered something to him, and closed the door as quietly as she could. She came around to his side of the car and said something else to him, but he just smiled and she started up the stairs. Half-way up, she turned and waved at him as though to shoo him away. He waved back at her but just sat there, smiling.

She reached the top step, opened the door and entered the room, looking quickly around for me. She put her finger to her lips and came towards me. "He's going to sit out there all night." She shook her head in disgust. She went to each window and pulled the shade all the way down. Then she went back to the door and locked it and threw the bolt. "You don't suppose he'll try to come up?" I shrugged my shoulders.

She came to me and threw her arms around me and kissed me. "At last. I've been waiting to do that all evening," she whispered. I put my finger to her lips. "He's not going to ruin my night." She kissed me again. "All the time at that silly party, I kept looking over at you and saying to myself rather smugly, 'Enjoy him while you can, because later on, he's mine.' . . . I've been so ready for you." And she kissed me passionately, and I felt suddenly afraid and without passion. I had wanted to share this moment of hers, respond, lead her on, play, enjoy. But now my feelings were so confused with guilt and self-disgust that a sudden panic that I might not respond to the occasion, to "her night," seized me.

I moved away from her to the bedside table and gave her the box with the stone in it.

"What's this?"

"Your opening-night present. I got it in Boston."

"But I have your lovely flowers." She went to the small table where the lamp was and picked up one of the carnations from the bouquet I had sent to the theatre. "I've been clutching this all night, and I'm going to press it and keep it forever."

"Open it." I listened for footsteps on the stairs.

"Such a beautiful box! What is it?"

"Open it!"

She came over towards me, undoing the ribbon. "I don't want anything more from you. You've already given me so much." As though she were embarrassed to open the present, she kissed me again and held me as though she would press me right into her. "You shouldn't give me things from jewelry stores."

"Come on. Open it." Perhaps her pleasure in the sentimental nature of the gift would awaken something in me.

She finally opened the box, after elaborately smoothing out the paper wrapping and folding the ribbon. She took out the stone, looked at it and looked at me as though asking, "What is it?"

"It's another stone for you to keep, to remember tonight . . . and everything else."

She took it to the light. "Oh, it's beautiful. What is it?"

"I don't know. It's not valuable. It's just the idea of the stone." I came up to her and touched her shoulder, hoping her closeness would stir me.

She placed the stone with some ceremony among the other stones on the table, then turned and kissed me. "Thank you. How dear you are! Thank you for everything, for making this whole time in my life possible . . . and for being here and letting me share. What an incredible time for me! All of this together!" She kissed me again, her strong arms pulling me to her. I embraced her, but felt nothing but a sullen, frightening deadness.

Another car pulled up outside. We stood there listening. "If that's another one of them," she whispered in irritation. A car door opened and closed. Marianne moved to the light and turned it off, then moved to the window and peered down from behind the shade. "It's the constable." We could hear muffled voices, angry but kept low, then nothing. Then a car started up and raced away. A few moments later another car door opened and closed, and then the car pulled slowly away.

Marianne raised the shade a little so that the light from the streetlight came in the room. She came over to me, put her arms around my neck, giggling. "We must thank the constable in the morning."

"I feel a little sorry for him."

"I don't." Playfully she toppled over on the bed, pulling me along. Why couldn't I trust her? Tell her what I was feeling, my guilts and anxieties. That I wanted to be with her. Help me. But with her feelings about Fran and our marriage—I suddenly thought, "Ruth may tell her."

Panic deadened me further. But I started to go through the motions, lying close, caressing her breasts through her thin sweater, nuzzling at her neck. Perhaps if I shut my mind, just let the sensations pass through my fingers to my nerve centers. I remembered Fran's first night home after her first operation, and how she had wanted desperately to be loved, and how I had done just that, shut my mind off and "performed." Now Marianne's sensuous movements under my fingers and lips mocked my own deadness.

She sat up and quickly stripped her blouse over her head and reached for the buttons on my shirt. I made it difficult for her by bending over her breasts, trying to find some response in myself with my lips and tongue. She playfully tugged at my shirt and finally pushed me away so that she could finish taking it off. Then holding me down and giggling, she kissed my nipples and then her hand reached to undo my trousers. I moved in such a way that she couldn't reach the zipper, moved in such a way that it seemed an ardent response to her.

How gladly I had welcomed her undressing me when I had been rigidly and arrogantly ready for her. But now. I pushed her back, and my tongue flicked at her breasts while my hand went under her long skirt. I was glad she had not removed her skirt. Perhaps the eroticism of her half-dressed body would bring me around, the memory of adolescent fantasies of reaching under skirts.

She wore nothing under her skirt, and as she had said, she was ready for me. Where normally this would have excited me beyond endurance, now it only panicked me further. Perhaps she would come with just my fingers. If only she would go along with it . . .

But she wouldn't. She moved, and again pushed me back and put her hand on my crotch, saying, "You must let me do something. You always make me feel so selfish."

There was no comment, no gesture, no look of surprise when she found no erection. I closed my eyes. It had seemed to me, the few times it had happened, like a calamity, and to Fran, a sign of rejection.

Marianne methodically went about peeling off my trousers and shorts, not saying anything. Then she started at my belly and worked down, kissing, nuzzling, making friendly cuddling little sounds. I lay there, making my mind a blank, waiting for sensations. None came. She did not add to my embarrassment and distress by redoubling her efforts. She crawled up beside me, and half covering me with her body, kissed my cheek lightly. "I'm very selfish. I've been thinking only of myself. This must have been a terrible night for you."

I was touched and kissed her and almost felt some response in myself. How intimately all the feelings and reactions are bound up together. If it had been just a terrible night with reference to Fran and the opening, her thoughtfulness would have aroused me. But it had been a terrible night in a more complex way, and responding to her sympathy seemed only the most unbelievable hypocrisy.

"I've been so involved with myself . . . with us, that I forgot." And she stroked my face and held me tenderly. "I shouldn't have asked you to come here."

"Yes. Yes. I wanted to come." I kissed her and my

hand moved to her breast. She put her hand over mine to keep it from caressing her, to quiet me.

"Waiting here, and then that silly boy. I shouldn't have gone to their party, but I had to. Let's just lie here. It's good just being here with you."

She was saying all the right things, and no doubt she meant them, but such things were meaningless to me. The only thing that mattered was my lack of response and the reasons for it.

"This was bound to be almost the most difficult night for you. I should have insisted you not come to the theatre."

"No. No. It was a terribly exciting night." I kissed her hair. I wished I could go, get away. Everything she said was right and meaningful, but it all sounded like her excuses for me, and I could not relate to them otherwise.

I wanted a drink, several drinks. But Marianne wouldn't have liquor, and to ask if she did, would again only point up the problem. This dear, dear, affectionate, desirable girl nestled beside me. How understandingly she was handling the whole thing. But I couldn't help but resent her at the moment, compounding all my complex feelings of guilt and loathing and unworthiness.

It was not as though we hadn't been together before, and successfully.

"Nobody has ever excited me as you have, or pleased me as much." She kissed me on the side of my face for emphasis, summoning up all the comforts and reassurances. I patted her for thanks.

"It's all bound to be so . . . complex for you for a while. It's complex for me too. My feelings for you."

"Of course."

"I told you I had such a feeling of pride at the party because of us. I wanted everyone to know that that charming impressive man, well, that he and I . . . It's the first time, you know, except at college, that I've seen you in public, seen you with people, and I could tell the way they felt about you, and I wanted them to know, somehow I wanted them to know about us. Selfishly. It would make me feel more important. But then I knew what they might think, of me. 'Who do you think you are?' 'The man doesn't go with the scholarship, young lady. This man is still married to one of the really remarkable women.' I couldn't explain to them what there is between us, that I'm . . ." She stopped. She pressed her head against my chest, and I stroked her hair.

Then she said, "Bring me my letter tomorrow. I feel it's mine now." I hugged her to me, and kissed her hair. But still was numb.

She moved her head away and looked at me, smiling, "You looked very handsome, all dressed up."

"I felt very old."

"Why?"

"I don't know. As long as I was messing around the cottage in my old Navy chinos and sneakers and a T-shirt, I somehow didn't feel much older than you."

She suddenly drew away and looked at me. "Is that what's bothering you?"

"No."

"You are so much more attractive and handsome *and* sexy than all those boys down there."

Reassuring me again. Now that she felt that my problem was perhaps simpler, susceptible to her attentions, she let her hand wander down my body again. "You must tell me what you like."

I felt her fingers, but they did nothing. Nothing.

Suddenly I shifted up and away from her, and in a great wave of activity scampered around on the bed, kissed her breasts, her belly. She giggled and squirmed. Then turning back her skirts I kissed her knees and legs and buried my face in between her thighs, kissing, nipping, mouthing, tonguing.

"Don't! No, please!"

But I kept on, wanting to hear nothing, wanting only to bury myself in the moist and pungent warmth between her legs, seeking there something which would arouse me. Marianne, whom I had treated with such affection and delight and gentleness, I now wanted to rape. An impotent rape with my tongue and mouth, hoping that the violence and the humiliation of it would appeal to some part of me and arouse me. It had been one way for a quick rearousal after a first orgasm. What was there about it? Something forbidden, something strange that aroused when other more usual means did nothing.

"Please, please! I wish you wouldn't!"

I reached up one hand and found her breast, and fondled it roughly at the same time I held her down. I muttered compulsively, "I want to. I want to." At first I thought her movements were in response to my tonguing, but then she stopped and lay there motionless. I pressed on with more force, more urgency, trying not to think of anything, of Fran or Marianne, or Jean or my guilts and anxieties and deadness. I was irrationally angry with Marianne for rejecting this way of making love. Part of me said, "I will show her. I will make her like it. Teach her." Another part of me just wanted to bury myself between her legs, to find some feeling there that would bring some life to my body.

She sobbed. I stopped, but did not move, hiding my face now where a moment ago I had been violently mouthing and devouring. We lay like that for minutes. Her small sobs stopped. My shame kept me down there away from her.

She sat up and reached down and pulled me up alongside her, covering us with the spread which had fallen to the floor. She held me, cradling me. "I'm sorry. It's my fault. I just can't . . ."

[295]

"No. I'm sorry," I muttered, still not opening my eyes, ashamed to look at her.

She stroked my cheek. "I'm all right. I'm fine. I don't need anything. Really!" How generous of her to ascribe my violent burrowing to an effort to bring her to orgasm. "Look at me!" I opened my eyes, and she was smiling. I managed a small smile and shook my head. "What?"

"I don't know."

"Are you angry with me that I can't do it that way?"

"Of course not." I kissed her. "I shouldn't have done that. I knew."

"Maybe someday . . . when everything's right."

Incredible girl. This we could discuss. This was a simple matter of personal preference which might be adjusted one day under proper conditions. We couldn't discuss what had really happened.

I knew she wouldn't send me home. She would wait for me to say I had better go. And when I said it the first time, she drew me to her. There was still some healing to be done. She had to convey that she still wanted me there in spite of everything.

"We're having a call for notes at eleven tomorrow. We should be through by noon. Can I come to the cottage then," her large eyes wide open, twinkling with innuendo.

I kissed her for wiping out the present by making pleasurable plans for the future. "Yes."

"I'll call first to make sure you haven't been overrun with people."

"All right."

Then with a sudden rush of concern, "Or do you want to stay here with me? It's going to be awfully lonely at the cottage, feeling the way you do tonight."

I didn't know what I wanted. I only wanted not to know. Anything. To sleep. To disappear from this confusion and depression. But I knew I couldn't stay. I couldn't leave in broad daylight.

"We could set the alarm for five."

"I'll be all right." I sat up.

"I hate your going, feeling like this. Why don't I come down with you? If you can get out without being seen, we both can."

I reached out and touched her cheek. "You're sweet." I didn't want to go back to the cottage, but I wanted to be alone. "Now that people know I'm there, they might come stumbling in at dawn."

She frowned "It's going to be difficult, isn't it?"

"Yes, but we knew that. We'll manage." I leaned over and kissed her, then got off the bed, found my shorts and trousers where Marianne had thrown them. She didn't watch me, but found her blouse and put it on and went to the mirror and brushed her hair.

"I love my stone."

"Good."

"And my flowers. Do you know anything about pressing flowers?"

I came up to her. "No. Put it between the pages of a book. Something like that . . . Good night." I put my arms around her and kissed her. "You were fantastic."

"Oh . . ."

"You'll see in the papers tomorrow. Bring them with you when you come."

"What will you do now?" There was that worried look of concern in her eyes.

"A few drinks and a sleeping pill, and it'll be morning."

"I should lay in some liquor."

"I'll bring some."

"I think this place is wrong for us, always listening for footsteps. I hate the idea of your having to sneak in and out."

"We'll work out something."

She came to me and put her arms around my waist and looked in my eyes seriously. "You want to, don't you?"

I put my arms around her. "I want to very much. Tonight was . . ." I left it hanging, letting her supply her own reasons.

"I know."

"I told you that I wasn't always the way I was the other day."

"Why should you be. Anyway, tonight was . . ." She moved to the window and looked out. "As far as I can see, okay."

I went to her and kissed her on the cheek. I was going through the motions. I had forced myself to try to do something I had no wish to do, and I had failed and I was depressed by my guilts, my lack of openness and by my failure. "Tomorrow should be a lovely day for you. I'll be able to say, 'I knew her when.' " She smiled and pushed me towards the door.

As I drove towards the cottage, I knew I didn't want to go there, to stay alone there. There was a motel up the shore. I would have to wake them up. And I had no sleeping pills with me, no liquor; and I would never sleep without them. So I ended up going back to the cottage, and finally falling asleep.

FORTY-SIX

The telephone was ringing. I tried to wake up, to climb up through the stupor of two sleeping pills taken with half a glass of gin at three in the morning.

Somewhere I thought, "Marianne." I fumbled to pick up the phone, dropped it and picked it up again. "Hello."

"My God, I've finally reached you."

"Jean?"

"Yes, and I've wakened you. I'm sorry. I waited till what I thought was a reasonably civilized hour . . ."

"What time is it?" I was trying to orient myself.

"It's just after nine. And I'm at the hairdresser's, of all places. It's the only time I could get an appointment. It's a silly place to be calling you from after all these years, but I wanted to wait for a decent hour. I've been trying New York and Connecticut, and it wasn't till I thought of calling your lawyer that he told me you were on the Cape and gave me the number."

"Yes" was all I managed to say. I was still half asleep and stunned by the call.

"I'm sorry to go prattling on like this, darling." The *darling* was not phony. She made it sound genuine. Her letters had always started "Darling Chris . . ." "How are you?" The concern was genuine.

"I'm okay."

"Did you get my letter?"

"No."

"I wrote to Connecticut. I was on location when I finally heard. Some place where no news could possibly penetrate." Then gently, with that incredible voice, "You know how I feel. I said it in the letter, which you'll get one day . . . Just a second, darling, I'm sorry. There's a terrible noise going on here."

There was a pause. I tried to come fully awake.

"There! That's better. Chris, I'm only going to be in New York today and tonight, leaving for the Coast tomorrow. Is there any chance of your getting down here?"

"Yes." I said it automatically. Whenever Jean had said "I'm suddenly free for lunch. Can you make it?" I had always said "Yes" and broken any appointment I might have had.

"Good. I've got a tentative dinner date because I didn't know if I would ever be able to reach you. But if you can come . . ."

"Yes. I'll drive to Boston and get a shuttle."

"You sound dreadfully tired, and this is a terrible imposition, but I want to see you."

"There was a party last night at the theatre. Very late."

"Oh, my darling, it must have been a rough go for

you. I'm so anxious to talk to you. Lots to say, but this is not the place to even start. That damned noise is starting up again."

"I'll call you when I come in this afternoon."

"What? I'm sorry."

"I'll call when I come in this afternoon."

"Good. I'm staying at the Pierre. I'm terribly anxious to see you."

"I'm anxious to see you."

"It's been too long. So much to say. Call me."

"Yes."

"Good-bye."

"Good-bye."

I hung up. I looked at the clock. Though Jean had told me what time it was, I couldn't remember. Nine-fifteen. I lay back, still drugged with the pills. God, would I ever sleep again without pills!

I tried to sort out what happened. I had said I would be in New York for dinner with Jean. I had not even thought of Marianne. I had just said "Yes." Something in me which always jumped to say "Yes" to Jean, which needed to say "Yes" to Jean.

But what about Marianne? For the moment my still groggy, struggling mind was involved only with the logistics of it. I had to go to New York. Marianne would be coming down here.

And then everything behind the logistics began to seep in. Marianne would come cycling down when she got through the cast meeting for notes, eager to make up for last night, to reassure me, "to come running."

Last night I had lain impotent in Marianne's bed and had hated Jean. No, hated having loved her. No, hated people knowing that I had loved her. While I had been seeing Jean, I had simply shaken my head and tried not to think about it. I suspended moral judgments on myself; one of those absurd arrangements one arrives at to survive.

Scandal isn't scandal to the people living it. It only becomes scandal when it's spread all over page three. And now I was getting ready to go to Jean. I didn't understand it.

I got up and shaved and showered and found my heart beating with the tension of trying to get out of the cottage before Marianne arrived. I was ashamed of rushing, but somehow I knew that if she came, it would all be worse. I couldn't simply say "I have to be in New York in a few hours" and run. And yet I had to go. So I had to get out before there was any chance of her coming. She might even come down for a moment before rehearsals!

I could call her. But she was probably still asleep, and the whole business of leaving a message with Mrs. Grader. I would leave a note at the theatre. I sat at the table and wrote:

Dear Marianne:
        I have to go to New York City on Estate Business. You were still asleep. I will be in touch. Congratulations again!

                  Love,
                  Chris

I should have said more. I looked up and saw the envelope and letter I had passionately scrawled to her in the restaurant a week ago. She had said she now felt it was hers.

I didn't know what I felt. I just felt an urgency to get out of the cottage before I had to face anything. I would think about it driving and on the plane.

At the theatre I left the envelope in her mail slot. I noted that someone had already posted one of the reviews. Headline: BRILLIANT DEBUT BY YOUNG ACTRESS. I took the note out and scribbled on the back of the envelope "Congratulations on the great review."

As I drove out of the village, safe at last from being stopped, questioned, faced, I stopped myself. I drove off the side of the road along the beach, turned off the motor and waited till my heart stopped racing.

What was I doing? Why did I just automatically say "Yes" to Jean? Marianne would understand the note, would not be hurt. That wasn't the thing. Why this uncontrollable rush? What was I rushing to?

Jean. But with what expectations? For a long while I couldn't think. I just kept shifting my eyes from the beach to the water to the road, expecting to find some answer there. My mind simply would not function, could not begin to analyze this compulsion. I just knew I was going to New York, for whatever reason.

I started the car and drove on, sensing I was doing something totally irrational, but I was doing it. Had I done anything rational since Fran had died? Did I somehow feel I had some privilege not to think of anything beyond the moment?

On the road I suddenly saw a greenhouse and a florist. I pulled too quickly off the road and parked. I would send Marianne flowers. As I was placing my order, I saw a large bunch of white roses in the case. Jean. Never anything but white flowers. Before I had asked her never to write to me again, the terrible night when she wouldn't come to me, I had bombarded her with every conceivable kind of white flower. On arrivals in New York, London, Paris . . .

When I finished ordering Marianne's flowers, I ordered some for Jean, "to be delivered at once. The Pierre, New York City. Only white flowers. They must all be white."

In the plane, finally, I leaned back and stared out the window . . . It would be good to see Jean again. How intricately she had been involved in that whole period of my life. She knew more about me and my real feelings than anyone. She had once said "One of the most important things in this world is to have a passionate friendship with someone." She had been my passionate friend to whom I had said "everything," had written "everything," love, sorrow, disillusionment with marriage. And she had said "everything" to me. ("Sometimes when Perry starts making love to me, I wish there were some aphrodisiac I could take.") She had always understood so much more than I understood about myself. I could talk to her now. She would talk to me now sympathetically of Fran's death. She would not say, "Oh, come on now! How can you feel so desolate about her death when you wrote me those letters about being sick of marriage and devoted to me?" She would understand what could not be understood.

FORTY-SEVEN

I called Jean from my apartment. "Where would you like to eat?"

"No place fancy, please. Isn't there some little place where nobody goes? I don't feel like being on exhibition tonight."

I told her about a small, dark little place on the East Side where I'd eaten once. "I'll meet you there at seven-thirty," she said.

"I'll come around and pick you up at the Pierre."

"No. I'd rather meet you there. I'll explain."

I was disappointed. I had hoped that we would have had a chance to have a drink in her suite, and talk.

I arrived at the place ten minutes early. It was as I had

remembered, dark, not unattractive. Only a couple of tables were occupied. I decided to wait outside on the sidewalk. In a few minutes a taxi pulled up. It was Jean. I rushed to pay her fare. She laughed. "I forgot about you. Always paying for my cigarettes, Kleenex. I carry money, you know."

As the cab drove away, I kissed her on the cheek. "You've dyed your hair."

"It's a wig." And we moved into the restaurant.

"I don't think I would have recognized you."

"Good. That's the idea."

We were shown to a table. The waiter lighted the candle and waited for our drink orders.

"Still vodka and tonic?"

She smiled. "Yes. God, what a memory. And the white flowers! Thank you."

When the waiter had gone, I leaned towards her. "You still wear Vent Vert?"

"You're impossible. How can you remember every damned thing?"

"I just do." I looked at her and took her hand. It was as though we had never stopped talking, confiding, commiserating. "It's great to see you again. You look wonderful."

"Still a few good years left. You look tired, but . . . You always looked like such a boy. Now"—she appraised me—"different." She paused a moment. "I wish you'd wired me, written me. I know I was 'banished,' and I understood, but . . ."

"A lot of things I do or don't do . . . I don't understand. I just do or don't do them. I started to wire you, and just saying to the operator 'Fran died Thursday' broke me up, and I hung up. I never tried again."

I just looked at her and shook my head in wonder.

"Now we mustn't start doing this. I probably should have written you a letter or something and not seen you, but I felt I had to. And I probably should have had you up to my rooms in the hotel to talk to you, but everything I do is dangerous."

"How come?"

"You apparently haven't been reading the papers, the more lurid ones."

"I've been in hiding on the Cape, very much involved with my own thoughts. Tell me."

"Well, Perry is getting a divorce."

"Perry is getting it?"

"Yes." She looked at me, pained. "I do wish you had read it all in the newspapers. It would have been easier than telling you."

"What?"

"Well, you always said that we'd split up one day. And I doubted it. And you said someday someone would come along and I'd want to split up. Well . . . he did." She looked at me a moment, then touched my hand. "We wouldn't have been any good together." I shrugged and smiled. "Anyway the whole thing was very messy. Like a bad French farce. Only it wasn't funny. And Perry is being very ugly about the whole damned thing . . . In a way, I don't blame him. He's had a miserable life with me off and away months at a time, flying here and there to be with the family over holidays, adapting his schedule to mine, hearing rumors drummed up by publicity agents that I'm having a 'thing' with each leading man. Don't smile. In spite of what you think, I'm a very good girl. You, of all people, should know. Anyhow . . . it's ugly, and there's a messy fight going on over the custody of the children."

"Bastard!"

"No. I can understand it."

The drinks came, and we said nothing till the waiter left. I raised my glass. "Well, I'm sorry I wasn't the man in the French farce. But happiness." We drank.

[307]

"You don't really mean that. You just like to say it. I think you'd like him. He's an English lawyer."

"I loathe him, sight unseen." I felt empty. I was here with Jean again, had come at her beck and call. I felt frustrated and ashamed.

She put her hand on mine and frowned. "We mustn't talk like this, really, because what I've got to tell you is very ugly and is going to upset you. And I'm desperately sorry, but there's nothing I can do about it." She turned and looked at me, examining my forehead, my eyes, my chin, and back to my eyes.

I hadn't the slightest idea of what she was going to say. "Well?"

She looked down at her drink and spoke very quickly. "Perry has gotten hold of those letters you wrote me, and he's bound and determined to make use of them in this custody fight, and they'll probably end up in all the papers."

I shut my eyes and shook my head. "Oh, Jesus!"

She held onto my hand, which I was instinctively drawing away. "I'm sorry. It's just God-awful. But he's hysterical, lashing around, trying to find and say anything that will hurt me."

For the moment I couldn't think of Jean and Perry. I was thinking of Fran and "people."

"The alternative was to let him have custody of the children. And I won't do that."

I realized then that my letters, the outpourings of my misery and loneliness, might cost her her children. "Could those letters make the difference? I mean . . ." I looked at her, incredulous.

"I don't think so, but . . ."

"God!"

"It's just his vicious hysteria, his wanting to get anything on the record and into the papers that will damage me. It's ironic. Everyone knows that Perry has slept around the last five years. I've known it, and I haven't cared, because I felt guilty for making him lead the kind of life he has had to lead. But now my lawyers are involved in the sordid business of trying to get some kind of affidavit from some of these girls that they did indeed sleep with him. It's ridiculous and sick-making. Something that made absolutely no difference to me now has to be researched and documented and brought forth as evidence that he is unfit to have custody of the children. It's disgusting."

We just looked at each other for a few moments. "When do you think this all might happen?"

"I'm surprised it hasn't happened already. I've been trying to reach you for days."

I didn't say anything. I just sat there shaking my head and looking out into the dark room. The consequences were so enormous and varied, I couldn't begin to think of them.

"I'm dreadfully sorry to drag you down here to tell you this. I didn't want to tell you over the phone or in a letter. It was stupid of me to have kept the letters." She paused and looked at me. "It was also stupid of you to have written them." I looked up at her. I didn't like being scolded by the woman to whom I'd poured out my heart and soul. "I'm sorry. I understand you had to write them. That it helped you in a difficult period . . ."

"You make it all sound so therapeutic," I said bitterly.

"It has always been difficult for me to talk to you honestly, without making you angry, without hurting you."

"I'm sorry. I realize you were doing me a big favor to receive the letters and read them and answer them . . ." I stopped. I was ashamed of my tone. It was a flashback to the many lunches we had had at similar restaurants years ago. "You don't love me."   "I can't love you."

"It's my fault that he got hold of the letters. I'd had them in a safe place, and then over the years, I'd forgotten about them, and when I was on location, the painters were in, and things got moved around and cleaned out, and he came across them."

"How long ago was this?"

"Oh, quite a while ago. He didn't say a thing about them then. Just kept them. I didn't miss them because I hadn't thought about them. It all came as a complete surprise when he threatened to drag them into the situation."

I ordered another drink for both of us. The waiter wanted to know if we were ready to order. I looked at Jean. Neither of us had an appetite. I said, "Later."

"I tried to explain to him about the letters, that there had been nothing . . . really nothing between us."

I looked at her. One of the things we had always argued about was just that. She had always denied that she had really felt strongly about me. I had constantly and insensitively kept reminding her of the first night when we would have been in bed if the child hadn't cried. And there it had always stayed. But now the combination of being reminded that there had been "nothing" and the knowledge of what that "nothing" might do.

"I feel so God-damned cheap. Not the letters where I told you how I felt about you, but the letters running down my marriage." I shook my head.

She put her hand on my arm and looked at me, a look of such compassion bordering on love that it was impossible to accept that there was "nothing" behind it. "Where is Perry?"

"On the Coast."

I closed my eyes. "If Fran were alive, I'd kill him to keep those letters out of the papers." I turned to her. "They can't just print a man's letters, can they?"

"I don't know. Maybe they can't print them, but if they get into the case, newspapers print what goes on. I don't know. I just know that some way he'll let people know."

I remembered Ruth. "Last night at the opening I saw Ruth Campbell."

"Oh?"

"She'd seen Perry, and she said that he told her that I had been in love with you. I wondered how he knew."

"Well, that's one way he's doing it. He'll do it. Don't worry."

"My son will have a field day with this." I was angry that this actual piece of half-truth would add fuel to whatever resentments he felt against me, for whatever reasons, all these years. This together with his suspicions about Marianne. And what would Marianne think, feel?

But the most important thing finally was not what "they" would think. Not what David or Marianne would think. What did I think?

"It's so ironic. The last three years, Fran and I . . ."

"I heard what fantastic care you took of her."

I shrugged this off, embarrassed. "But we really found something again. Her needing me like that. You know, she so rarely let me know she needed me. Once, on the road, a technical rehearsal, and a piece of scenery fell, not heavily, just floated down, but it struck her on the head. I was sitting in the theatre, and she turned when she was hit and called out into the dark theatre 'Chris!' It was one of the few times she let me know.

"But those last years, we grew very close. We had a marriage again, in some strange way. She was needful, and I could be responsible . . . Perhaps before that she didn't let herself go, turn to me more, because she wondered if I would really be there to catch her. I'm a very responsible person. Famous for my responsibility. But I wonder if I would trust me—I wonder if she would have trusted anyone—I don't know. Thank God she's not alive to hear about these letters."

"Chris, listen! I'm the one you wrote the letters to, and I'm the one who knows you loved Fran, certainly more than I've ever loved anybody. You loved her. You still love her. You'll always love her. And you'll worry that love like a dog with a bone . . . all your life, defining it, wondering if it was, or if it wasn't. Why couldn't it have been this or that? I won't think about Perry, why it didn't work. I loved him, of course, and there have been some pangs. We made mistakes, were cruel or mean. So, too bad. The difference in your case is that Fran died, and you're left with all the mistakes and no chance to sort them out and make up for them and forget them."

I listened to her words, but they didn't comfort. "I just . . . it just makes me out as such a fucking hypocrite. I'm sorry. Everything I've written about Fran is true. About me and Fran. It's just not the whole truth. And who the hell tells that? And those letters . . ."

"Chris, darling, people will understand those letters. They all know it was a tough time for you. Fran, sick, dying. People have some compassion, you know."

"A lot of those letters were written long before I knew Fran was going to die. Let me be honest about that, at least."

"But people won't know that."

"I know it. If I went around saying, defending myself, 'Oh, it was a rough time. I didn't know what I was saying, what I was doing, what I was writing . . .' A lot of those letters I wrote long before Fran was dying. I was sick of my marriage, and I adored you. It may not have meant anything to you, but I adored you."

"You exaggerated your feelings for me. You only like strong feelings. Adore. Hate."

"Maybe. But I adored you."

"I don't know why."

"Does anyone ever?"

"It was a series of circumstances."

"Fran and I had had bad times before, but I had never looked at anyone else before you. You can keep insisting that you had no feelings for me, if you want to, but I loved you." Here we were back again. I had come to tell her I loved Fran, to have her tell me I loved Fran, in spite of everything. But I was telling her I still loved her.

"It was awful not to be able to come to you that terrible night."

I was embarrassed. "I was disgusting. Emotional blackmail."

"No."

I was suddenly eager to tell her other things I was ashamed of. "I found someone else. Not that night, but later."

"Good."

I shook my head. "Someone meaningless."

"I'm glad you weren't alone."

I looked at her. "So often when I wanted you, I went to see her, and so felt doubly ashamed and guilty for using her when I wanted you . . . and for Fran."

"I'm sure the woman didn't feel that way."

"Again, it's really a question of what I felt. Those last years when Fran was really sick and, for the last year, an invalid, shrinking away to almost child-size, those years were like our first. Death brought a certain urgency. Oh, they weren't perfect, of course. *But* . . . It's as though we were both trying to make up for a lot of mistakes. Of course it wasn't entirely that way. Sometimes I hated taking care of her, and sometimes she must have hated me. She begged a couple of times to be taken to the hospital, just to get away from me, I think . . . But anyway, what I'm trying to say is, I wouldn't have—I don't *think* I would have written those letters during those three years. I don't know." I looked at her. "Yes, I would have. It's so hard not to lie. But if I don't lie, it's all so impossible to live with . . . Many times down at the cottage, when she would be sleeping exhausted on the couch, fallen asleep while I was reading to her, I would sit for hours on end and look at her and think about everything there had been between us and wonder about what love really was."

Jean was quiet for a few moments. "I said you loved her, always will, and you'll always wonder about the nature of the relationship and love . . . and . . . and . . . and."

"I suppose selfishly I'm very concerned about what people will think about me. I don't know why I'm so reluctant to be known as just another husband who loved his wife sometimes and sometimes didn't. But it's what it will do to Fran. That's hard to explain. I guess I can't. I have some mystical feeling that she lives on in me. Our marriage lives on. She is, after all, my wife. Dead, but my wife. And it's as though this thing wasn't happening five years ago, when I wrote the letters, but is happening now, to our marriage. She had such great pride, you know. It really destroyed her for anyone to know anything about her private life. A private, private person." I shut my eyes.

"Time . . . time."

"Yes, I know. Funny. I've never liked to pay my bills, and now . . ."

"You shouldn't have to pay for the little I gave you." Again she put her hand on my arm and smiled. Then a few moments later, "I suppose we should eat something."

"It is going to be rough on you. If you lose your children . . ."

"I won't lose them. And"—she looked at her menu for a moment—"bizarre as it all is, and ugly as it will all look in the papers, nobody has ever written to me like that before, or is ever likely to again." She looked up and smiled. "I hope you find someone to write to soon. It's very important for you to be in love." I smiled, but made a ducking, demurring motion with my head. "It's too soon, of course. But again, time. Let's all go to sleep and wake up next year."

I was on the point of telling her about Marianne because I could stand no more lies, but I didn't. We ate

[314]

something and drank some more, and as we caught up on the last years, I kept looking at her and knowing that I somehow was still in love with her.

As we left the restaurant, flashbulbs went off. The manager had recognized Jean after all and couldn't pass up the possible publicity for his place. I hurried her towards a taxi and was about to follow her in when she reached out to close the door. "Give me a ring and tell me how it goes." She closed the door as the taxi pulled away from the photographers.

I stood there, feeling hurt and ridiculous. I wanted to break the cameras and smash some faces, not just because they had intruded on a very private meeting, but also because people like them would soon be broadcasting my letters for the delectation of all. Instead I darted into the next cab and disappeared.

FORTY-EIGHT

I climbed the stairs to our apartment in a daze. I turned on the air conditioner in the living room, poured myself a drink, and sat on the couch and stared at nothing.

I was hurt and humiliated by Jean's closing the door in my face. I understood it completely. She had panicked at the flashbulbs and had instinctively thought to make it look better by leaving me in the middle of the street, not "going home" with me. Still, understanding it all, the abruptness left me feeling sick, to be left on the street with all the cameras clicking and the photographers smirking behind the lenses.

I had never left Jean's company except with a sense of incompleteness. "Then you shouldn't see me any more."

But I did. I always came back, the incompleteness a nagging challenge.

I looked aimlessly around the room, this room in our apartment which had been so much a part of our lives, which I wanted to keep because I wanted to have it for a retreat. Everything was still in this apartment—the triumphs of opening nights, the nursing, the screaming pain as she was carried down the stairs for the last time, but they did nothing to me. Flat. Facts.

In some way what Jean had told me about my letters and their possible publication had locked me out of this apartment, "our" apartment, and to a large extent from "our" life. While before I could slip warmly and comfortably, if sadly, into recollections, now the door seemed barred. It was almost as though Fran had found out about the letters and had slammed the door. My sense of loss was enormous.

The phone rang. I answered it quickly, alive now to what each call might mean. It was Jean. "I want to apologize for that dreadful thing I just did to you, running off like that."

"It's all right. I understood."

"It's not all right. I just panicked. Ever since this damned thing has hit the papers, there have been photographers. It's as bad as the *paparazzi* in Rome. But, darling, I didn't mean to do that to you."

"I understand. But it was nice of you to call."

"When I got to the corner, I couldn't believe what I had done, but it was too late."

"You're in a tough spot. We do these things."

"I'm just a selfish bitch. Perry always said so, and it's true."

"No."

"Yes. And no one knows it better than I do. You've always idealized me. I've loved it, but it isn't true."

Of course I knew she was right. I exaggerated everything out of some compulsion. All the time I was talking about how wonderful it would be to be married to her, some part of me knew it would not be wonderful, that what we had would be destroyed by marriage. Possession would be loss. The idea was everything. Yet I could never bring myself to say this or admit this, though perhaps she might have felt more comfortable with me if I had.

I almost said, "What are you doing now? Can I come over?" I didn't want to be alone. I wanted to talk about love and marriage and what they were. I wanted to "worry my bone."

But I knew that I would leave her, as always, more miserable and frustrated. I was through having fantasies about Jean coming around the corner of the cottage, coming up the stairs of the brownstone to be with me. She was a woman who operated on a very realistic level, though she was a fantasy figure for millions of men. "If you hear anything about what we were talking about, let me know."

"Are you staying in town?"

"I don't know. At the moment I'm just sitting here thinking. I'd like to disappear, to hide."

"I can understand. I'll call you if I hear anything."

"Thanks. It was great seeing you." There was genuine feeling in my voice, though it had been disastrous seeing her, had left me miserable and more lonely than ever.

To disappear. I realized that in a sense I had already disappeared, or was about to disappear. I had once had a friend who said she had no identity of her own. "I'm Paul's daughter, John's wife, Ted's mother." I was suddenly, in a way, being cast adrift from my identifying relationships. Fran's husband. Marianne's . . . what? In some way I felt that the letters to Jean made me unfaithful to Marianne too.

David's father. Well. I had disappeared as that long ago, at his own unexpressed request. I shook my head, thinking what he would say. "I always knew he didn't love my mother."

Perhaps if I called Marianne. I looked at my watch. She would be at the theatre. If I told her everything before it came out. It might be face-saving, no more. A little late. Why? Does one necessarily go around talking about . . . ? But I had allowed an impression to go uncorrected.

If I were to tell her and she were to understand. Understand! Shit! What is there to understand? I wanted forgiveness. And only Fran could do that. No, not forgiveness! And suddenly I found myself getting angry at Fran. If only . . . if only she hadn't gone away on that tour, there wouldn't have been Jean. I was left lonely and miserable and susceptible. I was immediately ashamed at my anger. I had gone away as often as she had, to do research, to write in seclusion.

That was too simple: it wasn't just being "away" physically. She had gone, *we* had gone "away" in more important ways which I didn't understand.

"Chris needs to be alone a lot for his writing. It works out well for us."

Starting to go over the old hurts, accusing, defending, blaming, arguing, trying to justify my attitudes, I felt ashamed and sick.

Ten o'clock. If I caught the midnight for Boston, I could be in . . . But I didn't want to be in the village when the news broke. After the festivities last night at the opening! Where did I want to be?

I wanted to be nowhere.

FORTY-NINE

I stayed in New York for two more days, darting out to get the latest editions of the newspapers, scanning them quickly for any accounts of Jean's divorce, then settling back into the same kind of morbid dialogue with myself.

The morning following my dinner with Jean, our pictures appeared in the *News*. How ironic it was that we should be "exposed," as it were, three years after we had meant anything to each other and because my love letters might be mentioned in her custody suit.

Roger called about the picture. "I think it's tasteless of them to have printed that picture, knowing how you feel at the moment, involving you by innuendo in that messy business out there." I almost asked him if I could come to see him, to tell him the truth. But I didn't. I knew I was making it more difficult for myself when the news broke, that he would feel hurt that I had allowed him to go on and on about how wronged I'd been.

I went to the movies to try to take my mind off what was going on. I walked miles and miles at night, and I bought the papers.

I did and did not want to call Marianne. I didn't know what to say. I knew that her feelings for me were very much involved with her feelings for Fran and our marriage. I somehow felt that to call her and talk as though nothing had happened would be a deception. I would sound false. She would be able to tell with her extraordinary feel for honesty.

The third afternoon I sat in my apartment feeling nothing. I had exhausted all the touchstones of my feeling. It was like the end of a day of writing, when the mind finally "surfaces," the flow of associations stops, and I would just sit there with my eyes closed, seeing nothing, thinking nothing. Blank.

David? It would be impossible to talk to David after the story came out. Or before, for that matter. But I had an obligation there. How little I had been thinking of myself as a father! Husband, lover, unsuccessful lover, widower . . .

The evening papers had nothing. I finally came to the conclusion that I might rescue a little self-respect if I talked to David, told him whatever I could tell him. I did not arrive at this decision easily. It came about after a supper of soup and cheese and crackers. I had been talking to him in my mind, trying to make him understand how much I loved his mother, and how those letters . . . well . . . He had made me angry with his surly answers, and I had found myself jumping up and pacing and answering

him and trying to get through to him, till finally the imagined scene was no longer any good. I had to talk to him.

I threw some clothes into the suitcase and left the
apartment, feeling better at least to be moving, going
somewhere.

FIFTY

I was on the plane before I realized that I hadn't called David, didn't know whether or not he would be in. I would call from the airport in Boston. "David, could I . . . ?" What? Come over? I hadn't thought of that. I wanted to talk to him, but I hadn't thought where. In front of Gretchen? Ask her to leave her own apartment? Gretchen would probably be more sympathetic than David. Talking to women was always easier for me than talking to men. Why? Mother? Father? Their willing suspension of disbelief?

I decided it would be poor taste to drag Gretchen in on this. It would be up to David how he wanted to handle it with her. It might seem as though I were trying to dull his reaction to have her there too. So, where? In the airport? A bar? I had thought of driving on down to the Cape if we were through in time. The hotel. I hated summoning him to a hotel, but perhaps it would be better. Something unattractive about going to his apartment to . . . confess? Also, if he came to me, he would be the free agent, able to leave when he wanted.

What was I going to say to him? I began to think that perhaps it was all a bad idea. What if Perry never revealed what was in the letters? I reacted strongly to this cringing behind a technicality. I would feel better if David knew. *I* would feel better. Was that so important? He might respect me for coming to him before it was published. Respect? Is that what you want? "Dad, I broke the garage window with the baseball." I could hear my father saying, "I can understand a boy doing something wrong, but I can't understand his lying about it when his father asks him."

I was tired of trying to figure out my motives for anything. I knew what I was going to do. I seemed to have a compulsion to confess and be judged for this so that possibly the judgment and punishment could stand for all my other offenses, real or imagined.

What was I going to say to him? The truth? What was the truth? You see, there was this time when I was miserably lonely . . . That sounded disgusting. Every time I put anything in words, it sounded self-serving and disgusting. Fran was a wonderful and remarkable woman, and I was a shit. Was that true? It all suddenly sounded that way.

Maybe nobody would be very surprised when the letters were revealed. Maybe everyone thought I was a bastard right along, and I was just fooling myself that they had thought I was a fine fellow and a good husband.

I reached David from the airport. Gretchen was out at a dance class, so he was free to come to the hotel. On my way up to my room, I picked up the papers and glanced at them. There was nothing about the letters, but there was a picture of Jean and me on the inside pages of the *Record*. David would have heard about it or seen it. Nothing in the *Globe* or *Herald*.

I took a drink from the bottle I had brought along and put it on the dresser. Then I picked it up to put it on the shelf in the closet. David used to watch me drinking. Say nothing, but just look. Obviously, he thought it a hang-up of the older generation. I put the bottle back on the dresser. To hell with it!

A few minutes later David arrived. He was clearly uncomfortable at being summoned. He was wearing blue jeans and a work shirt. "They almost frisked me downstairs."

"You'd think they'd be used to it by now." He had always disapproved of my choice of this hotel. "I stay here because I can get a room the last minute, and it's comfortable." Why the hell should I apologize for my hotel?

"I thought you were in New York. I saw the picture." He motioned towards the papers on the bed.

"The Boston papers are a little slow picking things up. Jean called me on the Cape, wanted to talk to me." I wasn't ready to get into it all, but here I was offering a lame excuse for being with Jean Hamilton.

He flipped the paper open to the picture. "You look as though someone were about to zap you." I had instinctively thrown up my hand to block out the flashbulb.

"The flashbulbs." I looked again at the picture. It was different from the one in the New York paper. Jean and I both looked terribly guilty, ducking, shielding ourselves.

"Pretty woman." David had immediately established the offensive. He seemed pleased. There it all was in the papers. He didn't have to say anything. He could just stand there with his arms folded and wait to hear what I had to say. And whatever it was, it proved him just right.

He didn't go so far as to say, "Are you the next Mr. Jean Hamilton?"

"Can I order you some wine?"

"No. I want to be back when Gretchen comes home." In other words, get the hell on with it!

"Sit down, David." I sat in one of the small easy chairs. David perched on the edge of the bed, reaffirming that his stay was temporary.

"This . . . uh . . . picture is meaningless, David. We were having dinner, and she's in this divorce mess with her husband, and they follow her everywhere, and . . . that's it."

He sat there, nodding his head as though to say "Yeah, sure" and fixing me with his eyes. It was a maddening situation. I was about to get rid of his suspicions by admitting something infinitely worse. When would he understand what I was talking about? When he was forty-three, as I had only come to understand each phase of my father as I passed through the same phase myself?

"As I said, this picture is meaningless. The truth hasn't been in the papers. It rarely is, but she is going to marry an English lawyer when she gets her divorce from Perry."

David's face shifted almost embarrassedly into neutral. He had lost some of his assurance.

"However, as you may have read, it's been a messy divorce business."

With sarcasm, "I hadn't really been following it."

I took a deep breath. "And I am likely to be involved in it, sooner or later. That is why she wanted to talk to me, why we had dinner."

David frowned.

"Five years ago."—What should I say? How should I put it?—"I met Jean while your mother was on tour"— For Christ's sake, don't go giving that as the reason!—"and I fell in love with her. She didn't have any real feelings for me, but I was . . ." Don't say miserable and lonely! "Anyway, I fell in love with her. It didn't amount to much. I wasn't a very persuasive lover." I tried a smile. David wasn't smiling. "We never got very far. *But* . . . I wrote a number of letters, rather passionate love letters, and more than that, full of the unhappiness I was feeling at that time with our marriage. It was a strange release. As I said, nothing ever really happened between us. I mean . . ." What did I think I was proving by emphasizing that technically we had never been lovers? "Anyway, it was brief, all over a long time ago. *But* Jean's husband, Perry, somehow got hold of the letters. She had forgotten she had them. It had been so long ago and so meaningless, really, for her. And she was on location, and he came across them and didn't say anything at the time, but just kept them. Then when she met this man, this lawyer, and the whole marriage went to pieces, Perry got ugly, and as you see, well, you haven't seen, but he's been making quite a custody fight for the children, and Jean wanted to tell me that he will probably use some or all these letters to try to prove that . . . I don't know what you prove by such things, but something. Just to make it messy for her." I looked up at David. His face was tight. Contempt.

"Did Mother know anything about this?"

"No. There was really very little except these letters." He stared at me, nodding his head, not believing. "Oh, a few—" I meant to say "kisses," but I couldn't get the word out in front of my son. "Some long luncheons and suppers. Your mother was away on . . ." I stopped. I knew that such simple-minded excuses would disgust him as they disgusted me. The truth, whatever it was, wouldn't disgust me, or possibly him, if I could find it out by going over and over our relationship. What I had done did not disgust me at the time, though it had made me sad. "Things happen in life. It's very difficult to explain, even to oneself. Perhaps when . . ." I stopped.

"I'm older?"

I was angry at his tone, yet I understood. The important thing was that I had told him. I had not waited for him to read it in the papers. I was obviously getting no credit for this. "If you don't know that I loved your mother, nothing I can say will prove it. Like most marriages, we went through some . . ."

"You don't have to defend yourself to me." He stood up.

I could see that he was straining to hold himself in. Tears, anger. I was surprised. I hadn't really thought at his age it would make that much difference. Perhaps with Fran away so much, she had become a kind of idealized figure, the power of his imagination and longing making up for what he often missed.

"Is that all?"

It wasn't all, but I wanted to spare him breaking down in front of me or lashing out at me. And I wanted to spare myself the semi-justifications I would have thrown back at him, all of which might have crisscrossed in a jagged path back to his conception and birth.

"It's not all. But I know you want to go. Thanks for coming."

He turned quickly and left.

I had not expected understanding. I had not gotten it. But nonetheless I was angry at his contempt. It was a relief from my shame.

FIFTY-ONE

I left the hotel at eleven o'clock that night. I felt foolish checking out a few hours after I had checked in, but having told David, I was now eager to tell Marianne and get on with my life.

Driving down, I speculated over and over again what her reaction would be—hurt, disappointment. She had given herself to me, I knew, in the name of Fran and our marriage. In a sense, she had been the Fran who wanted to but could not be there to hold and comfort me.

As I turned off the main road down to the village, I wondered what I should do. I wanted to see her. I desperately wanted to go up to her room and crawl into bed beside her and whisper "We'll talk tomorrow" and just go to sleep holding her.

But something inside me said strongly that I should talk to her almost before I touched her again. She should know. She should have the option. I had a momentary drowsy fantasy that she might be at the cottage, asleep in our bed, waiting for me. Then I thought of the picture in the paper which she would have seen. I had written in the note I left her that I was going to New York to take care of something in Fran's estate. Then the picture of Jean and me. And I hadn't been in touch with her.

I had drawn in on myself this time, hidden in the cave, not turned to someone else for help and comfort.

I stopped the car at the side of the road and picked up a small stone from a chink in a wall and drove on.

There was no light in Marianne's room. Two-thirty. I drew the car up in front of her steps, hurriedly put the stone on the third step, and got back in the car and drove away. I was too tired to care if I had been seen. I did not even take the precaution of not slamming the car door until I had turned the corner.

It was after ten when I awoke the next morning. I went to the bathroom, put on chinos and a sweater, and went to look for Marianne's bicycle. I could see it through the window, propped against the shed. Where was Marianne?

She was in the kitchen sitting at the table drinking a cup of coffee. She was wearing a shirt and a pale-blue denim skirt. She looked up at me with a completely different look from any I had seen before. A kind of sad smile. Something had very definitely changed. I kissed her on the side of the head. "You should have wakened me. I was exhausted." I pressed her to me gently. She seemed to draw away slightly. But she did touch my hand.

"How was New York?"

[330]

Obviously she had seen the picture in the paper. "Complicated." I poured myself some coffee.

"Did you get the estate thing finished?"

"I didn't go for estate business. I saw Jean Hamilton. And that's a long story."

"You don't have to tell me." She seemed deeply troubled.

"I want to tell you. I went to Boston last night to talk to David, and I drove down here right after to talk to you. But I was too tired when I arrived." I looked at her across the checkered tablecloth, the morning sun coming in the window behind her. How vulnerable she seemed. She sat there willing to be brave about what she thought she was going to hear. I reached over and put my hand on top of hers. "Thanks for coming down."

She smiled. "I got your stone."

"I'm sorry I didn't call from New York or get in touch. Sometimes I'm a bastard that way. I don't quite understand why. Sometimes I reach out, and sometimes I draw into myself."

"I understand. I do that myself."

This extraordinary girl. I didn't want to sit there and talk and tell her things which might separate us forever. I wanted to move to her, take her hand and put it on my body. I could persuade her that the picture with Jean was nothing, apologize for not being in touch. A few tears, and then the delightful comforting and coming together again in bed. For a few more days, until the story broke. But I felt somehow cheapened, not the deserving, bereaved man of two weeks ago. My image in relation to myself, to Fran, to Marianne was shaken. "I used to know Jean quite well, about five years ago."

"Ruth told me." She looked up and smiled sadly. "I think she sensed there was something between us, and partly because of what happened opening night, she wanted to hurt me."

"And partly because I wouldn't go to bed with her that same night." She shook her head. It was hard to know what was going on in Marianne's mind. For the moment it seemed that she was simply hurt because she felt I had taken up with an old romance. Perhaps I had been wrong. Perhaps she wouldn't feel hurt as Fran's surrogate, that my whole relationship with her had, in a sense, been built on a lie.

I looked across at her, hoping to give her assurance that I was telling the truth. "Five years ago I was very much in love with Jean. She was not in love with me. It didn't amount to much." I had a very strange feeling from the way Marianne looked at me, as though I had been diminished a little because Jean had not loved me. *She* had loved me. Why hadn't Jean? "It only lasted a few months, then Fran got sick, and it just all ended . . . No. No, that's not quite right. It didn't end just then. I pleaded with her for comfort and compassion . . . almost blackmailed her with my sorry situation. Then it ended, about three years before Fran died. Everything I've told you about Fran and me during that last period is true. I think we were very much in love again. But I had written letters to Jean. And she had kept them, and forgotten about them. And when Jean fell in love with a man, a lawyer in England, whom she's going to marry"—I looked up, hoping that point at least would be clear—"a custody fight started, and Jean asked me to come to New York so that she could tell me that Perry, her husband, might use my letters to mess things up for her, might bring them into court, and they might get spread all over the papers." I put my hands on the table. "That's it."

She shook her head. It was impossible to know what she felt. "Did Fran know?"

"No. But I wanted you to know before it broke, and before we . . ." I meant to say "went any further," but I didn't. "I feel doubly ashamed. Obviously as far as Fran is concerned. But as much as far as you are concerned. I know your feelings for me were based very much on your feelings about our marriage." She half shrugged, as though to deny anything so childish.

She stared at me a long time, smiling, then serious, then smiling. Finally, "Confession time."

"I don't know how I could have told you sooner, though I suppose I should have."

"No. No." She looked at her cup and then up at me. I reached over and touched her hand, took it and held it.

She smiled and gently took her hand away. Then she said very simply, "Larry, the boy you saw me with at college, drove on from Ohio the day before yesterday, and I slept with him that night and last night too. I wasn't home when you left the stone. I was in a motel. I saw the stone when I came home this morning." She started to cry, burying her head in her hands. I got up and went to her and tried to comfort her.

"Don't. Don't."

And again I pressed her to me. I was trying to think about what she had said and murmur comfort to her at the same time. I had never asked about this boy. I knew he existed. I had thought perhaps it was over. I reached out and drew my chair alongside hers and sat down, keeping my arm around her. She finally looked around as her tears subsided.

"I don't understand it. We argued violently before I came down here. He hadn't written, and . . . that makes it all sound so small and nothing . . . I don't know. I *was* upset by what . . . No, that wasn't it. I didn't believe what Ruth said." She suddenly put her hands to her face and smoothed her cheeks and stared at me. "I don't know. It happened."

"Is he still here?"

"He left for Boston early this morning. He'll be back tomorrow. He's going to get work near here for the rest of the summer."

"Do you love him?"

"I don't know."

I reached over and kissed the side of her face, just to be close, to touch. She brought up her hand and stroked my face. Comfort? What? I knew I wanted to comfort her. These complexities were new to her.

And I knew I wanted to make love to her. A new closeness had been reached by our confessions. She suddenly seemed beautifully older. Each ambiguous gesture and touch and look of hers led me on, compassion blending with passion. Also some hurt, some male sense of wanting to reaffirm my own claim.

I didn't force anything. I just stayed there, holding her shoulders, touching her cheek.

After a few moments she drew back and looked at me. I kissed her lips lightly. She looked at me very seriously, almost pleading. "I never said I loved you."

I was touched by her sweet effort to straighten out her feelings, her sense of honesty. "No."

"You don't love me."

"Yes, I do. I do!" I had said it and kissed her before I had thought. It was half reassuring, half sincere. She smiled and shook her head. "Yes." I moved closer to her.

"It was the situation. Everything. Not me."

"Everything including you. I know you felt it was the situation, and I was afraid to disturb it, to upset anything." She looked at me, wondering, and finally kissed me, a friendly, touching kiss between two people who have been lovers but are to be no longer.

I wouldn't let her take her lips away, but held her gently. She didn't move away. My hand moved to her breast.

"No!"

"Yes. Yes. Please!" I closed my eyes against the word. Please. I was begging again. It had been so lovely only a few days ago, both open to each other. Now this begging, as with Jean. But at the moment I knew no shame. I wanted her.

She pushed and moved her chair away and looked at me, troubled. "I don't understand. How can you want me? I've just told you that only a few hours ago, I was . . . Doesn't that . . . ?"

I looked directly at her. "Don't you want to be with me?"

She rose and moved to the living room.

I followed her quickly, only knowing that my body needed her body, wanted to be close to, in, her body. Only feeling that if we could be together at once, we could get over this moment. I was exposed, not just physically but in whatever shamelessness it took to say I didn't care if she had just been with someone else. I had made a terrible declaration with my body and my words, and her not being able to understand it seemed to make me more intent on proving to her that I didn't care what the conditions were. I wanted her. I reached for her and brought her against me. "Please! Please!"

She pulled away and ran out onto the deck. "I don't understand. I don't understand."

She started off down the beach, after a few steps removing her sneakers. I watched her for a few moments, then turned and went to my bedroom and lay on top of the bed, trying to understand what I had been doing.

How overpowering her presence was! Yet I had not called her. Away from her I had not sensed her as a force in my life. If I had called . . . That's too flattering. This boy, this "puppy dog." But to be with her again! My God, how lovely! To be without her . . . She was clearly torn, had based it all on her not being able to understand how *I* could be with her, after the "boy." Not whether *she* could be with me.

How could I be? The idea of Fran's having had a lover before me had made me sick. But now? The idea of repossessing her, quickly, making her mine again, and then the "boy" would be out of my mind because she had come back to me. I tortured myself with images of her and the "boy." I suddenly wanted her primitively, to blank out the images. If we were together, and this time in every conceivable way, he would not exist. I would have purged him from her body.

And it would leave her in tears. She had once said very simply, "So far in my life I can answer to my god for everything I've done." And I was the one who only a few days ago had been enraged by the other boy and what he had attempted or done. It would not be the "What." It would be the doing it.

If she came in here, to this room, she would remember. It had obviously been an important time for her too. What we had done. Would memory, that most potent aphrodisiac . . . ?

And then what? Could we try to rebuild the relationship on all we now knew? Could we ever regain the simplicity of what we'd had?

I looked and saw my reflection in the full-length mirror on the closet door. I had forgotten. I had been thinking of myself as a young man, or rather, ageless. Together, catching glimpses of ourselves in the mirror, holding, loving, we had been two ageless bodies.

She came through the door from the deck. She stood at the foot of my bed, smiling sadly. I knew it wasn't possible for her to stand there and look at the bed and not remember and be tempted. Perhaps unconsciously it was why I had come in here.

"Everything happened so fast with us. You don't

know me. I don't really know you. Somehow it's all different. We had such a lovely time here *alone*. And then everything rushed in."

"He went away before!"

"And you'd just stay here waiting?"

"Do you find that shameful?"

"I don't understand it."

"I have no pride. Pride is a luxury a lover can't afford."

She smiled. We both sensed the almost too glib nature of the remark.

"I can't believe you love me. People just don't love that easily. You like to say so. You like to say the words, write the words." I was hurt that she was belittling my feelings. "May I take my letter with me?"

"A souvenir of my writing?" It was a cruel and unnecessary thing to say.

She sat on the edge of the bed. "It's a beautiful letter. Everything you've said to me has been beautiful. Everything we've done."

"It's just that I heard those words from Jean a few nights ago—'You like to say the words.' "

"I can understand why she kept them, the letters. If they use them, I suppose it will be terrible for you in a way, but if they're like mine . . ."

I looked at her for a few moments. "The letters were not all like the ones I wrote you. Oh, some were, inevitably. There are only so many words." I paused for a moment, then somehow I had to tell her. "But there were other letters telling her how disillusioned I had become with my marriage."

She looked at me with that same concern there had been in her eyes the first day we had been together here. She reached out and took my hand.

"Fran never wanted to be married." I brought Marianne's hand up and kissed the palm and kept it against my face, remembering that she, too, never wanted to marry. "But we had had such a wonderful time those two years just being together, I couldn't imagine being away from her. And I had a great longing to commit, to escape from the lonely center of myself. When I begged her to marry me, told her everything would be all right, she would look at me, the way you did when you said that about the 'words,' doubting, wondering. Maybe in some way she knew that I would not be a very good husband. That I liked being a lover too much, that I was a giver, not a sharer. Or perhaps she sensed I had the desperate need but not the capacity for sustained closeness . . . I don't know. But in the end I convinced her." I smiled. "When my sincerity is doubted, I redouble my efforts and sometimes in the winning, lose."

Marianne's fingers tightened on my hand.

"I don't know what it was. Something in both of us . . . You know, one day a little before she died, when she was all trussed up and in traction, I got something for her—a glass of water, a cigarette, something—and she looked at me a long time and finally said, 'You know I never wanted to be dependent on anyone. It's as though God had had to teach me a terrible lesson.'"

I closed my eyes and shook my head. "We did terrible things to each other. I adored her . . . but I hated marriage." I opened my eyes and looked at Marianne. "I hated Fran too. Sometimes." I turned away as the tears started. Marianne moved quickly up alongside me and put her arms around me and covered me. "I *hated* her sometimes!"

As we lay there, saying nothing, it was as though Fran and I were at last talking honestly. No "What's the matter?" "Nothing" And I felt closer to her, more open, more honest, more loving. And I thought, "If I had been this honest, this trusting, she would be alive. I would have told her about the small lump in her breast, and we would have been in time." It was irrational, but somehow the idea swept over me with force and conviction. Why had we been so closed off from each other? So loving, yet so closed off?

Marianne didn't say anything, just lay there, protecting me, shielding me until the tears stopped, every now and then leaning down to kiss my cheek, or my eyes, warming me with her body. I couldn't open my eyes. I was with Fran. Ashamed. Open at last, but ashamed. "I'm sorry."

"Shhh." And she drew me closer and pulled the blanket over us.

Sometime later we made love for what I knew would be the last time. Quiet, sad, comforting, saying nothing, without taking off our clothes.

And when I woke up from the deepest sleep I had known in months, she was gone. The letter was gone too.

FIFTY-TWO

That afternoon I packed Fran's things in boxes and cartons, looking out the window from time to time, thinking I had heard Marianne's bicycle bell. I answered all calls, wondering if one might be Marianne, but knowing it wouldn't be. She had gone as she had come, suddenly, cleanly. Our time had passed, an unreal time, as unreal and intense as the last years of Fran's dying. We would undoubtedly meet again somewhere, sometime. But everything would be different, except that we would look at each other in a special way, remembering.

I couldn't spend another night in the cottage. It was doubly lonely there now. I put the boxes and cartons in

the station wagon and drove all night to get home. And for
the first time since Fran's death, I slept in our bed.

The next morning there was a telephone call from
Jean's lawyer in California. Jean had had to hurry off to
England, but my letters were on their way to me, registered mail. They would not be used. And Jean had her
children.

I closed my eyes and breathed deeply, sensing a mix-
ture of relief and disappointment. Somehow, subcon-
sciously, I had wanted my guilt known, to be punished and
to move beyond it, not to have to live with it alone, to
deal with it alone. However, to be spared the embarrassment, and for Fran to be spared, was good.

Later I got in the car and drove out the back road to
the cemetery. I parked and walked through the woods to
the back side of the hill where the plot was. I sat leaning
against the old elm, unseen from the road.

For a while I didn't think about anything. I was simply there. I looked across the fields to the Catholic cemetery on the side of a distant hill. I looked at the simple
stone marker which had been placed for Fran, flush with
the earth. Grass was beginning to grow, and someone had
planted small flowers at one side of the stone. Who had
done that? I felt very still, very quiet.

I thought about my "guilt" now to go unresolved, un-
punished, and I remembered in some discussion, somewhere, a friend had said of someone, "He's suffering a guilt
that denies what we are." Which is human, fallible. It had
sounded very comforting. But when does being human
stop? How wide a range of failings are we allowed before
we feel legitimately guilty? And someone else had said,
"Well, we all have to learn to live guilty."

I finally brought myself to think of Fran, quite literally, as here in the grave, dressed in her prettiest dress,
forever in these New England hills. "Let me go! Let me

go!" Another voice, "Fran is dead. It's over. It's all over."

But somehow I knew it would never be over. I would go away soon, to God knows where. Try to look to the future. Fran did that. Fran would have done that. A quick kiss, a smile, then turn and stride off, never looking back.

But I knew that for many years, perhaps the rest of my life, no matter where I might be, I would be standing here waving good-bye, and wondering.

ABOUT THE AUTHOR

ROBERT ANDERSON has been a distinguished playwright in the American theatre for twenty years; *After* is his first novel. Born in New York City, Mr. Anderson graduated from Phillips Exeter Academy and Harvard University, where he also received his master's degree. In 1953 Mr. Anderson's first Broadway play, *Tea and Sympathy*, was produced by The Playwrights' Company, of which he became a member. His most recent plays are *I Never Sang for My Father* and *Solitaire/Double Solitaire*.

Mr. Anderson has frequently taught, most recently as a member of the faculty of The Salzburg Seminar in American Studies. He is married and lives in Connecticut.